"An intriguing glimpse at the decadence, debauchery, and prudery of Baroque-era Venice."   —*Kirkus Reviews*

"The eighteenth-century world of Venice and famed composer Antonio Vivaldi come to life in this novel. . . . Like Tracy Chevalier's *Girl with a Pearl Earring* . . . this book has great appeal, especially for teenage girls; it also offers much to those readers interested in the composer and his influence on Venetian society in the early 1700s."
—*School Library Journal*

"*Vivaldi's Virgins* is a beautifully written story. There are some sentences that are so lovely and . . . that beg to be reread over and over again, but apart from that, the story will draw readers immediately into Anna's life. The setting—eighteenth-century Venice, Italy—is lush, mysterious, and extravagant. It is the simple things like a girl getting her first period or falling in love for the first time that will make readers recognize themselves in Anna and the other women of the Pietà. Secondary characters are well developed, intriguing, and add greatly to the story. . . . *Vivaldi's Virgins* is a story not to be missed and perfect as summer gives way to autumn. I highly recommend it."
—*Romance Reviews Today*

"Author Barbara Quick brings a sharp, artistic eye to the proceedings, describing the subtle details of Venetian fashion and society down to the last pearl on the hem of the dress to the last drops of blood in the aristocratic bloodline. Quick is animated by a deep love of and appreciation for the lost past of Venice and the city's rich romantic heritage. It is her talent in bringing the insular world of the Ospedale della Pietà alive that keeps the story going, and it is her disciplined historic research that keeps the reader enthralled. With that combination you can get away with a good deal, but you can also produce a lot—in this case, a fine novel like *Vivaldi's Virgins*." —BookReporter.com

"Behind the masks of Carnevale and the musical scores of Vivaldi, eighteenth-century Venice comes brilliantly to life in this passionate novel. The plot takes several twists and turns that will enthrall the reader. The details of history are well researched and the imagery sensational. The prose is lyrical and mesmerizing at times. Quick has included a glossary at the end to help the reader with Italian words and phrases. At the end, she describes what is historical fact and what she created from her imagination. This is a complex tale that will appeal to lovers of Italian history as well as to fans of Vivaldi and his music. Barbara Quick has written a truly enduring coming-of-age story."

—Historical Novel Society (Editor's Choice)

"An entertaining tale populated by some of the major figures in eighteenth-century European culture. The depiction of the implausible Venice of Vivaldi's day is somehow completely convincing." —John Schaefer, host of *Soundcheck* on WNYC

"As we travel with Anna, we can hear, see, and almost touch her world. This is the perfect novel to read for visiting Venice."

—Elaine Petrocelli, president of Book Passage

"Lovingly researched and lovingly written—a captivating and poignant novel."

—Sarah Dunant, author of *In the Company of the Courtesan* and *The Birth of Venus*

"Richly imagined and lyrically composed, *Vivaldi's Virgins* is a sublime feast for the senses. On this compelling journey behind the cloister walls and inside the intrigue of eighteenth-century Venice, readers will be serenaded, seduced, inspired, and moved."

—Elizabeth Rosner, author of *Blue Nude* and *The Speed of Light*

"In this thrilling, evocative novel, Quick brings the decadent atmosphere of Baroque Venice vividly and convincingly to life—the sights, the smells, but most of all the sounds. Seen through the tantalizingly restricted gaze of a convent dweller, we experience the imagined life of Vivaldi's most talented pupil, an orphan girl abandoned to the care of the Church as an infant. Quick's narrative skill keeps the drama alive from beginning to end, drawing us into her characters and their adventures. *Vivaldi's Virgins* goes far beyond the standard coming-of-age novel in its loving recreation of an era, its attention to historical detail, and its ability to reveal the essence of a life imbued with music."

—Susanne Dunlap, author of *Lizst's Kiss*

"The writing evokes Venice and the love of music and the longing of young girls so beautifully! I read some passages with tears in my eyes. At one point when music may be lost to Anna Maria forever, it was so poignant I had to put the book down a few times. . . . I marked many passages to read again. Some sentences I had to reread several times before going on. They were truly music."

—Stephanie Cowell, author of *Marrying Mozart*

"*Vivaldi's Virgins* is historical fiction at its most alluring. Though the compelling voice of Anna Maria dal Violin, a foundling and extraordinary violinist, members of Vivaldi's famous La Pietà orphanage players, we virtually live in Venice during the decadent but culturally thrilling eighteenth century. . . . *Vivaldi's Virgins* is extremely well researched, with a fascinating historical note." —*Jewish Book World*

© 2007 by Margaretta Mitchell

About the Author

BARBARA QUICK is the author of six books, including the novel *Northern Edge*, which won the Discover Prize. A full-time writer and avid *sambista*, she lives with her teenage son, Julian, in the San Franciso Bay Area. *Vivaldi's Virgins* has been sold for translation in twelve countries.

VIVALDI'S
VIRGINS

Also by Barbara Quick

Northern Edge

VIVALDI'S
VIRGINS

A Novel

BARBARA QUICK

HARPER

NEW YORK · LONDON · TORONTO · SYDNEY

For my father, Hal Tritel

HARPER

A hardcover edition of this book was published in 2007 by HarperCollins Publishers.

HarperCollins books may be purchased for educational, business, or sales promotional use. For information please write: Special Markets Department, HarperCollins Publishers, 10 East 53rd Street, New York, NY 10022.

FIRST HARPER PAPERBACK PUBLISHED 2008.

Designed by Leah Carlson-Stanisic

The Library of Congress has catalogued the previous edition as follows:

Quick, Barbara.
Vivaldi's virgins : a novel / Barbara Quick.—1st ed.
    284 p. ; 22 cm.
   ISBN: 978-0-06-089052-0
   1. Vivaldi, Antonio, 1678–1741—Fiction. 2. Ospedale della Pietà (Venice, Italy)—Fiction. 3. Child musicians—Fiction. 4. Violinists—Fiction. 5. Composers—Fiction. 6. Venice (Italy)—Fiction. I. Title.

PS3567.U285 V58 2007
813'.54 22
2006050988

ISBN 978-0-06-089053-7 (pbk.)

22 23 24 25 26 LBC 11 10 9 8 7

[D]uring the renovation of the Pietà as part of the observances of the tercentenary of the birth of Antonio Vivaldi, the Venice Committee of the International Fund for Monuments discovered a massive collection of documents relating to wards of the Pietà. The archive, in a chaotic state, was long believed to have been destroyed at the time of Napoleon's invasion in 1797.

—JANE L. BALDAUF-BERDES, *"Anna Maria della Pietà:*
The Woman Musician of Venice Personified"

AUTHOR'S NOTE

*T*ry as I might to make this book historically accurate, it is, by design, a work of literary fiction. Some small fragments of conversation between historical personages depicted here came to me by way of historians and memoirists of the time. The rest are the product of my own imagination.

—*BQ*

CHAPTER 1

ANNO DOMINI 1709

Dearest Mother,

Since I was first taught to dip a quill and pen my ABCs, I have imagined writing to you. I have written many such letters in my mind, and you have read them. They made you weep. With the power of exquisite music exquisitely performed, they called you back to this place to claim me.

Have I ever been in your thoughts, as you have been in mine? Would my eyes remind you of the infant I was when last you saw me?

When I happen on my reflection in a dark window, I am sometimes startled to see a young woman's face looking back at me. How much more surprised would you be to see the transformation wrought by Time?

Here, within these stone walls where you left me, I have grown like those plants that are cultivated indoors, with shallow roots and always turning toward whatever sunshine can be stolen from the day outside.

I have heard that children often resemble their parents. I have looked at my long-fingered hands and wondered, are they like your hands? Is my profile like yours? Do you have fair hair that seems not to belong with your dark eyes? Is there also a hunger inside them?

Until this morning, I had no hope that any letter of mine could ever reach you—nor any assurance beyond the promptings of my own imagination that you even lived.

Today all of that has changed.

Who you are, where you are—both are as much matters of darkness to me as before. But I pray to the Holy Virgin, even though I have never seen her. I play my violin for God, even though I cannot know if He has ever listened. Why can I not then write to you? Sister Laura has never, as far as I know, lied to me before. And today Sister Laura told me to write to you.

But I must explain.

On this one day a year, the figlie di coro—*the daughters of the choir, as both the singers and instrumentalists are called—are allowed to visit whatever blood relations on the outside are willing to welcome them. Girls look forward to it, plan for it, dream about it, and then spend the rest of the year hoarding every detail of it, like squirrels with their treasure of nuts, until the next year's visit comes around.*

Last year on this day, while servants beat rugs and shook out draperies, I sat beneath the arch of my favorite window, near the rooms occupied by the privilegiate *of the coro. The window affords a splendid view, through the iron grating, of all the life that moves upon the water below. I sat on the little bench there, in the silvery storm of dust that danced in the light, my arms wrapped around my violin. I heard and then watched Maestro Vivaldi climb the stairs.*

He has been my teacher—and one of the very few men who has ever seen my face or spoken to me—for nearly half my lifetime. I was only a girl of eight when, newly ordained as a priest, Antonio Vivaldi, native son of Venezia, was hired by the governors of the Pietà to be our master of the violin.

I can remember the day when Sister Laura brought me before him. Don Antonio sat in the sacristy unwigged, his hair as red as the branding irons they would use to mark the infants when they were left here—just like the one that marks me on my foot, a small, ornate letter P to designate a foundling enrolled at the Pietà.

"What's this?" Don Antonio asked. Looking up from the papers and quills that lay in disorder on his writing desk, he protested that he was hired to teach the advanced students, not the piccoli.

Sister Laura pushed me forward, even though, with all my heart, I longed to turn away and run. The color of his hair frightened me—it put me in mind of the flames of Hell. And the impatience in his voice bespoke a man who had no love of children.

But Sister Laura urged him to hear me play.

When I was done, he took the instrument from me and examined my hands, turning them over in his. He tipped my face up so that he could peer into my eyes, and it was then that I could see the happiness my playing had given him. He asked me my name.

"They call me Anna Maria dal Violin," I told him.

Sister Laura explained to Don Vivaldi that none of the foundlings is allowed to know her surname, if she has one. Many of the babies brought to the Pietà are sent out to the country after they are enrolled, to be nursed and raised by a foster mother until they return, at the age of ten, to complete their education. But I was one of those suckled by a wet nurse here (we still had wet nurses, nenne, then, who lived on the premises). My musical training was begun as soon as I was able to hold a violin.

I hoped she'd explain further, for my benefit as well as his. But she only stood there beside me, with one of her hands resting on my shoulder. That hand was trembling. Sister Laura was my teacher until Maestro Vivaldi came to the Pietà.

"Anna Maria dal Violin," said this red-headed priest. "You will be one of our fourteen iniziate, an apprentice musician in the coro. Work hard!" He turned back to his papers then, dismissing us with a wave of his hand.

I felt myself fill with happiness like the water that fills the empty bucket when it is dropped into the well. Sister Laura told me that she had never heard of an eight-year-old being made an iniziata. It would mean classes and rehearsals with the girls and women of the coro, *under the direction of Maestro Vivaldi.*

Imagine now, if you will, dear Mother, the passage of five years. A girl, unusually short of stature, is pulled and pinched like bread dough into a new shape and size. Thirteen years old, her eyes filled with tears, her heart filled with bitterness, she looks down from her solitary perch beneath the window at the unfamiliar sight of a priest climbing the forbidden stairs to the third floor.

I wondered if someone was dying. No men, not even the priests, are allowed on the third floor unless a girl requires Last Rites—and even then he must be accompanied by two of the governors. But I was the only one left here that day. Every other member of the coro *had somewhere else to go. I had the distinction of having no one on the outside willing to claim me.*

When he got closer, I saw that it was the maestro. It is not unusual for him to ignore the rules. But he had never broken this particular rule before. He walked toward me, searching through a sheaf of papers he had tucked in his robes. "Ecco!" he said, handing a page of music to me. He was breathing hard from his climb, and there were beads of sweat on his brow.

It was the solo part for a new sonata. The ink was smeared in places where his fingers had touched it before it had dried. There was a dedication inscribed across the top of the page: "Per Sig.ra: Anna Maria."

Before I could give voice to either my pleasure or surprise, Maestro Vivaldi had already turned and started back down the stairway. He paused at the first landing, looked up, and waved to me. I waved back at him. And then he crossed himself and continued climbing down, jabbering to himself all the while and humming beneath his breath as he does sometimes, sounding as mad as one of the inmates of the Incurabili.

I sat and studied the music, hearing the notes, as I read them, on the violin God put inside me.

Of course, I wondered if the maestro had actually composed this sonata with me in mind. Or whether, as an afterthought—perhaps at a whispered word from Sister Laura or one of the other teachers—he'd hastily written my name across the top of the page.

I decided that it didn't really matter. I practiced my part over and over again until I'd committed it to memory. Staring out through the grille at the gondolas going by, I played with all the feelings I found inside the music—feelings I hadn't been able to feel before when I sat there in silence, watching the people carried along to all the places people go when they live on the outside.

This year there was no new sonata to take my thoughts away from the other girls and all the delights awaiting them. The embraces of cousins, the special dishes cooked for them by aunts and grandmothers, the whispered secrets and shared tears. The person who would notice and remark, "How you've grown since last I saw you!"

I sat, as I always do, by my window. But I wasn't playing. I sat and stared down at the canal, and I felt wretched to be, once again, the only figlia di coro *with no one to visit.*

The other girls had no call to pass by my little bench at the window. But I could watch them as they twittered out from the dormitory and down the staircase in chattering groups of twos and threes, dressed in the red robes we wear whenever we perform or otherwise venture outside these walls—red for compassion, which is what the governors hope the sight of us will inspire in all who behold the foundling musicians of the Pietà.

Only Marietta bothered to seek me out and say goodbye—Marietta, who has, since last Easter and rather to my surprise, declared me to be her best friend. "Poverina!" she said in her sweetest voice, bending to kiss me. "Imagine, having no family at all!" Her pitying looks couldn't hide the satisfaction she feels in at least having a mother, no matter that Marietta returned with bruises up and down her arms after her visit last year. Some of the girls here have a mother or a father, but none that has the means or moral rectitude to raise them. Or, if they have the means, they still do not dare compromise their social position by claiming an illegitimate child.

I made myself smile until after Marietta had turned on the landing and waved goodbye to me.

When I found myself alone, the tears raced past my resolution.

And then I heard the rustling robes of Sister Laura. Although outwardly the same as those of the other teachers, her garments make a particular sound as she walks. I am convinced she wears a silken petticoat beneath them. I tried to wipe the tears away, even though I knew it was impossible that she had not already noted them.

Sister Laura looked straight into my eyes, as if measuring something she saw there. Then she told me to follow her.

I have followed Sister Laura up and down these stairs since the days when I was so small that I needed to use my hands to help me scale them. I walked behind her in the central pathway where the stones have been polished smooth, where the steps dip slightly, worn away by the footfalls of all those who have lived and died inside these walls.

We walked in the pale light of early morning, along the hallway that looks down upon the bacino, to the hidden hive of rooms where the teachers take their rest at night, locked behind a carved wooden door. In one of these she sat me down at a little writing desk, a pretty piece of furniture that looked out of place among the austere furnishings of the room—the small bed in its white clothes, a plain wooden washstand, and the walls unadorned except by a wooden crucifix at one end and an ancient-looking icon of the Holy Virgin at the other.

Sister Laura opened the desk and brought out an inkwell, a bottle of sand, a quill, and some paper. "Here," she said, smoothing the paper on the desk and placing the quill in my hand. "Write to your mother, Annina. Tell her of your life here and everything that is in your heart."

At the sound of her words, my heart raced like one of the maestro's most difficult passages. I asked her if she knew where you were—or who you were.

Sister Laura touched my cheek with her dry warm fingers, calloused from playing the violin for all the years she, too, has lived here. "God knows everything," she told me. "And He will make sure your letter finds its way to your mother's heart."

In truth, I didn't believe her. The Prioress reads every letter that leaves this place, unless it leaves by secret means. I've heard that the six months of revelry during Carnival are the best season for finding a visitor, safely masked in anonymity and willing to serve as courier for an uncensored letter passed from sleeve to sleeve through the grille of the parlatorio. But who knows how many of these letters reach the person to whom they are written? The intimate thoughts of cloistered virgins are said to be so prized by monachini, the men who find pleasure in courting nuns, that such letters are sometimes bought and sold. Well, we are not nuns, but we are kept from the rest of the world in exactly the same way.

Every letter vetted by the Prioress has passages blacked out that might prove an embarrassment to the Pietà. Many letters written *by the inmates here make a short passage from words to smoke in the hungry fire that burns most nights in the Prioress's office.*

No, such a letter as this one would never be sent. I looked at Sister Laura with new eyes, wondering if I had misjudged her all these years, taking her for one of those exemplary members of the coro *whose gravest infraction of the rules is the secret wearing of a silken petticoat.*

She simply looked at me, an unaccustomed fierceness in her eyes, and said, "Don't ask!"

And so I write to you, although I cannot know if or when or how this letter will ever reach you. When I try to imagine you reading my words, I see only darkness where your face should be.

There is a particular window on the second floor, at the turn of the grand stairway, where one can look out and see the scaffetta, the niche in the church wall where people leave their babies. Everyone always looks down when they pass, just to make sure the niche is empty.

Maestra Bianca—she is singing in God's choir now, but she was the one who looked down from the window on an autumn night some fourteen years ago, just after she'd said her prayers. As Sister Laura tells the story, the clouds parted long enough for moonlight to spill over their edges onto the canal and up onto the church wall. Maestra Bianca saw that the niche had something inside it. And just as she looked, the bell started ringing, the bell that people ring when they abandon infants there.

Maestra Bianca ran down the stairs in her nightclothes and told the portinara to unbar the door and light her way to the scaffetta.

And that is how I entered the Pietà—first stuffed into the wall of the church, like a swallow's nest. And then plucked out and carried upstairs by Maestra Bianca, her famous golden hair un-

loosed, shouting so that her voice echoed in every archway and corner, waking all the foundlings: "A baby! God has brought us another baby!"

But it was not God who brought me to the Ospedale della Pietà.

I have tried to imagine it a thousand times, tried to will myself to remember. When I close my eyes and get very still, I can feel the dip of the gondola as the gondolier holds your elbow and you step across onto land. Usually you are clothed in black like a proper Venetian noblewoman, and you are masked (as is the gondolier), because it is one of the months of Carnival. At other times, when I've been unable to sleep at night, you have been a washerwoman or a courtesan or a Jewess from the Ghetto who wished for a musical life for her child. Sometimes it is not your foot that dips the gondola, but the gouty foot of a cardinal shod in red silk. Or the clodhopper of a farmer's son, terrified because he has been in Venezia only once before and feels sure the gondolier is planning to rob him, hit him over the head with an oar, and drop him into the canal. Sometimes it is four brothers and five sisters, all younger than I am now, who pull back the cloth that covers my head. They kiss me, one by one, passing me from youngest to eldest so that in the end my face is wet with their tears, my family's tears.

Fourteen years ago, you held me in your arms and gazed down upon me. I like to think that you looked down on me with love, glad that I was born.

When I play well, I play for you. My greatest wish is that someday, at the end of a performance, I will see a beautiful woman rise up from the audience. (I always imagine you as the most beautiful woman there, even though I myself am not beautiful.) There are tears shining in your eyes as you hold out your hand to me. "Anna

Maria dal Violin," you say in a voice both sweet and low, "it is
time to go home."

The bells are ringing for Vespers. I will write to you again when
Sister Laura lets me. I will hold you close to my heart till then.

Your daughter,
Anna Maria dal Violin,
student of Maestro Vivaldi

CHAPTER 2

ANNO DOMINI 1737

*T*HE PRIORESS ANNOUNCED the governors' decision today: I've been named *maestra di coro*—concert
mistress and leader of the orchestra at the Pietà.

Would that I could reach out to my younger self, put my
arms about that desperate girl and whisper, "Anna Maria, *sii
coraggiosa*—be brave!"

Her letters—my letters—now yellowed with age, are spread
out before me on my writing table, a beautiful piece of furniture inlaid with rosewood and mother-of-pearl, commissioned
from a master of his craft by the Doge and given as a present to
me.

I haven't looked at them for a long time, these missives
spilling over with my girlish hopes and fears and needs. But
today, after the announcement at dinner, I took them out of
their silver casket lined with pale blue silk and untied the
darker blue ribbon their recipient used to bind them together
so many years ago.

I have in my possession not only the letters, but also the part-
book containing all the violin solos Vivaldi ever wrote for me:
twenty-eight of them, plus two for the organ. All are marked
at the top, "*Per Signorina Anna Maria*," with his notes scribbled
throughout and little changes we made inked on fresh scraps of
music paper, carefully stitched over the altered passages.

Sometimes he and I were the only ones who could play the fast sixteenth notes in the ledger lines. He would mark them, just for me—"*Più allegro che possibile,*" faster than possible. The book, bound in soft brown leather and stamped in gold with my name, is the only token I have of him. It is worth more to me than all the gold and jewels of any noble house of Venezia.

He treats me as a friend now and has even confided in me more than I would wish. But during my girlhood there was so much more that I wanted from him than he was ever willing to give. I craved his special notice—which, in all fairness, he often gave me. But I also wanted his protection from those who wished me harm—from la Befana and, in those days, Bernardina.

When the maestro was traveling, we were often given over to Maestra Meneghina, who had a moustache darker than Vivaldi's and hit us when we didn't play to her satisfaction. We called her la Befana, for the ugly witch who rides her broom to give either presents or lumps of coal to children at Epiphany.

I used to wonder at the incontrovertible fact that la Befana could not have come into the world as a bitter old woman, but must have been a young girl at some point, not all that differ-ent from any of my peers among the *figlie di coro*. It made me shudder to think about it—because if she was once young like me, then I could end up old and horrible like her.

Children are incapable of believing that they will ever really grow old. It's their special trick of believing only in the present. It's a trick I would love to learn to recapture. But old people, as far as I've been able to see from those around me here who are even older than I am—old people live only in the past.

I suppose I'm showing my age by writing these notes at all. The past! We are either dwelling in it or fooling ourselves into believing that we are still as young as we were then. Growing old still seems to me to be something that happens to others but will never happen to me.

Giulietta and I would talk about it sometimes—and we would always end up rolling on the floor, holding our sides, vying with each other to see who could paint the more horrific picture of the other's old age. But, really, when we were done laughing—as I looked at Giulietta's rosy cheeks and bright blue eyes—it was impossible to believe that any such horrors could ever come to pass.

One of our favorite pastimes in the dormitory was to act out a play in which a nobleman had come to ask for la Befana's hand, having fallen in love with the beauty with which she played her violin. (We knew she must have been among the best musicians of her generation to have been made a *maestra,* even though she never performed, and picked up the instrument only once in a while, and only then to demonstrate how to do right what she felt we had been doing wrong.)

The play had two endings. In one, la Befana and the nobleman swore eternal vows—and when she lifted her veil, demanding a kiss, he threw himself upon his sword. In the other version, the bridegroom caught sight of her face before the wedding and ran off with her best friend.

Whoever says that girls are kind has never lived among them.

La Befana saved her special wrath for me, although she only dared show her feelings when the maestro was away. Either I was playing with too much brio or not enough, too fast or else too carefully. There was no pleasing her. I never bowed my head, as the others did, when she railed at me, which infuriated her all the more. I didn't give her the satisfaction of seeing how she hurt me when she hit me with her baton. Never on the face or hands or arms, but always where the marks would be hidden from the world's eyes. I knew nothing then of the special reason she had to hate me.

Giulietta begged me to give in enough so that la Befana would leave off me. "It is a sin, Anna Maria, to be so proud." Giulietta was ever a true friend to me, pretty Giulietta who clasped her cello between her legs as if in practice for the lover who would eventually carry her away.

It was not pride, though, but anger that made me hold my head high, that kept my face frozen while la Befana beat me. I stared ahead of me and prayed to the Virgin to appear before us in all her glory so that my teacher would fall to the ground in fear and shame, hiding her pockmarked face from God. In my dream, the Virgin extended her hand to me—"Come, Anna Maria. The angels are weeping."

Sometimes it was not the Virgin but a veiled lady who would take my hand. I couldn't see her face, but I knew who she was. "Come, Anna Maria," she would say to me in a voice that I remembered as one remembers a lullaby unheard since infancy. "Come out from these walls so that all of Venezia can know who makes these heavenly sounds."

And then la Befana would hit me again.

If Vivaldi passed by on his way to the sacristy to get a new supply of quills or rest between lessons, he merely smiled and waved without really looking at us. "Play on, my angels!" he would call over his shoulder.

And I would ask myself, how can a man who notices so much when his own reputation is at stake—who can hear the smallest omission, the tiniest cheat in our playing—walk through the rest of his life as one who has neither ears nor eyes? How can a man whose music cracks open the hearts of all who hear it have so little room in his own heart for anyone apart from himself?

In those days, before the arrival of Anna Girò, his only allegiance was to his music.

Nothing was more important than his own ambition then. Even God had to wait His turn while Vivaldi composed. People still love telling the story about how he would abandon his place at the altar during Mass because some musical idea had struck him. He would leave all of us waiting while he hastened off to the sacristy to write it down.

This only had to happen a few times before the governors excused him from saying Mass altogether. It was an easy thing to find another priest to lead us in our devotions, but quite another to find a composer of Vivaldi's prodigious merit. From the first years when I thought to notice such things, I noticed that the governors seemed to value the musician without much liking the man.

We loved him, though. He was always by far our favorite teacher. There was no one's love and praise we craved more than his—perhaps for the very reason that he didn't give it lightly.

I've given much thought to this in my years as a teacher here. Vivaldi asked more of us than anyone else did. I think we were willing to work so hard—well past what we would do for any other teacher—because the maestro believed in our greatness. We *were* angels for him, heavenly messengers who delivered his music to the world.

The bells are ringing to mark the interval of rest before we carry on singing the Divine Office and once again preserve the Republic from the wrath of God. Venezia's sinners will have another day and night to go about their pleasures in peace.

A fire crackles in the grate here in my room—yes, at this point in time, my allotment for wood is always generous. And I have only to raise my eyes from my desk to gaze out upon the *bacino* and the life I no longer have any cause to envy.

Venezia—*la Serenissima*, the most serene—immortal that she
is, has hardly changed at all since the day when I wrote that first
letter. It is only when I look down at the map of my own hands
that I can trace time's passage.

How is it possible that so many years have gone by? How
can I have nearly reached the age of forty-two? When I chance
to see my face now in a darkened window, I can only wonder at
the identity—and the boldness—of the stranger who stares at me
with such a look of knowledge in her eyes, as if she were able to
see straight inside my soul.

Every time, that reflection fools me. I have taken to averting
my gaze from the windows after darkness falls. Far better to look
at all the fresh young faces round about me here than to com-
mune with my own decay.

No matter. My hair may be fading from blond to gray, and
my cheeks may be less plump and pink than they were before,
but my fingers still work well. I can still send a cascade of notes
heavenward from my violin—or, for that matter, from the cembalo, cello, *viola d'amore*, the lute, the theorbo, and the mandolin, as the writer of doggerel wrote in yesterday's *Palade Veneta*.
Six full stanzas of his silly poem were devoted to me, the self-
same Anna Maria who wept bitter tears twenty-eight years ago
because no one knew her and no one cared.

How many moments I stole from sleep to go searching
through the lightless passages of memory! But sleep always
overtook me before I had traveled far enough to find out what
I longed to know. It mattered so desperately to me then. Who
were my parents? Why had they left me here? And what sort of
life would I have if I found them?

The secret files of the *scaffetta* are filled with notes about each
baby who was ever placed in the niche of the church wall, down
to the last detail. Some of the foundlings are put there dressed in

velvet and lace, and others have nothing more about them than filthy rags. Sometimes a token is found in the swaddling clothes or clutched in a tiny hand, and it is always half of something: half an elaborate drawing or half of a rare coin or medallion—so that someday the parent who possesses the other half can come back and reclaim her child. It has happened only twice in all my time here, but it is something that every child of the Pietà dreams of and hopes for more fervently than they hope for Heaven.

The earliest memory I was ever able to grasp was before the time of speech, but well after I had been tucked into the *scaffetta* and left there. It was spring. I know it was spring because I could smell something wonderful, which only much later I learned to connect with the purple wisteria that scales these walls and hangs about these windows with a determination as great as that of any lover bent on wooing a virgin of the Pietà.

I can remember the sound of rain on water outside the windows that give on to the canal. It was definitely before what Maestra Emmanuela, the Prioress then, called the age of reason—I thought the music I heard came from the stones of the *ospedale*. There was always music, so I concluded, with a child's logic, that the stones could sing. Later, when I saw the orchestra, I thought the girls' bodies were part of the instruments they played. After all, they were part of their names: Beatrice dal Violin, Maria dal Flauto, Paola dal Mandolin. There were also girls without instruments attached to their names but heavenly sounds that issued directly from their bodies: Prudenza dal Soprano, Anastasia dal Contralto, Michielina d'Alto. I remember the moment when someone told me that, no, they weren't angels. They were girls made of flesh and blood like me.

Even after I had become an *iniziata* in the *coro*, my childish mind found much to distract it from the rigors of lessons and prayer. In all my classes with Vivaldi, I would ever marvel at the   ·

color of his hair—how it seemed to burn more furiously when someone played a false note or failed to play fast enough. *"Il Prete Rosso,"* everyone called him behind his back, as they refer to him even now: "the Red Priest."

Sometimes he would make us play so fast and practice so long that our fingers bled. When we held up our hands to show him, he only nodded and said, "Good. It is good to bleed for music. Girls shed blood all the time for far less noble reasons." We would blush when he said such things.

There were those who predicted that Vivaldi's red hair would bring him to a bad end. But I always believed in him as one beloved of God. Not because he was a priest—for, in truth, even then I knew that priesthood is more often a livelihood than a calling. I believed in Vivaldi's grace because he wrote music for us that was fit for God's choir.

He is still doing so. The choral music he's just lately begun to produce for us is, in my opinion, among the most celestial of his compositions—and most expressive of his nature, his real nature, which he keeps hidden from almost everyone. It overflows with the part of him that—quite apart from being a priest—truly is a man of God.

They come from all over Europe to hear us perform his music: poets, philosophers, princes, popes, and kings. We watch them trying to peer beyond the grille that shields us from their eyes, past the veils that make each of us appear to be, at least potentially, beautiful and young. They press gold into the hands of the Doge: "For the orphans of Venezia."

And gold I had in my hands without seeing what I held. Poor Anna Maria! If you knew then what I know now! If you could have but glimpsed the future, you would have found such comfort there. But my suffering younger self can't hear me, no matter how many words I scribble in this little book, nor how many secrets I reveal. I can read her words, but she can never read mine. She's caught in that past of hers, abandoned and alone.

ANNO DOMINI 1709

Dearest Mother,

Sister Laura says that I must try to calm my passions by writing to you. When I asked what I should write, she told me to tell you my history—because you would know nothing of me beyond whatever I wrote in my last letter. I told Sister Laura that if you had been interested in my history, you surely would have enquired about it before now or found a way to write back to me. I was sent to the Father Confessor then, and made to say a hundred Hail Marys upon my knees.

How can I believe in a mother who refuses me even the most basic comfort of letting me know that she lives? And yet wanting to believe that you do live—and that you are, somehow, listening—makes me willing to write. If there were even the smallest chance that these words will reach you, then wouldn't I be a fool to abjure writing them?

I am, if truth be told, calmer now, although it does not please me to be locked in this room while all the others are eating their supper. A letter—not just a hasty letter, but a long one, filling many pages—is the only key, I am told, that will unlock this door.

I am hungry—and so I will tell you of my history and my life here.

For the first five years after I entered these walls, I had only my given name, Anna Maria. I was schooled with the hundreds of other children of the comun. *The boys and girls take classes side by side until, at the age of ten, the boys are sent out to apprentice in a trade. The girls are kept here for further instruction as lace makers* and seamstresses, cooks, nurses, pharmacists, or maids, depending on their aptitude. The priests see to our souls, and our teachers keep us ever busy.

I liked my classes when I was a figlia of the comun. And I had good friends among the boys and girls my age. We were much given to mischief when our teachers weren't looking.

I certainly had no expectation of being plucked out of this crowd at the age of six to participate in classes with the coro.

In truth, I was astonished when a student teacher held me behind after Matins one day and told me to sing for her. Before I had sung more than a few scales and trills, she pulled me by my ear and brought me over to the clavicembalo, where Sister Laura had just finished teaching a class in solfeggio.

I was sure I was about to be punished. The other girls, all towering above me, smirked and whispered among themselves. After Sister Laura dismissed them, she took my face in her hand and spoke to me kindly. I remember how mild and calm her eyes looked, like the summer sky that shows above the courtyard.

She had me pick some notes out from the air with my voice, and then asked me to copy what she played at the keyboard. It seemed a delightful game to me—especially since I was apparently very good at it. Then she showed me how to hold my arm and my chin and placed a violin between them.

From then on, the instrument has been both part of my name and part of my body. It is my voice.

I have studied with all the sottomaestre—the student teachers. Only the best among the figlie di coro are allowed eventually to teach classes. And the very best among these—the privilegiate—are allowed to take on private, paying students of their own. Thus the lessons of Maestro Vivaldi are learned by all the string players here, even if only some of us are taught by him directly.

Most recently I have been working on the maestro's first concerto in the series he says he will call L'Estro Armonico. *He told us that only he and we will know that he has named it thus for the way in which this entire institution hangs upon the monthly moods and bleeding of its female population—l'estro, for the time when female animals are in heat.*

The maestro boasts that he can predict within a day when we'll all come undone with cramps and crying fits, because two weeks before, we always play with the most fantastic frenzy and fancy— our own version of l'estro, *as he chooses to call it. His eyes sparkle with wickedness when he says such things. And yet we know the maestro values our skill nearly as much as he values his own. Certainly because we are the only means by which his music can reach the ears of the world—and the music the world hears will only be as great as our performance of it.*

Unlike the internal teachers, who see us as their wards and treat us like children, the maestro looks at us first and foremost as musicians. I don't think he ever gives much thought at all to our age.

He has been pushing us especially hard to perfect our performance of twelve sonatas he recently finished writing. We are to play these on some as yet unspecified date for a highly exalted personage whose name the maestro refuses to divulge. To hear him speak, the entire future of his career as a composer—to say nothing of the future of the Republic—is in our hands. And we are lazy, and vain, and we laugh too much, and God will punish us if we don't play the music as it's meant to be played. The maestro prays and rails at us and then begs and cajoles us, and brings us sweets and pulls funny faces. But by the end of our rehearsal, he has more often than not squeezed the music out of us that he wants.

Yesterday, Bernardina—who is one of the best among the

younger violinists, despite her one blind eye—begged off rehearsal because of cramps. The maestro was in a froth of aggravation.

Taller than I by a handsbreadth, Bernardina delights in look-ing down on me—though I have twice won out when we have all been set to play against each other. Her freckled face turned bright red both times, and she looked as if she hoped that God would strike me dead.

I know that when my elders speak about becoming a woman they are speaking of this business of frayed tempers, cramps, and blood. It happened earlier this year to Giulietta, who is my best friend, despite Marietta's claims to that position.

I heard Giulietta's cries before I'd chased away the night's dreams. "I am dying! I bleed—oh, I am wounded!" I threw back the covers and both saw and smelled the brownish red blood on the bedclothes. Although I thought we had both been wounded, I felt no pain. And then I saw with horror that the blood was coming from between Giulietta's legs.

A few of the older girls roused themselves from their beds and then gathered round us with sponges and water and clean robes. "You are not wounded, Giulietta, you silly goose," they told her. "You are a woman now. Say your prayers and put these rags in your knickers!" They went away to breakfast, laughing and talk-ing as if this were something perfectly normal.

Pretty Giulietta, with her creamy skin and soft brown locks that curl all on their own, clutched her belly and said that she was sure she had been poisoned, because her insides ached so.

Every month now, Giulietta bleeds. She and all the other older girls and all of the women here who do not yet have hair on their chin. All of them bleeding at the same time. All of them, in the days just before their blood, scowling and short of temper and weeping without reason.

And all because Eve bit into that apple so long ago! I feel sure that if Eve had only a hint of the grief she would visit upon her daughters, she would never have allowed herself to be tempted to that first bite, but would have foresworn apples forever.

I do not look forward with gladness to my womanhood. Just last week, Prudenza—one of the older, prettier members of the coro *and one of the most celebrated sopranos of all the* ospedali—*was brought to the* parlatorio *of the orphanage for the sort of interview each one of us both dreads and dreams of.*

The parlatorio *is the great vaulted room where you would come to visit me, if you came to visit. It's much the same, I'm told, as the visiting room of any convent. Divided from the rest of the ospedale by a lacelike metal grille, it is our window to the outside world. We can see and be seen there, but touching is forbidden.*

Having learned that she had relatives at the convent of San Francesco della Vigna, Prudenza petitioned the governors last year for permission to take vows. None of us believed they'd let her go. She is a well-known singer whose presence accounts for the rental of many chairs at our concerts—and her beauty is so fabled that many in the audience come in hopes of catching a glimpse of her as much as to hear us perform.

The Prioress herself brought Prudenza to the visitors' side of the parlatorio through a secret door. There she was unveiled before a masked stranger, an obviously ancient gentleman with bent shoulders and silver hair.

The governors had decided to grant Prudenza's request. But then one of them—Signor Giovanni Battista Morotti—thought that perhaps he would offer the Pietà's star singer a different kind of veil. While this graybeard looked on from a distance, his entourage of female family members told Prudenza to turn this way and that, examined her hair, and even pried her lips open to look at her teeth before the gentleman finally bowed and thanked her.

We heard the whole story whispered in between mouthfuls, and interleaved with the day's sacred text, during supper. Yesterday the Prioress called Prudenza to her office and presented her with an offer of marriage from Signor Morotti. If she wishes to keep the dowry of two hundred ducats provided for each of us who marries, both Prudenza and her aged bridegroom—who is noble but not particularly rich—must give their signed promise that she'll never again perform.

I swear to you that I would sooner promise to cut off my hands. It is beyond my understanding how any one of us could make such a promise. Who will Prudenza be without her golden voice? How will God hear her?

Giulietta thinks my first blood is coming, and that is what gnaws at me. But it is the second movement of the maestro's new concerto that crawls through my belly like the serpent who tempted Eve.

After the maestro had shamed us with his talk of monthly bleeding, I made a solemn oath to the Virgin to learn to play my part with skill that would keep him from ever again speaking of us in the same breath as animals.

The first movement went beautifully well, the notes yielding, sweetening as my fingers found their hiding places and called them into the air. They followed my bow as if I were the leader of a great army of musician warriors: I made them sing.

That was the first three days, one blurring into the next. I only knew it had been three days because Sister Laura said I had better stop and do something else for a while. She urged me to come into the courtyard, where Signora Olivia's peonies have begun to bloom. The sun hurt my eyes. I did not want to smell flowers or play badminton. I longed to be inside the echoing stone walls again. I wanted to work on the largo.

Again, I felt the strength to fulfill my promise to the Virgin. It was as if my fingers, not my eyes, were reading the flurry of notes that danced across the page, scrawled in haste in one of the maestro's fits of inspiration. Only someone like myself, well used to reading his hand, could make out the notes from the blots of ink where he'd broken his quill.

Giulietta and I saw him composing this concerto in the sacristy. We had been spying on the maestro, because he is so odd and amusing to watch while he composes. He pulls his cap off and buries his fingers in his red hair and sometimes weeps as if it were as hot as its color and he were a martyr in the flames. He writes and writes, dipping his pen and wiping his eyes, a great stack of quills before him, the broken ones flying over his shoulder as if flying back to the birds they came from. He coughs, especially in the months of fall or spring, clutching at his chest with one hand while writing with the other. Then he stands before the clavicembalo, picking out the notes he has written with the most terrible look on his face, like a prisoner who is about to get a beating. And then something happens, something invisible to us but very real to him, by the look in his eyes. It is as if the invisible jailor has unlocked the chains binding the maestro to his prison walls. As if Christus himself has reached out His hand and touched the maestro's tears. He weeps again, but this time for joy. Then he picks up the violin, closes his eyes and plays.

Of course it is hateful to him if we do not play the music the way he has heard it, whispered to him by angels. The color drains from his face. He mutters things, terrible things, about fanciulle, virgin girls. How can a gaggle of cloistered virgins possibly understand music that springs from the loins of a man? We know it is a sin for him, a priest, to speak this way. And yet I know he speaks without knowing how he wounds us. "Virgins!" he shouts, looking heavenward and sweeping out of the room, his black robes like a storm cloud racing across the sky, bringing rain.

And there we are, the famous orphan musicians of the Pietà, not daring to look at one another. Ashamed that we have failed him yet again.

It was because of my solemn oath to the Virgin that I kept trying and trying to play the third movement, the allegro, as an angel might play it. An angry angel. I played until the pain in my bowing arm was so great that tears spilled out of my eyes. I saw them, like drops of rain, on the beautiful wood of the violin. I think it was Giulietta who went to call Sister Laura, who gently but very firmly unclasped my hand from the neck of the instrument and took it away from me. "But the allegro—I have not found it yet!" I cried, as mad as the maestro himself.

Again, I could not sleep that night, last night. There was the pain in my shoulder that kept me awake. But more than this, there was a sense of—I don't have any words to describe the sensations that kept me from sleep. Demons, perhaps. A sense of unworthiness so staggering that I could not keep myself upright under its weight. And yet I could not sleep.

I didn't touch the bowl of polenta that Giulietta brought to me from the kitchen this morning, even though she'd drizzled it with honey and cream just the way I like it. Sister Laura came in then and sat by me. She didn't say anything for a long time. Then she spoke in that voice I have come to know so well, as low and familiar as the bell of San Marco that signals the beginning and end of every workday for all those who live outside these walls. "Maestro Vivaldi composes some of the most difficult music that has ever been composed for the violin. You must not fault yourself if you find it difficult to play."

I started crying then.

She lifted my chin and made me look into her eyes, so blue and mild. "God himself would have trouble with that allegro."

Even after she let go of my chin, I kept my eyes locked on hers, looking for the secret thing that allows her to always be so steady and calm.

Oh Mother, if this letter has truly reached you, hear me! Would that I could ask for your help not in words, as clumsy and ugly as the flies that gather in the corners of the windows in summertime, but with the notes of my violin.

I write to you now a girl, still a girl. A virgin who cannot find the key to playing music that comes from a man's loins. Who cannot play the allegro.

I beg you to pray for me.

> *Your daughter,*
> *Anna Maria dal Violin,*
> *Student of Maestro Vivaldi*

I had an answer to my prayers that autumn. A new girl was brought to the Pietà—not an unwanted child, but a paying student from Saxony. She had excellent training and already played quite well.

Even now, there is usually at least one such girl every year, sent to board with us until she reaches the age of seventeen. They are not, as we are, bound for ten years to perform and teach in exchange for the charity bestowed upon us, and to train two replacements if and when we choose to marry or take the veil. For these students from the outside, the Pietà is only a way station on the road to an advantageous marriage and the production of heirs.

These girls bring with them a breath of worlds unknown to inmates of the *ospedale*, worlds where music is not necessarily at the center of one's existence. They come with their talk of fashion, families, and stolen kisses.

Claudia, as a violinist, was placed under my special care.

I taught her every trick I knew of the Italian style, helped her with her grammar, and acquainted her with our routine. But I was ever more her student than her teacher.

Although only two years older than I, Claudia was already womanly and wise in the ways of the world. I remember how it startled me to see how the maestro clearly took note of her bosom. I was uncomfortable thinking of the maestro—or any priest—as a man. I cannot say that I am overly comfortable with the thought now, even though I know full well that it is a fact of life. It is their very manhood that makes their vows of celibacy both necessary and so difficult to achieve.

It was Claudia who told me, in her imperfect Italian, how important it is to remember that all men—whether noblemen or beggars, priests or procurers—have the same one thing in common, to which they are commonly in thrall.

Shortly after her arrival, the maestro had one of his fits of temper, during which he tore at his hair and wept at the innocence that keeps us from playing with the passion demanded by his music. I looked over to see how Claudia would react. To my surprise, she sat there with an enigmatic smile on her face, looking well satisfied with herself.

That night was particularly cold. Most of us were sleeping in twos, as was our wont in wintertime, even though, the year before, we had each earned the right to our own bed. I was just drifting off, with Claudia's arms wrapped around me, when she whispered into my ear.

"Anna Maria, I can teach you the secret of this passion your maestro wants you to feel."

My eyes were still half closed with sleep, and sleep had come only with difficulty because of the cold. "I am a virtuous girl," I muttered, resentful at being wakened.

"And you can remain one. I promise you! Your virtue will

be unsullied. But you will bring your maestro great joy." She propped herself up, leaning back on her elbows.

I turned to look at her. "You speak in riddles," I said crossly. Even though the darkness was impenetrable, I could sense Claudia's smile.

"Here, let me show you!"

"Show me? Here? In the dormitory?"

"There is no better place."

She sat closer still, speaking in little more than a whisper. "Every woman, Anna Maria—and every girl—has a secret place on her body. If you stroke it in just the right way, it makes the body quiver and make music like the strings of your violin."

I lay back down, angry to be mocked in this way. "Go to sleep, Claudia! We need to be at our best for the rehearsal tomorrow."

She shook my shoulder. "Which is exactly why I am telling you this tonight, Annina."

"Don't call me 'Annina,'" I said. I thought about how I used to believe that the music made by the *coro* came from the girls' bodies. I couldn't guess how this Saxon witch came to know of my childish folly.

"Look." She pulled me upright again. "Here, do what I do."

My eyes by then had begun to grow accustomed to the darkness. Claudia positioned herself as if playing the cello, her knees splayed. "It's here," she said, reaching under her nightclothes. "You have one, too. It's like—I don't know the word in your language." She took her hand out and then cupped her other hand around her finger, pantomiming a bell. "The little piece that makes it ring. Can you find it?"

I reached under my nightclothes. How was it I'd never noticed before? When I touched it, it was exactly as if I were a violin. I felt the touch of my fingers vibrate in every part of my body, but especially the tips of my breasts and the arches of my feet.

I saw that Claudia had closed her eyes. I did the same.

"Can you feel it?" she asked me.

"Yes," I said, gasping a little, because my breath was suddenly labored, as if I'd been climbing stairs.

"Stroke it just as you stroke the strings of your violin, Anna Maria dal Violin."

"The strings of my violin don't grow wet when I stroke them."

"Think of the sonata we're playing tomorrow—of the allegro. And when we're playing the allegro tomorrow, think of this!"

I could not answer her. The urge to keep stroking was suddenly larger than everything else, so large and so loud that everything else disappeared. I forgot where I was; I forgot *who* I was. There was only the urgent need to—I knew not what. And then—oh, blessed Mother of God—my body rang with the joyful force of all the bells of *la Serenissima* on Easter morning.

It was as if I'd fallen into the sea during a storm and been washed up on the shore, half drowned, half dead, but like one who has seen the face of God.

When I woke the next morning, I wondered if it had all been a dream. But there was Claudia sitting over me, smiling her little catlike smile.

I smiled back at her.

"Don't forget to think of it while you're playing today."

"I will think of nothing else!" I assured her. "I must tell Giulietta. She must think of it while she is playing her cello today!"

I told Giulietta (and drowned in that sea again in the telling), and I think Giulietta must have told others in her turn.

When we all gathered for rehearsal, it was a pale-faced, fever-eyed group of girls who faced the maestro. "What's this?" he muttered. "Have I misread my calendar?"

From the moment we began playing, it was clear to all of us—but most of all to him—that everything had changed. We played with brio. We played with passion. We played with urgency. We played so that we were panting at the end, and I would not be surprised if some of our bells were ringing.

The maestro lowered his hands and stared at us with disbelief. "I'm dreaming," was all he said at first. And then, with an expression of rapture filling his eyes: "How did this happen?"

All of us just sat there and smiled with the same little half-smile that Claudia wore.

CHAPTER 3

I SIT HERE holding my next letter, the first one written from jail in the depths of that famous winter of anno
Domini 1709. If Sister Laura had told me to write to the Virgin
herself, I would still have poured out my heart to her, so desperate was I to have someone—anyone—hear my cri de coeur.

Casting myself back in time, I think the real beginning of my
life of trespass was that winter night when Marietta and I sat
on the cold stone floor between our two beds, our nightgowns
pulled over our bare feet.

I was fourteen and had not yet seen my first blood. Marietta
and I were both keeping half an ear open for Sister Giovanna,
who was patrolling the halls as the *settimaniera* that week. I
whispered, as loudly and harshly as I dared, "You're completely
pazza!" Marietta had taken it into her head that she would
become an opera star. But, of course, opera was then and is still
forbidden in every cloister of Venezia.

With a voice that spanned three octaves, Marietta could move
up and down the scale so lightly and quickly that a flea would
seem ponderous by comparison. She had the rose-petal skin, in
those days, of a Botticelli angel, and the devil's own fire in her
eyes. Dressed in velvet and taffeta, draped in jewels, her pretty
little feet shod in silk, she was made to be Venezia's favorite
prima donna. She knew this, and it was burning a hole in her
heart.

I reminded her that she would not be allowed to perform in

an opera without foreswearing her home at the Pietà, as well as her dowry.

Marietta's eyes are still as green as the most sluggish canals of Venezia at the height of summer—and sometimes just as full of poison. She made them bore into me, there in the half-light of our dormitory, as she said that she would foreswear both in an instant for the chance to sing on the stage.

In the rest of the room beyond us, the other girls were sleeping and snoring. Marietta managed to make her whisper sound like a clarion call as she announced to me and whomever else might be listening, "I must see and hear a real diva sing—in a real theater!"

Even a commoner's *bollettino di passaporto*, in the pit of the theater, cost a third of a ducat, which is more gold than girls our age then could save over months of stinting ourselves. I asked Marietta how she—a cloistered *figlia* of the Pietà—proposed to lose herself in such a crowd, with agents of the Grand Inquisitor everywhere, impossible to recognize or run away from. Did she think she would just sit herself down among gondoliers and thieves and knaves and all manner of men who would see her as nothing more than a rare and delicious comestible?

I reminded her of the veritable war at the Ospedale dei Mendicanti over whether the cloistered musicians could perform an opera there. The Mendicanti's governors merely censured the choir nuns who advocated in favor of opera. But then one of the most outspoken among them—one Sister Justiniana, herself renowned as a soprano and mentioned by name more than once in the *Palade Veneta*—was, to the great scandal of all Venezia, fished out of a well.

I asked Marietta to think of poor Sister Justiniana.

She gave me that superior look of hers, and shook out her curls. "What I'm thinking of has nothing to do with any nun!"

Someone called out from her bed, "Will you two please shut up? We're trying to sleep!"

Marietta dragged me out into the hallway. The wick of the oil lamp on the wall was smoking, and the smoke cast weird shadows around us. "Tonight—it must be tonight!" she whispered, leaning so close that I felt her lips on my ear. "That new soprano from Napoli is singing at the Sant'Angelo—the maestro told me."

Although I was—I have to admit—a little afraid of Marietta then, I planted myself squarely in front of her and crossed my arms. I asked her how she would find her way to the theater, even if she did manage to get out.

"Unlike certain people who have spent their entire lives inside this crypt, I can make my way around Venezia, thank you."

I assured her that she would never be able to pass there undetected. The maestro—who was performing then as a soloist in the Sant'Angelo's orchestra—would find her out in an instant and see that she was brought back and given a good beating.

Marietta expressed her opinion—which I largely shared—that Vivaldi cared little enough about the rules. Her words awakened in me the resentment I felt about the latest rumors circulating, that the maestro had begun composing an opera in hopes of having it staged at the Sant'Angelo.

As *inserviente della musica*, we were his servants, too—vessels always ready to be filled with the holy oil of his musical fantasies. Why would he spend his talents on others—and others, at that, who worked not for the good of the Republic but to fatten their own purses and flatter their reputations?

Marietta understood Vivaldi and his ambitions much better than I did then.

She turned the full grace and charm of her looks upon me. "I will persuade him to write us an opera disguised as an oratorio—

one that will be so magnificent that the theaters will sit empty while people flock to hear us. And then the governors will change their rules. But I must have a chance to study these divas first, and learn their ways."

"And will you fly out these walls on the wings of a dove?"

"Matteo's rheumatism is bothering him tonight."

"What does this have to do with you?"

"Signora Bettina will resume her post as *portinara* when the bells ring for Compline. We can leave when Matteo leaves."

"We?" In the silence that followed, I could hear my heart pounding with the noise of a kettledrum.

Matteo was a hugely fat old man who had started his life as a foundling of the Pietà. He was said to be too feeble-minded to be placed as an apprentice, and so continued on here, performing tasks that no one else wanted to do. The regular *portinare* of the *coro* called on Matteo whenever they grew tired of sitting hour after hour, guarding the door.

I thought of the oft-rehearsed dream of my mother appearing before me, extending her hand, inviting me to leave. It took me a moment to find my voice. "How?"

"Under his cloak."

I'm sure my face reflected the disgust her proposal inspired in me. Matteo looked like he may have bathed once or twice in all his years, but at no time recently. He kept stale crusts of bread in the folds of his robes, as well as hunks of dried fish that he chewed on while sitting on his stool in the doorway. We all believed him to be almost completely deaf. It was said that he was allowed to work among us for this reason, because he would not be tempted to lust by the beauty of our voices.

"I would sooner be carried out with the contents of our chamber pots!"

"That's the trouble with you, Anna Maria, living your whole

life here as a hothouse flower. You've never known the stink of life on the outside."

I tried to look as much unlike a hothouse flower as I possibly could. "The canals stink horribly in summertime."

"That's not the same."

Marietta knew whereof she spoke. Her mother had worked in the dankest alleyways of San Marco, sometimes as a chambermaid, sometimes as a whore. One day when she was sober enough to see clearly, she noticed how men had begun to look at her eldest daughter, who was earning bread for them both by singing in the perfect musical venue formed by the vaulted spans of the Rialto Bridge. That's when Marietta's mother took her to the board of governors, and had her sing for them. They offered to take her in at the Pietà, even though she was already so old. They would clothe and feed her and pay her dowry, if she served out her ten years and trained two others to take her place.

Marietta wept and wailed without stopping for the first week she was at the *ospedale*—she was put in a room by herself so her cries wouldn't keep the rest of us awake, but we heard her anyway. She cursed her mother's name, and then she begged the Virgin to make her mother change her mind and take her back again. Even the worst family is better than no family at all. That's what Marietta never tired of telling me during her first years here—until she decided to make a friend of me.

I looked into Marietta's jade-colored eyes, and I could tell that she knew from the start I would agree to go. She gave me a kiss on the cheek, I suppose to show me how glad she was I'd given way to her. That girl gave out kisses like a queen scattering coins.

I clutched at her arm, more to steady myself than out of affection. She shook my hand away, done with charming me. "There are two woolen cloaks under my bed—get them, and wait for me at the bottom of the stairs. I have an errand to do in the kitchens." She turned and scampered off, leaving me alone in the hallway.

I thought of abandoning her to her foolish scheme and simply tiptoeing back to my bed and climbing under the covers. And yet I was also filled with curiosity and excitement at the prospect of such an adventure. I let myself believe that perhaps, with all her knowledge of the world, Marietta could make this happen in such a way that we could go and return undetected.

I had quite convinced myself by the time I slipped back inside through the darkness of the dormitory, feeling my way along the cold marble floor.

The air was thick with the exhalations of the fourteen girls who slept in our room, each one floating in the murky stuff of her own dreams. I got down on my hands and knees and swept my arms under Marietta's bed till my fingers found the rough wool of the cloaks.

It never ceased to amaze me how Marietta was able to make things work for her that worked for no one else. Woolen cloaks were closely guarded and hard to come by. But then I remembered having seen Marietta more than once in conversation with Maestra Andriana, who was the *dispensiera* that year, in charge of all our supplies. A theorbist as well as a singer, Andriana was one of the nine *cariche* among the eighteen *maestre* entrusted with the most delicate tasks of responsibility at the Pietà.

It was rumored—and now I know that it was probably true— that Maestra Andriana had been imprisoned for misdeeds when she was younger. I can say from my own experience here that the Pietà's prisons have often been the nurseries for its leaders.

I gathered up the cloaks and then stood in the shadows of the doorway, looking up and down the hall and peering as best I could down the stairs before venturing out again.

Shrinking into a shadowy corner at the bottom of the stairs, behind the balustrade, I waited for Marietta. Finally, after what seemed like hours, she emerged from the passageway to the kitchens and larders, carrying a bottle of wine and what looked like half an uncooked turkey under her arm.

"If we're caught," she said as she thrust the wine into my hands, "I'll lie and say that I made you come with me."

"As well you did," I murmured—but she was already halfway down the portal stairway, as fleet of foot as she was of voice. I had to rush not to be left alone in the hall with the stolen cloaks and wine.

There were torches burning in the portal. Matteo's fat face lit up when he saw us. "Ah!" he sighed, but whether he sighed after the victuals or Marietta, I couldn't tell. He pressed his finger against his lips and beckoned us to join him in a dark corner.

And then—in truth, I feel sick with the memory—he lifted up his voluminous robes, settling us under them with the little shakes and sounds of contentment of a mother hen.

It was all I could do not to drop the wine. The odor of the uncooked fowl was overpowered by the most intimate smells of Matteo's body—not just the smells of elimination and sweat, but another, terrible odor, previously unknown to me, which I knew instinctively had to do with his manhood. I shrank from it as I shrank away from the most noxious sores and pustules in the hospital on the days when we were made to tend the beggars there—days that were fewer and farther between as I rose in the ranks of the *coro*.

"Matteo!" we heard Sister Giovanna's voice trumpet from the stairs. "Where are you?"

Apart from la Befana, Sister Giovanna was the worst of our keepers when it was her turn to patrol the halls at night. All the choir nuns of Venice, of course, come from the ranks of the nobility. But some have a religious calling, whereas others are given to God against their will. Sister Giovanna was one of these, interred here by her parents so that they would have sufficient funds to marry off her younger, prettier sister to another of Venezia's noble families. It seemed to be Giovanna's purpose in life to make others suffer for the injustice visited upon her.

"Did you call me, Reverend Sister?" said the doorkeeper as he began to shuffle out into the room.

"Are you ill, Matteo?" She was much closer now. We could see her bulky shape silhouetted through the brown cloth of the doorkeeper's robes.

"It is my rheumatism, Reverend Sister. I can hardly move."

"It is no wonder, Matteo. You have grown so fat!"

"The pain is always worse when it rains," he whined. "My sister-in-law has made a poultice for me. But Signora Bettina will sit tonight and keep the angels safe."

"God keeps the angels safe, doorkeeper. Your job is to keep the angels in." I had never before heard her speak of us in this tone, as if she spoke of felons rather than angels.

The bells began tolling in the same moment that we heard the tap of Signora Bettina's stick on the flagstones. Although Signora Bettina was nearly blind, I was sure she would nonetheless see us beneath Matteo's robes. She used to tell us that her stick had an eye upon it that could see even through walls—and then she would point it at us and narrow her eyes, so that we always felt naked before her.

"Ah, there she is now," said Matteo, patting his clothing so that his hands fell upon our bodies. "Goodnight to you, Reverend Sister! And to you, Signora—and may God bless you both!" There was the sound of the door being unbarred, and then we felt the rush of cold air as it was opened and Matteo continued to shuffle out into the night with us holding on, by necessity, to his hairy legs.

He was surprisingly agile for such a large man. "That's right, my poppets," he murmured when we'd crossed the threshold. His robes ballooned in the wind, sheltering us from the rain.

"Can't we get out now?" I pleaded with Marietta.

Much to my surprise, because I'd spoken in a low murmur, Matteo answered, "Not yet—the old bat will be watching from the window until we reach the embankment. Stand closer to it, Marietta—there's a good girl."

It was a great confusion in that noisome place beneath Matteo's robes. But I saw how Marietta, while holding tight to the turkey drumstick, shoved herself up against the doorkeeper's fat thighs. I felt the shiver that ran down his folds of flesh. I have, I told myself, died and been sent to Hell for my sins.

As soon as we turned the corner, Marietta flung his robes aside and we burst out, gasping, into the storm. Matteo's face was suffused with a look of ecstatic torture, his eyes rolled back and the whole of him trembling like a leaf in the wind.

Marietta thrust the turkey into his arms, wiping her hands on the front of his robes, which were wet from the rain. Much more tentatively, I handed him the wine.

Putting up the hood of her cloak, Marietta looked him up and down and then spat. "I will not thank you, Matteo, as it is you who are in my debt now!"

*M*arietta knew the way so well that I wondered how many times she had already left the *ospedale* under Matteo's robes. We had no torch, and there was no moon because of the storm. In fact, we were not much more noticeable

than two brown rats would have been, scuttling from one alleyway to another and through the greater darkness and momen-
tary respite from the rain of a covered passageway. The wind
howled and the rain soaked us, seeming to come up from the
ground and down from the sky at the same time. I was so utterly
lost that I could not have found my way back to the Pietà if my
life had depended upon it (which well it might have if Marietta
had decided, in one of her moments of supreme selfishness, to
abandon me). I clung to her with all the force of my fear.

It was easy to stay in the shadows, for there were only shadows. Despite the weather, there were people abroad in the night,
mostly merrymakers, all of them masked, their torches smoking in the rain. We huddled down into our cloaks and walked as
quickly as we could, although it was hard to see.

We were far from the Grand Canal then, in a district that
seemed inhabited principally by cats, rats, and noxious
smells. Marietta dragged us into an alleyway and pounded on
a disreputable-looking door. She had to pound and shout for a
long time.

Some ladies—I use the word guardedly—leaned out of a window above. When they saw no one but two poorly dressed girls,
they emptied a pot of slops that landed not an arm's length away
from us, then shut themselves in again, ignoring Marietta's
curses and cries.

I had heard tales of errant maidens who were drugged and
stolen away only to wake in a harem of Arabia, there to be robbed
of their virtue by a dusky infidel with hundreds of wives. In the
past I'd dismissed these tales as fables designed to frighten us
into obedience. But now, as Marietta pounded on that door, I
sensed that I may have made the greatest error of my short lifetime.

At length, the door opened and a horrible hag appeared before us—a witch with a toothless mouth and eyes that gleamed yellow in the darkness like a cat's. I crossed myself. Her clothes were rags; she reeked of spirits. Holding a candle up to our faces, she laughed then turned to lead us inside.

"Come!" Marietta said as she urged me into the passageway.

"I won't!" I cried. "You are the most wicked girl I have ever known!"

"Don't be an idiot, Anna Maria! There's nothing to be frightened of."

I turned to run, but she and the old hag held on tight to me. When I started to shout, one of them covered my mouth. I tried to bite, but was soundly slapped.

"What's wrong with her?" rasped the old woman.

Marietta answered through gritted teeth, "She'll be fine. Just get her inside!"

They pushed and shoved me down a dark passage and through another door and into a chair. After barring the door, the creature threw her loathsome arms around Marietta.

Marietta suffered herself to be embraced, and even kissed the wretched creature. My face streamed with tears and I asked myself how many gold ducats I'd been sold for to put this Judas with dimpled cheeks and lustrous curls in such a loving mood. Finally breaking away, Marietta said in the humblest tone of voice I'd ever heard her use, "Anna Maria, I would present to you my mother."

Suspended halfway between relief and horror, I ducked my face and mumbled some polite words. When I stole another look at the wretch, I could see something of Marietta's verdigris eyes in that face that otherwise seemed as different from hers as a privy is from a throne.

Marietta was also scrutinizing her, but with a look of expectation. "Well? Do you have them?"

"Of course, of course I have them, *figlia mia*. Somewhere ..."
She looked about uncertainly. Her room, lit by the light of a single candle, was the filthiest I'd ever seen. Following her unsteady gaze, I saw that some of the bundles stacked against the walls and both on top of and under the furniture were children, all of them apparently in the profoundest slumber.

"So little I ask of you!" Marietta burst out.

The poor wretch picked at a sore on her head, examining the blood on her finger and then licking it absentmindedly. "*Ecco!*" she cried out, as if the taste of her own blood had restored her powers of recollection. "Here they are!" She moved a child (who stirred but didn't wake) and rummaged in the pile of clothing that made its bed, handing Marietta two lumpy sacks, each held together with a length of rope.

Marietta undid first one and then the other, dumping their contents out onto the floor and cursing in a manner she would never have dared use at the Pietà. Each sack contained a none-too-clean set of men's clothes—not a nobleman's raiment, but the most common sort of garb: leggings, a tunic, and thick shoes. Marietta was shaking with wrath. "You drunken fool! You thief!"

"Marietta, my pet—"

"Two ducats! Two gold ducats!"

The old woman gestured around the room. "I have many mouths to feed."

"And an endless thirst!" Marietta began to weep. "They were to be women's clothes! Proper clothes!"

"*Pace, bella!* You and your young friend will be much safer dressed as men. And look—look, my pet! I bought you these!"

She rummaged in another pile, moving yet another apparently unwakable child. "Here—look at these beauties!"

She held up two masks of the type the Jews of Venezia are supposed to wear when they go abroad during Carnival, with noses as big and pendulous as the bananas I have seen on the vegetable barge passing by. Others also wear them—as a joke, I suppose—during the months of merrymaking.

Marietta, quite beside herself, stamped her foot. "I have never hated you more than I hate you now!"

"Hush!" I urged her. "It is your mother to whom you speak!"

"Would that I had no mother!"

The canny woman clutched at her heart and groaned.

"What now?" said Marietta. But I could hear the concern behind the coldness in her voice.

Steadying herself against one of the more precarious pieces of furniture, Marietta's mother stumbled, sending a child, in the process, tumbling from its perch with a cry. She shouted at it to be quiet. Then, making sure she had our full attention, she recovered her balance and spoke in a voice overflowing with the tender strains of self-pity. "I take comfort knowing that my requiem, at least, will be well sung."

Marietta laid her head on her mother's breast that seemed so in need of laundering, and shook with sobs.

"I spent the money on medicine, *carissima*."

This was too much even for Marietta. Raising up her head, she said, "You spent it on drink, old liar!"

And suddenly both mother and daughter burst out laughing.

Marietta noticed me then. "Come change your clothes, Annina! Why are you making that face at me?"

Marietta tugged a set of clothes on and tucked her hair under the hat that came with them. "There!" she said, stuffing her own clothes and shoes from the *ospedale* into the sack.

I was so relieved to know that I wasn't to be sold into slavery. It was with a light heart that I did as Marietta did and changed my clothes. "You're much too pretty to be a boy," I told her.

"And you, Annina. If I were not a boy myself, I would fall quite in love with you."

I put the mask on. "Kiss me, then!"

In the commotion that followed as we chased each other around the room, several of the children wakened and began to cry.

"Now see what you've done! Go back to sleep, you naughty beggars! You have a long day ahead of you tomorrow." Marietta's mother, who had fully regained her strength and vigor, hustled us out the door.

"I'll have my ducats, old whore!" Marietta just managed to shout before the door was closed in our faces.

The wind and rain, before ending their duet, had put a hard, bright polish on the stars. I watched one fall but took note too late to wish upon it. Marietta, raised to be so much more alert to opportunity than I, had closed her eyes and whispered a prayer while I was still adjusting to being out in the night again. She looked so funny in her costume. But, then, I imagine I looked equally droll.

"Are they all your brothers and sisters?" I wanted to know.

"Brothers, sisters, cousins, and a few strays she's picked up here or there."

"How they sleep!"

"She works them hard. Believe me—I know!"

"How can you bear it, Marietta?"

She looked at me, shaking her head with an irony intensified by the leering look of that horrible mask. "How do we bear any-thing? How can I bear having such a mother? How can you bear not having any mother at all? We are alive, *bellina*—and I for one intend to make the most of it!"

CHAPTER 4

*M*ARIETTA PULLED ME ALONG through the sparkling night, our heavy shoes ringing on the cobblestones. There were more people abroad now, and the streets were full of their laughter and snatches of song.

The farther from her mother's abode we walked, the less certain Marietta seemed of her way. We twice passed a sign that read, CALLE DELLA MANDOLA, but I failed to see even one almond tree. When I asked Marietta about it, she laughed at me. "*Mandola, bambina*, for the shape of a woman's sex. Those are the only almonds to be found in this part of San Marco."

As a group of men came up behind us, she pulled me into the shadow of a doorway under another sign that read, CALLE DELLA CORTESIA, and I was able to understand then without Marietta's help that this was a district of courtesans and their transactions. From the safety of the shadows, Marietta raised her mask and looked around. I could tell she was lost. "*Terra dei assassini*," she read out loud.

"For the love of God," I said, "where have you brought us?"

She led me away from that place, onto an alleyway that ended suddenly on a canal, beneath a sign that read, RIO DI SAN LUCA. We flattened ourselves against the gritty stones of a building as first one gondola and then four others glided by, filled with laughing people dressed in masks and evening clothes.

"I knew it!" said Marietta. "They're on their way to the theater."

"It could be any theater! And unless you plan on swimming there, we cannot follow them. Ask someone the way, Marietta! How can you be so stubborn?"

"All right—*pace!*" She pulled me into the shadows again. "But we must choose with care. Any one of these people might be a spy."

Of course, she was right. The agents of the Inquisitor were then, as they are now, notoriously clever in their disguises. "What about him?" I whispered, pointing out a passing juggler who seemed at least to be young. He was scurrying along with his head bent low, walking as fast as he could without running. I reasoned that a spy would be walking more slowly and looking carefully about him. And it also seemed to me that a juggler—a real juggler—was bound to know where the theater was.

Marietta cleared her throat. "My friend, good evening!" she sang out in a voice well below her normal range.

The juggler looked like he was about to jump out of his skin. "What ho!" he said in tones that sounded as strained as Marietta's.

I didn't dare open my mouth, but dug at Marietta's ribs with my elbow. "The Teatro Sant'Angelo!" she said in a voice that started out as the girl she was and ended in a fake even deeper than the first one.

The juggler walked close up to us, looked us up and down, and then suddenly lifted Marietta's mask, whereupon she covered her face with her hands. But then, with a laugh, the juggler lifted his mask as well.

"We *are* well met," said the fair girl beneath it. She was as lovely as a painting, all creamy skin and rosy cheeks. "Here," she whispered, "come away from the light!"

Once safely in the shadows, I lifted up my mask and we all three had a giggle together. "What ho!" Marietta said several times, in her best imitation of a *basso profondo*.

"But, seriously," said Marietta, quieting her own laughter, "whoever you are and whatever your business may be, do you know the way to the Sant'Angelo from here? We took a wrong turning..."

"I know it well—my family has a box there. And, as it happens, I am passing that way."

"Will you guide us then?" I asked her.

"I will do so gladly, but only if you swear a solemn oath to tell no one you saw me."

We stood in a tight circle. "We swear. *Giuriamo!*" Marietta and I both said at once.

"It must be a solemn oath," said the girl, who was perhaps a year older than Marietta and even prettier, although I hadn't thought such a thing possible.

"What can we swear by?" I asked her. Neither of us wore a cross, ornamentation of any kind being strictly forbidden at the Pietà.

The juggler opened her tunic and laid bare one of her round white breasts with its rosy nipple just catching the moonlight. "Do as I do!"

Marietta and I looked at each other. Then we each unbuttoned our tunics as well. The juggler put her hand on Marietta's breast, Marietta put her hand on mine, and I put my hand on the juggler's.

"Giuriamo!" we all said at once. "Now say," the juggler added, "'if I tell anyone of this meeting tonight, may my breasts grow as withered and brown as prunes!'"

We exchanged another look, sighed, and repeated the juggler's words. Then we all hastily put our clothing and masks to rights again.

"Follow me—we're not far!" The juggler took off at a smart

pace in a different direction than we had gone before. Looking over her shoulder, she added, "I am to be married tonight!"

"Or so he has told you," said Marietta—and it was an odd sight hearing these words pass between a juggler and a Jew in the nighttime.

I had heard more about the strange encounters of Carnival than I had ever seen: senators dressed as washerwomen, ladies dressed as sultans, lovers hidden together in the folds of a single silken robe.

The juggler stopped at Marietta's words. "He would never lie to me!"

"Wouldn't it be more prudent," I hazarded, catching up so that I could speak the words quietly, "to marry with your family's blessing?"

"My father would have me marry his old business partner! I would sooner drown than give my virginity to him!"

"And this other?" asked Marietta.

"We knew from the moment he first came into my father's house that we were destined to love one another."

"Men will say anything."

The juggler waited for Marietta to catch up with her. "You are far too young to be so sour. Do you believe in nothing?"

"I believe in the oath I swore," Marietta said without stopping. "And I believe that men—even good, godly men, even men with the eyes and lips of angels—will tell lies in the service of their loins."

We all paused in the shadows under a bridge to catch our breath. Marietta lifted her mask again. "Marry your father's friend and then keep this boy as your intimate companion—your cicisbeo. His name can be written into the marriage contract, *cara!*"

Even now it amazes me how much knowledge Marietta had of the world. How did the daughter of such a mother as Marietta's come to know about this ultra-refined practice of the aristocracy, the cicisbeo—the wife's official lover and best friend, sanctioned by her husband's family? But Marietta's fine ears were ever attuned to more than only music. If she had been a boy born into a noble family, she would surely have become a senator or a judge. "Spare your parents' hearts," she advised the bride-to-be with the sagacity of a lawyer, "and spare yourself a lifetime of suffering and privation!"

"I will never suffer as long as he loves me!"

As impressed as I was with Marietta's worldliness, I envied this girl for being so much in love. The most I had ever done was sigh in secret over the beautiful body of San Sebastiano in the painting that hangs in the West transept, wondering what it would be like to kiss those places where the arrows puncture his perfect skin. Such thoughts always sent me running to the confessional.

I lifted my mask, lifted the juggler's mask, and planted a kiss on those rosy lips. "Then may he love you forever!"

"Amen," said Marietta, although I heard both pique and impatience in her voice. "Which way now?"

The juggler bride turned and pointed. "There's another little bridge after this one. Cross it, then take the first turning to the left. It will open into the *campo* of the theater."

"*Grazie mille!*" I told her. "And may the Holy Virgin bless your love!"

"And may Santa Cecilia look down upon you both tonight, and keep you safe!"

"*Addio!*" we all said at once, clasping hands. Then she continued on her way to meet her lover, while we set off to find the second bridge.

I wondered how it was that she had thought of invoking the patron saint of musicians. I was about to ask Marietta's opinion on the matter when the narrow passageway opened out onto the square and we saw the throng of men and women there, surging up the stairs, talking and laughing, and buying refreshments from vendors who hovered about the place with their wares.

There was a shrunken Gypsy fortune-teller in conversation with a giant, who bent down low to hear his fate from her. Perched at the top of one of the booths was a monkey sucking on a lemon and screaming at the people below. A baker on stilts circulated with his tray piled high with delicious-looking cakes and buns and *biscotti*. A Turk was selling coffee, and a woman with a limp was selling flowers. A man with a net on a long pole slung over his shoulder proclaimed to anyone who would listen that he was equally good at castrating cats and brewing love potions.

I had seen crowds of people before, but usually in church and from the vantage point of the choir lofts, where we peek out through the grille upon our audience, well above them and safely apart. Here, though masked, we were right in among the press of bodies—nobles and merchants, courtesans and clerics, and common Veneziani who, as everyone knows, love music more than any other people in the world.

We were almost at the doors where people were handing over their tickets before being let through. "Now what?" I asked.

"Keep your mouth closed and stick close to me!" Marietta took my arm as we were pushed up to the ticket taker.

"Allora?" said the fellow, holding out his hand and wriggling his fingers. "Hurry up, you Hebrews—if that is what you are. Have you not heard of the curfew for your kind?"

"Sir!" said Marietta, bowing low. I did the same. Her man's voice was more convincing this time—or perhaps I had merely grown used to it. "We have an urgent message for Maestro Vivaldi."

"What business has the Red Priest with the Ghetto?"

Marietta leaned close to him and said, "Believe me, sir, when I tell you that the maestro is highly concerned with this business and will take the greatest interest in our errand!" She rubbed the fingers and thumb of one hand together in front of her face, then dropped it suddenly, perhaps fearing that the smallness of her hand would give away our disguise.

But she need not have worried. It was a theater, after all, a place of illusions.

People were pushing behind us and began to shout for us to go through or else depart. The ticket taker looked at the sacks we carried, little guessing that they contained nothing more than the clothes of two convent girls. "I see," he said, lowering his voice to a whisper. "Has he lost all his money at the Ridotto, then? Ah, there's no respect in the world anymore. Come in with your moneybags—and be quick about it!"

We waded into that sea of silk and rain-soaked woolens: the brightly colored breeches and cap scarves of the gondoliers, with their white shirts and billowing sleeves, and ladies wearing velvet skirts as wide as a doorway. Every face was hidden behind a mask. "How in the world did you know what to say?" I whispered.

"A lucky bit of improvisation."

"Perhaps your mother chose our costumes wisely after all."

"Ha! That was a lucky bit of improvisation as well. Although I would give the contents of my bank account for a silk dress, a petticoat, and some pretty shoes tonight! Look at all the grandees who are here!"

There were many finely dressed people, both Venetians in their black costumes and foreigners in their brightly colored capes and gowns, all bedecked with jewels and feathers. "Come—let us find a place in the pit while we can."

We spotted two unoccupied stools and made for them. Marietta pulled me through a channel she parted with her elbows. I didn't dare open my mouth to excuse our rudeness. But underneath the mask I blushed with shame.

Still, they were good seats, and close to the stage.

The audience was so different from what we had been used to at our concerts in the church, where scandalous things no doubt went on, but with at least some pretense at keeping them hidden. Here there was every sort of scandalous behavior in full view. Men sat in clumps together, gambling over games of dice and chess. Young noblemen escorted beautifully got-up ladies of the night, with their naked breasts on display. There were old women hawking oranges and sweets, and the pips and skins of these rained down upon us from the boxes above, along with gobs of phlegm coughed up by foreign diplomats unused to the dampness of our city, and men with pedigrees too fine or pockets too deep to be bothered with using a handkerchief to catch the remnants of their winter colds.

The spit rained down and extinguished the candles people were using to read the libretto. Both men and women in the audience seemed to be vying with each other to see who could make the most ludicrous noises. Someone was clucking like a hen while someone else, in another part of the theater, was snorting quite convincingly with the sounds of a pig.

Although his red hair was well hidden by a snow-white wig, we spotted the maestro as soon as we were settled on our stools. He was unmasked, and it was clear from his expression that he was suffering a solo performer's usual agonies of self-doubt. He seemed to look right at us for a moment, wrinkled his nose in distaste, and looked away.

"Ha!" said Marietta at my side.

By then the crowd was stamping and shouting for the program to begin. A gob of spit landed on the back of my hand. Marietta hissed at me to be quiet when I cried out in disgust.

"Dio!" she breathed as a great buxom diva floated out onto the stage and the audience burst into ecstatic applause. "Oh, will you look at her!"

Although dressed in the costume of an Oriental slave, the singer made no pretense of matching her manner to her clothes. Even though the opera had not yet begun, she alternately bowed and held her plump and heavily bejeweled arms out wide to receive the tributes of the audience. A volley of flowers attached to, presumably, love notes and laudatory poems rained down upon the stage. In the middle of all this, a dark-skinned woman, who didn't seem to be part of the production, scurried forth from the wings to gather up the tributes in a basket and then scurried off to the other side, to the hoots and cheers of the men who sat with us in the pit.

The opera's composer walked out into a storm of applause. And then the music started and the curtain parted, revealing a set so rich and clever that the audience gasped and then cheered even louder. The diva, looking most annoyed at the shift of attention away from her, stood there tapping her foot and fussing with her wig of waist-length black curls.

Finally the audience calmed down. The diva collected herself and began to sing.

In the Carnival season of anno Domini 1704, the governors arranged for the *figlie di coro* to visit the opera. I was so young that my memories of it became entwined with the stories everyone told about it later on, until I could scarce sort out the reality from the dream. For all of us, though, it was an experience that awoke the most intense emotions. Several of the girls ended

up in the infirmary suffering from hysterics afterward, so great
was the impression that performance made on them—and the
experiment was not repeated. But tales continued to be told and
musical phrases repeated and scenes acted out by candlelight in
our dormitories over the years. Opera—both the music and the
event of going to the opera and being seen there—was the setting
for many an orphan's most delicious fantasies.

Although now I know that the diva of that evening's performance at the Sant'Angelo was probably a second-rate singer
compared with those who sang at Venezia's bigger theaters, she
seemed like no less than a goddess to Marietta and me. We had
never heard anything like this before. The agility required for
the trills and tremolos was very much like music created for the
violin. But whereas Vivaldi was always urging us to make our
instruments sing with human voices, here was a human voice
that sang with the intricacy and ornamentation of a violin.

We had never been given the chance to perform such music,
apart from the secondhand and half-remembered versions we
sang in our nightgowns. Old Gasparini—our *maestro di coro* and
Vivaldi's boss then—worn down by our begging and cajoling,
found ways to smuggle certain elements of opera into our sacred
oratorios. But these were still only a pale shadow of a real opera,
as I now saw. The costumes! The scenery! The strutting and pos-
turing of the singers!

I tore my eyes away from the diva to look at Marietta: she was
trembling. We had both lifted our masks to see better—but then
I shut my eyes so that I could more fully comprehend the sound,
undistracted by the diva's popping eyes and glistening teeth
behind which her tongue flicked like a snake in its cavern.

I was roused from my dream by a fight that broke out among
some gondoliers sitting behind us. And then a chess piece went
flying by my nose, hitting the back of the head of the man sit-

ting in front of me, who leapt up and waved his fist to a flurry of imprecations. I lowered my mask, but not before another man—this one sitting hard by me—reached out and pinched me on the cheek, making kissing noises. He said in a gravelly, garlicky voice in my ear, *"Una bella mozzarella!"*

I turned to Marietta and saw that she'd not only let her mask drop to the floor but had half-unbuttoned her tunic as well, exposing her neck and much of her shoulders. Her lips were parted and her eyes glittered. Her hand, when I touched it, was icy cold. She flicked my hand away as if it were a fly, never removing her gaze from the diva.

And then another scribbled tribute, this one weighted, it would seem, by a rock rather than a flower, hit the singer on the foot during the final note of her aria. Everyone could see her stop singing and shake her fist in the direction of the missile. And yet her note—an impressive A above high C—still shimmered in the air with ever more beauty and force and even more passion than before.

The audience laughed and cheered, and I looked in horror at Marietta, who had taken up the abandoned note and stood now, eyes closed, singing it with a sweet and shattering volume.

The diva stopped swearing, squinted into the footlights, and then opened her mouth in great embarrassment to take up the note again.

In the instant of recognizing what Marietta had done, I retrieved the cast-off mask and shook her arm, urging her away.

She opened her eyes like a sleepwalker who wakes to find herself in a strange place, far from the safety of her own bed.

"Oh *Dio!*" she groaned. "What have I done?"

I felt a heavy hand on my shoulder and turned to see two of the Inquisitor's officers. Marietta tried to put her mask and hat back on, but, of course, it was far too late.

"A nice bit of pastry here! Should we take them back to the Ghetto," said one of the guards, "or take them to jail?"

"Leave off your joking," said the other. "Can't you see they're scared out of their skins?"

I let my own mask fall, covered my eyes, and hung my head in misery and shame.

"Oh, come on ducky," the first guard said in a completely sympathetic tone. "The padre said we're to get you back to the orphanage lickety-split."

I shot a look over to where Vivaldi sat in the front ranks of the orchestra. He merely raised his eyebrows at me, but I saw an expression of humor there. In fact, he looked like his old self again.

Marietta blew kisses at the audience before the guards led us off to the water entrance of the theater, where a gondola was waiting.

I had never been in a gondola before, although I had spent my life watching them from my window. I was so entranced with the sensation of gliding silently along the canal that I didn't give any thought to the punishment that awaited us. I couldn't stop looking at the stars. It was as if the celestial blue of the Virgin's robe were showing through pinholes pricked in the black velvet sky.

I know the nighttime well now. But I have never ceased to be entranced when I find myself beneath the starry sky. In the state I was in that night—filled with the sounds and sights of the opera—the stars seemed too magical to be part of the real world. I gazed at them and thought I must be dreaming.

On Feast Days, when I was still a very young child, I walked through Venezia in sunlight and rain with the other boys and girls of the Pietà, all of us in our red robes, invoking the saints and singing psalms. One of the Sisters walked at the front, ringing the bell and calling, *"Per pietà!"* while a child—a pretty one was always chosen—held out the alms basket to every passerby.

Once our bodies began to grow womanly enough for gondoliers to throw us kisses and mutter compliments as we passed, we were barred from going out.

Of course, I had stared at the stars and moon from my window, but then I had seen only a scrap of all the glory I now beheld above my head, framed by the silhouettes of the *palazzi* along the Grand Canal.

The sky on a clear night is a living, pulsating thing. The stars are like musical notes turned to light, and, like notes, they shimmer and swell and fade and fall. The painters have never captured it—but they never will until some painter teaches his colors to dance.

When I stole a look backward at the gondolier, he winked at me. They are sworn to an oath of silence in their profession. None of them will ever give up a secret he has overheard while plying his trade, whether it concerns love or murder. If I ever run away from the Pietà, I told myself, I will do so in a gondola.

We arrived at the water gate of the orphanage all too soon, and only then did I think with dread about the consequences of what we'd done. Girls had been demoted from the *coro* to the *comun* for far less serious infractions. I pictured myself in one of the workshops, making lace or spinning silk for the rest of my life instead of making music, and I hated Marietta then. I hated her for what she'd made me do, even while my heart warmed to her for giving me one of the most wonderful experiences I'd ever had.

One of the guards had a fat tip—no doubt, courtesy of the Red Priest—to give the *portinara*. Maestra Bettina was nowhere to be seen by the time we'd climbed out of the gondola and stepped across the threshold. I wouldn't have thought that these guardians of our portals—always the oldest and most pious and often the meanest among our keepers—could be bought. But of course I've learned since then that all people have their price.

Barefoot and unmasked, Marietta and I ran up the stairs and through the dark hallways. We tiptoed with the utmost caution past the snoring form of Sister Giovanna, who sat propped up in a chair, perhaps dreaming of the life she might have had if she, instead of her sibling, had been the better favored of the two. We threw off our men's clothes and pulled on our nightgowns. Then, exchanging a glance but without a word, we stuffed the clothes given to us by Marietta's mother through the grille of the window. We could just hear the splash as they dropped into the Rio della Pietà and the evidence of our adventure was carried away to sea. I smiled at Marietta, feeling for the first time that night a bond of true friendship and a surge of respect for her.

My head no sooner touched my pillow than I, too, was sucked down into the obliterating waters of sleep, till I felt a hand on my mouth and woke to see Bernardina looking down upon me with her one good eye and the other with which she always swore she could see the future.

"Not a sound!" she whispered. And then, slowly, she pulled the covers down and pulled my nightgown up. The moon had set by then, but I'm sure she could still see all of me in the light from the stars and the faint glow from the sconce in the hallway. Her eye gleaming, she reached down and touched the almond of my sex with one long finger of her free hand—just a quick touch, as if it were hot. Then she smiled and put my clothes and my blanket to rights again.

I pushed her hand away from my mouth.

"Hush!" she said.

"Leave me be!" I hissed at her.

Bernardina was still smiling. "I saw what you did, the two of you—the going and the coming—with this eye," she pointed at the one that was sighted, "and with this eye." She pointed then at the one that was blind. "Guard well your place as the maestro's favorite, *bell'Annina mia!*" She looked at me then with such unguarded hatred that had she possessed a knife, I'm sure she would have plunged it into my heart.

But her hands were empty, and she smiled again. "Sleep well," she said, leaving me staring wide-eyed into the darkness, feeling more afraid—and more alone—than I ever had in my life-time.

CHAPTER 5

ANNO DOMINI 1709

Dearest Mother,

Clearly I need your guidance, for it seems that I am forever incurring the wrath of my keepers.

I had to crack a thin layer of ice in my water jug this morning before I could quench my thirst. It is, they say, the coldest winter in a hundred years.

La Serenissima has been transformed, frozen in time as surely as I am stuck here in jail. The canals and even the lagoons are all turned to solid ice.

Before this winter changed the view from our windows, I never thought about how Venezia, though made of stone, is a city in which even the most solid things are always in motion. The pink and gray marble buildings break into an infinitesimal number of shimmering blocks of color on the surface of the water. And that same shimmering movement is reflected in every windowpane, while the gondolas dart back and forth like swallows.

The view from the larger windows—from my favorite window— is so familiar to me that I can see it simply by closing my eyes.

I wish I could see outside now onto the water. But the one window in this cell is far too small and set too high in the wall for me to see anything but a patch of gray sky.

The water is moved by wind and tide. The stones of the Church and the fondamento and the distant tower of San Giorgio Mag-

giore move together and apart again across the waters in a mad dance of reflections. Nothing in this city, no matter how steady and solid it would seem, is ever truly still.

Oh, to write and write and never receive an answer! All these words. Do you ever read them? Do you live? And if you live, where do you live, and why do you hide yourself away from me? Do you look out upon this winter? Are you so cold that your fingernails have turned a pretty shade of blue? Mine have, and I can hardly write for the stiffness in my hands.

Once, in the hospital here, I tended a blind beggar woman. There were two milky white lozenges where the blue or green or brown of her eyes should have been. The ice sits in just the same way—dully, impenetrably—on the canals. Venezia, that queen who loves nothing more than mirrors, suddenly cannot see. Worst of all, she cannot see herself. And we, the foundlings of the Pietà, have been unable to play music in the presence of all that stillness, as if the notes themselves have been caught and frozen midair.

There has been such excitement over the condition of the canals. On the first day of the great freeze, girls didn't get out of their night-clothes or go to breakfast, but stacked themselves like prayer books in the windows, feasting their eyes. Much to our delight, three of the kitchen girls emerged out on the ice wrapped in cloaks and wearing masks. They slipped and slid, their arms outstretched, their faces lifted upward.

Using her elbows to make room among us at the window, la Befana crossed herself and said it was a scandal. But we cheered anyway when one of the girls fell on her bottom and slid between the other two, who tried to stop her so that she spun round and round like a weather vane in a windstorm. We pushed and shoved to get a better view when, miracle of miracles, we saw someone drive a car-riage across the Grand Canal, pulled by four white horses.

We begged to be let outside. But the dispensiera said there

wasn't enough warm clothing at the Pietà to keep everyone from catching their death. And then we shouted like a lot of five-year-olds, "We will run to stay warm!"

We'd given up our pleas by the time the maestro came for our rehearsal. His cheeks and nose were as flaming red from the cold as his hair. He'd brought a porter with him—a big strapping youth who was also red in the face, but for altogether different reasons, finding himself face to face with the famous girls of the Pietà. In the wicked mood we were in, we teased him. My friend Claudia, a boarding student from Saxony, wrapped herself up to the eyes and then let her scarf fall slowly from her shoulders. The young man was so discomfited that he placed the two cello cases he carried down on the floor and fled before collecting his fee. The maestro rubbed his hands together—though whether from greed or cold, I do not know—and said, "Good work, Fräulein." Claudia bowed.

The maestro looked upon us then with a supreme expression of mischief in his eyes. "These are very special instruments, angels, procured for you at great personal cost!" He opened the cello cases—and you'll never guess! One was filled with Carnival masks, the other with an assortment of woolen cloaks. We shrieked with pleasure before he hushed us, looking back toward the passage-way and lowering his voice. "Do you think I'd allow them to keep you locked up here on this glorious day, this once-in-a-century moment for la Serenissima, when she has been vouchsafed the knowledge of a fourth season?"

His face was radiant as he handed out the masks and cloaks, calling each of us by name, and choosing, it seemed, our masks with special care. Mine was the one called Winter. "Listen to the way it feels!" he whispered as he first held the mask before me and then allowed me to look through its eyes. "The cold and the wind, the ice under your shoes, the way the silence roars. Listen and remember!"

Matteo, who had been guarding the door, was nowhere to be

seen (and I suspect he could have been found at some tavern or other, spending the maestro's coins). Masked and cloaked, we ventured out the door two by two, holding hands, followed by the maestro, who was wearing the big-nosed mask of the Joker.

The cold—how can I describe the cold to you? For a moment, it was like falling into the canal: the sensation of it touched every part of us, pressed against us, as if looking for ways to get inside our bodies. We were too astonished to run around, but merely stood there watching our breaths transformed into little puffs of smoke, as if we were not girls in masks but small fire-breathing dragons.

Don Vivaldi in his silly mask ran among us then, urging us down the stairs, which were fiendishly slippery. Even the algae that covers them was glazed in ice. I've never felt so awkward before—and never did merely walking seem such a hazardous business to me. There was a good deal of hesitation among us, and shrieks of alarm every time someone lost her balance and grabbed at the air or the girl nearest to her.

The maestro held under his arm what looked like a rolled-up animal skin. "Careful, children—no broken bones, please. Crawl on your hands and knees if you must. But be brave—it may be another hundred years before Veneziani can walk on water again."

We all made our way out onto the canal, holding on to one another and trying to keep our feet under us. The maestro flung the leather skin onto the ice, fur side up. "Here—sit upon it! You and you." Two of the girls sat down on the skin, pulling their cloaks around them, so that they looked like two otherworldly birds perched on the ice. The maestro, who was far more adept than we at staying upright, pulled the skin this way and that. And then he let it go so that it slid with the girls upon it, screaming with laughter, their hands and feet in the air. "This, my angels, is what children do in wintertime. Mind your fingers, you string players—keep them under your cloaks!"

And thus we played till, despite the frigid air, we felt warm all over and our cheeks were blazing. Some of the bolder among us swooped across the ice, sliding on our boots and letting the maestro catch us in his arms on the other side.

He was more the Joker than himself, it would seem. After my turn, when he caught Claudia, he lifted her mask and kissed her, pulling her so close that her back arched like a sapling in a strong wind. It happened in an instant, so that I almost doubted the truth of what I saw. And then I looked up at the window from where la Befana had been watching before: there she stood. I prayed that she had blinked in that moment or turned away.

I wish I had not seen it myself. It does not seem right that the maestro, creator of such heavenly music, wears boots that are as soiled as those of any other Veneziano. I remember well what Claudia told me about all men, even priests, and their earthly preoccupations. But the maestro is made of different clay—I am sure of it. He plays with the world in the same way we play our instruments, to coax from it the sweetest harmonies, the most graceful flights of fancy. And surely there is both grace and sweetness in Claudia's smile. Perhaps the maestro was like a bee that, finding itself so close to a flower, could not keep from tasting its nectar.

Soon afterward he herded us all inside again. We were all sweating underneath the woolen cloaks. Our teachers clucked and complained, and upbraided the maestro for exposing both himself and us to the cold. He went off coughing, but with a smile on his face. The cooks wrapped us in blankets warmed by the kitchen fire, gave us broth for dinner, and then sent us to bed.

I lay awake for a long time, thinking about all I'd felt and seen. Knowing that the maestro would be standing at the clavicembalo, transforming the sensations of the cold, the excitement, and even the kiss into music. And knowing he'd reserve the most difficult and expressive passages for his instrument and mine.

What I would do for one of those heated blankets now!

The next morning, half asleep, I thought I felt his arms around me. And then I woke with a start, and realized that it was Claudia who embraced me.

I turned and saw that she was also awake. I tried to imagine her married, with a horde of children—with a grand house and servants, jewels and silk dresses, and a husband who might be years older even than the maestro.

Claudia let me rest in her arms while my thoughts drifted. I think I had just fallen asleep when she spoke to me. "I know where I came from," she said in a very soft voice, as if speaking to herself. "And I know exactly where I will go and what I will become. But you, Anna Maria—you have a special destiny in this world."

If only I knew how to unlock this destiny of mine!

I wish I could turn now to see your face and feel your hand upon my shoulder. Your eyes would be my book of answers.

I pray for a warm blanket, a window to the world outside, and the end to all illusions. I pray for light.

Your loving daughter,
Anna Maria dal Violin,
Student of Maestro Vivaldi

An end to all illusions! I lived by illusions, mixing them with every mouthful of bread, every bite of meat, every sip of wine, and every measure of ink I used to write those letters.

In the week before Epiphany of that year in which my life would change forever, Vivaldi unveiled his plan to dedicate the new set of violin sonatas to King Frederick IV of Denmark and Norway. This was the grandee the maestro had told us about without, at first, divulging his name. But now it was common knowledge—even among the cloistered *figlie* of the *coro*—that the king was traveling incognito in Venezia as the Duke of Olemberg.

It was an odd thing in the season of masks for him to be traveling thus with one identity hidden inside another. It puts me in mind of those nesting Russian dolls Rebekkah used to carry with her to distract the youngest girls while they waited their turn to be measured and pinned for their choir robes. What seemed a solid, elaborately painted doll could be worked open along a hidden center line; and there was another, perfectly painted doll fit inside her. Work this one open, and there was yet another—and so forth, until there was the tiniest doll at the center, no bigger than a bean.

We gave a grand concert in honor of the masked duke that held a king inside him—and I wonder now what sort of bean there was at his center.

Vivaldi so inflamed us with his desire to please the king that we played better than we ever had before. It was a joy to see the maestro's face suffused with love for us when the so-called duke announced his intention to pay a second visit to the Pietà—and this time, he said by way of his messenger, he hoped to hear us play in a more intimate setting than that afforded by the church.

King Frederick was not the first rich, powerful, or otherwise famous man who was judged to merit a command performance in which we were neither hidden behind the grille of the choir lofts nor veiled like little brides of God. Some of the governors themselves were complicit on occasion in thus bending the rules. But this time, Vivaldi acted on his own. Intent on dazzling the king's eyes as well as his ears, he selected a small group of us from among the youngest players who would still make a good musical impression. Some of the most accomplished instrumentalists of the *coro*—women well past their youth who were nonetheless at the height of their virtuosity—did a good deal of what I now see to have been justifiable grumbling.

But Giulietta, Bernardina, Claudia, and I were bursting with our own good fortune. Giulietta was lovely in all ways, as well as being a fine cellist. Bernardina, my rival throughout those years, was tall and slim and had pretty hair. Her one blind eye would not be noticeable if she was placed (as Vivaldi was careful to place her) at an angle. Claudia, as a *figlia di spesa,* was not even a member of the *coro.* But the king was not privy to such fine distinctions. She was a good enough player, and her youthful beauty had long before caught the maestro's eye.

Marietta was sick with envy, and regaled us in the dormitory with her curses of the maestro for not having written an oratorio instead so that the singers—especially she—could share in this opportunity to shine before such a person as the king of Denmark and Norway. Marietta was not alone in believing that if she could only be heard and seen at the same time, she would be plucked out of the *coro* and made a princess.

Maestro Gasparini provided us with oratorios with the same workmanlike regularity with which the *dispensiera* provided us with shoes and hose. But Vivaldi hadn't yet written any of the choral music that now fills these halls and thrills the people who come to our concerts.

The ambitions of individual *figlie* of the *coro* were certainly not among his preoccupations. His only goal at that time was to make himself shine in the eyes of the king. A patron of such wealth and stature could save the Red Priest from ever having to worry about money again.

Determined to control every last detail of our upcoming performance, he brought in his father, Signor Giovanni (a barber before he became a regular violinist at San Marco), to cut and coif our hair. Since of course there were none of our signature pomegranate blossoms to be had at that time of year, one of the maestro's sisters, Signora Zanetta, prepared sprigs of holly for our hair instead. God knows where she got them, but the effect was charming. When we nodded or laughed, the bright red berries trembled—although one had to be careful not to prick oneself on the leaves.

We played well. Bernardina and I both went out of our way to try to outplay each other—and, in fact, the maestro had chosen his E-flat sonata, which features a sort of duel between the two solo violins.

When we were finished and had taken our bows, the king declared himself besotted with the *figlie di coro*.

"Vivaldi," he said in the most affected voice imaginable, "I cannot possibly go to my next engagement without these angels in my entourage."

The king walked among us then, touching a cheek here or a shoulder there. Bernardina kept her gaze on the ground. We were all of us flushed from the effort of playing.

But the king was the picture of sangfroid. Beneath his curls, which were more elaborately coiffed than any of ours, his fleshy face was powdered a bluish white. Just below his right cheekbone, he wore the beauty spot that coquettes among the nobility refer to as "the saucy." Over the years, more than one member of the *coro* has shown up for a performance with a beauty spot stuck to her face in one place or another—there's "the man-slayer," "the passionate," "the rakish," and the "majestic," which is stuck smack in the middle of the forehead, between the eyes. I can't imagine anything sillier, especially as our faces—except on the rarest occasions—are always hidden when we perform.

After taking his tour, the king waved one of his heavily beringed hands in our direction. "My dear Vivaldi, can't you do something," he drawled, "so that they might accompany me?"

If the maestro had bowed any lower, he would have turned a somersault. He kissed the largest ring of the so-called duke, as well as the hem of his robe, as if he had been the Pope himself. "There are no rules that cannot be broken for your Grace, and there is nothing these angels won't do to please me." He leered at us then, so that we all moved back a step or two. Vivaldi could be quite disgusting when in pursuit of a powerful patron.

But the king took it all in stride. "Very well, then, Padre. Let us all hasten to the Palazzo Foscarini. But, wait—"

He looked at us more closely then, seeing for the first time, I think, the plainness of our red robes, which had been mended and washed a hundred times. Bernardina put her hand over her bad eye. The king peered with sad distaste at the sprigs of holly in our hair, and the fresh red berries seemed to shrivel beneath his gaze.

And then a smile lit his features again. "Never mind!" He clapped his hands, and half a dozen liveried servants appeared, surrounding him and bowing low. The king gave the grandest one among them instructions, and he in turn gave instructions to the next grandest, who minced orders at those below, all in French—which I suppose is considered to be the world's most elegant language. It is spoken, I have been told, as far away as the royal court of Russia.

A trunkful of jewels and another of silken garments materialized as if out of the ether. The rustic holly was stripped from our hair and replaced with strands of pearls. Our carefully mended robes were whisked away without regard for our modesty, replaced by corsets, crinolines, and frocks of the finest lace and silk brocade, all in shades of ivory, pink, and pale gold. Another trunk held the most delightful dancing shoes, cunningly fashioned of silk and velvet in the latest mode. There were enough shoes and of sufficient variety to accommodate all four of us. We were too busy swooning over these objects of fashion to mind being remade.

My heart, for one, was pounding at the prospect of not only attending a ball but perhaps being allowed to dance there. Claudia, our great ambassador from the outside world, had been teaching us all to dance by the light of a stolen candle beyond our bedtime. My longing to test myself with an actual man, rather than a girl in her nightdress, had been keeping me awake at night.

Finally, the king's majordomo opened a silk-lined silver chest to reveal richly jeweled Carnival masks, each one worthy of a princess. There must have been premeditation in this, although, at the time, I and all the others were quite happy to accept it as a miracle.

When we were thus ranged before him, the king nodded his approval. "Everyone shall wonder from what royal court I have absconded with these lovely ladies." We giggled and curtseyed as he left the concert room, and then looked at one another to marvel more fully at our transformation.

All four of us served as mirrors to one another as we turned and struck poses and admired ourselves covertly in our admiration of the others. It was all very much antithetical to what we had been taught about modesty and humility and behavior befitting a girl charged with the moral safekeeping of the Republic.

I felt that I had truly stepped out of my own body and into another. Every fiber of my being was excited by the secret trove of possibilities held by the night, as if the doors of life had suddenly been thrown open and a red carpet rolled out to receive us.

The maestro ordered some of the king's servants to stay behind and guard the passageway till we were all safely outside. But when he'd turned his back, I could tell that they were sneering at him and at us, as well. Perhaps their sensibilities were offended by the thought that we might be the children of beggars and whores. I have since learned that servants are ever more snobbish than their masters, living in constant fear, I suppose, of being exiled from the rarefied world vouchsafed them by their position.

But who could say that we did not belong in these rich garments? Giulietta was rumored to be the illegitimate daughter of a senator and one of Venezia's highest-born married ladies. Bernardina, like so many of us, hadn't the slightest clue about her parentage. She claimed to have a vague memory of living on a pirate ship and being blinded in a battle. But Claudia told us it was far more likely that Bernardina's eye was blighted in childbirth by syphilis. Claudia herself hailed from one of the richest families in Saxony. Her father and mother between them owned five castles and vast holdings of farmland. Such garments were probably her everyday wear.

And I? And I. There were no whispers about me, Anna Maria dal Violin. And yet there were whispers awakened inside me as soon as the jeweled mask was placed upon my face and from top to toes I was transformed. Was this, then, the true identity of Anna Maria, foundling of the Ospedale della Pietà? Were my orphan's robes my true disguise? And then I could not help but wonder—was it not possible that one or both of my parents might be there at the ball?

The *portinara* on duty had mysteriously disappeared. And all that was to be seen of Sister Celestina—one of our visiting nuns who came to the Pietà to further her musical studies—was the back of her robe receding down the dark passageway. I was sure I heard the jingle of coins in her pockets.

Thus resplendent, one by one, we were handed over the threshold of the water gate, down the stairs and onto the king's gondola, which was draped in red velvet and brocade and lit by hundreds of candles that cast a sort of golden daylight, even though the stars shone bright above *la Serenissima*. There was a crescent moon in the icy sky, and I swear it looked dipped in molten silver that night in honor of the king.

At first there was only silence as we glided up the Grand Canal toward the Ca' Foscarini, the star-studded mirror of the water barely rippled by the expert oarsmen, who gazed at us with lust and wonder.

But the splendor of that gondola ride was as a journey on a cart along a muddy country lane compared with the splendor of the Palazzo Foscarini.

As much as the king may have relished the notion of traveling incognito, there was no one in Venezia in ignorance about his exalted station, and no expense was spared to fête him in befitting style. I am sure I was not the only one among the orphans to have a moment of difficulty breathing when the doors of the Foscarini's grand salon were thrown open to us.

The mountainous chandeliers of Murano glass. The ceilings that seemed as high as Heaven, painted with gods and goddesses in the likeness of our hosts. The intricacies of the carvings. Everything gleaming, inlaid, bejeweled, waxed, and perfumed. Candles swathed in pink silk and light that would put the sun to shame for the plainness of its illumination.

The noble company—all masked, of course—parted, bowing low, at the entrance of the king and his entourage. We each of us held her head high, trying to look as regal and as foreign as possible—although I was careful not to meet Giulietta's eyes, as I knew we would both begin giggling if I did. The maestro, craning his neck to gauge the reaction of the crowd, was quite inflated with his own success and ours.

Then the musicians struck up a gavotte and the king, laughing underneath his mask, whirled away with the *procuratessa* Mocenigo, who was dressed all in black and diamonds and feathers. She had visited us before and even spoken with a few of us through the grille in the *parlatorio*, and I was sure she knew at once who we were.

It looked as if the king were dancing with a magnificent and dangerous bird of prey. Rumor had it that she was intimate with the Grand Inquisitor, and I wondered if the maestro was having any second thoughts about his boldness not only in secreting us out of the *ospedale* but also in exposing his folly to Venezia's highest and mightiest.

Kissing *la Mocenigo's* hand when the song ended, the king turned to find himself presented with Venezia's pride, Signora Caterina Querini.

Of course, I had heard of her, of her beauty and her riches. There were those among the adults of the *coro* at that time—as now—who were patronized by noble families, who would send them food and furniture, invite them to their homes to recuperate when they'd been ill, and include them on family outings during the *villegiatura*, when whole households are loaded onto barges and floated down to one or another country estate on the Brenta River. When in a festive mood, these senior members of the *coro* would regale us with riveting tales of the nobility and their way of life.

Signora Querini was a favorite subject of these stories. But now it seemed that her reputation did not do her justice. One could see her gracefulness even when she was standing still. Indeed the entire assembly stood absolutely still, like a thousand moths in the breathless moment before fluttering toward the brightest lantern they've ever seen. Even the king looked truly dazzled.

No one danced while they danced, which they did with an obvious and mutual delight.

And then an odd thing happened. We heard the sound of a harpsichord suddenly usurp the orchestra, a kind of playing I had never heard before, so fast did the fingers of that musician fly. Everyone looked to see who it was who dared upstage the king in his graceful dance with Signora Querini. And yet neither the king nor his partner was of a mind to be upstaged. They danced faster and faster, as if caught in a whirlwind, their heads thrown back, laughing. Oh, to experience that, I thought to myself. I heard the maestro mutter, "Good God, it is Handel!" And then a man's voice beside him laughed, "It could be no one else but the famous Saxon—or the devil himself!"

The maestro—and all of us around him—turned to see who had spoken. "Scarlatti!" the maestro cried. "Is it you? Is every musician in God's kingdom here tonight?"

But Scarlatti's answer—oh, he was dashing!—was drowned by exclamations of surprise and one would even say horror from the crowd as pearls began flying from Signora Querini like drops of water from a dog just emerged from a swim on a hot summer's day. *La bella Querini* at first tried to catch them, and then, holding her lovely arms out straight and throwing her head back, she whirled round and round till all the pearls from the broken threads of her gown lay scattered on the dance floor.

No one dared move, and the music stopped. And then the king himself dropped to his knees and began to gather them. He scooped them up in his hands and—with a bit of help from some of the other men ranged around, who discreetly kicked stray pearls in his direction—the king presented the pearls to the lady with a bow.

There was a moment of stunned silence, and then all of us, at once, broke into applause at the magnificence of this gesture of tribute by a king to *la Serenissima's* greatest beauty.

A commanding voice in the crowd shouted out, "Scarlatti, you must challenge the Saxon—for the honor of your countrymen!"

Claudia whispered to me, "It's Cardinal Ottoboni of Rome!"

Scarlatti bowed. "Your holiness," he said to the cardinal with a sly grin, reaching for the sword at his side. "Would you have me kill the great Handel, then?"

"Not with your sword, boy! With your bare hands." And then Ottoboni held up both his arms, which were clothed in white lace beneath the red taffeta of his robes. "*Signore, signori,*" he boomed from under his ruby-encrusted black mask, "the two greatest keyboardists of our time are here tonight. Let them do battle so that we can determine which of them to crown our king!" He bowed low to the king then, who kept up his charade by looking innocently around and applauding with the rest of the company.

Scarlatti bowed to the cardinal, to the king, and across the room to Handel, who sat at the harpsichord hidden behind the winsome white-and-gold mask of Harlequin. "I cede my place at this noble instrument to you, brother Scarlatti." He jumped up from the bench, gesturing for Scarlatti to come take his place there.

Everyone looked for an anxious moment at the king and *la Querini.* "Very amusing, utterly delightful!" he said to her in a voice loud enough for all to hear.

At that, Scarlatti bounded across the room, shouting with mock rage, "Out of my way, you Saxon dog!"

I looked at Claudia to see if she would take offense at Scarlatti's jibe. But she was gazing across the room with an expression I had never seen in her eyes before, like someone overcome with a memory of something incomparably sweet—although whether the look was directed at Handel or Scarlatti, I could not tell. I noticed that Giulietta, at my other side, looked similarly in danger of swooning. The maestro murmured, to no one in particular, "He normally wouldn't even *think* of playing in public!"

Scarlatti played fiendishly well, a capriccio in G major. There was a surge of cheers and applause when he'd finished. He strutted before the crowd, bowing and preening like a returning war hero. Claudia was shrieking so loudly I had to cover my ears.

Handel, his mask still beaming (although it was impossible to know what his real expression was), placed himself beside the cardinal, who inclined his head toward the Saxon to better hear his words. We all saw him nod then.

"*Signori, signore*—please, a little quiet. Scarlatti, you peacock, stop that!" Scarlatti had somehow got hold of a quill and was signing ladies' fans. He threw the pen over his shoulder and bowed to the cardinal.

"Ah, that's better," said Ottoboni, turning to the crowd again. "*Signori, signore.* Our distinguished young musician from Saxony has asked the favor of a second round—at the organ!" And then the cardinal shouted, "Let an organ be brought into the room!"

The fair lords and ladies of Venezia roared their approval like the bawdiest lowborn youths of Cannereggio. I saw money change hands in a frenzy of betting while the instrument was carried in, with great difficulty, by a dozen servants wearing the purple and gold of the Foscarini.

Handel bowed his thanks, then gestured to Scarlatti, offering him the chance to play first.

Scarlatti played, if anything, even better than he had before. I could have sworn that he was playing extemporaneously—a toccata in the key of F major. Two ladies tore their bodices open, baring their breasts to him—this with priests in the room!

Handel, whose entire person seemed to be grinning now, took his place at the organ. The room, which had been abuzz with laughter and jibes, grew silent except for the sound of the music he played—an allegro in D minor. Faster and faster, with a thunderous sound, so that several ladies—much to my distress, Giulietta among them—fell in a swoon. Someone cried out, "*Diavolo!*" and I saw the maestro make the sign of the cross.

When Handel finished, there was a moment of silence. And then the crowd began to roar again, shouting first one man's name and then the other's. "Scarlatti!" cried one group of supporters, while another shouted back, "Handel! Handel!"

Cardinal Ottoboni leapt up onto one of the tables laden with food and wine to address the crowd. "*Veneziani!*" he pleaded. "*Pace!* I have reached a decision."

There was the sound of breaking glass and ripping cloth before the crowd calmed itself enough to hear him out. "We have at least two kings among us tonight." At this, he gave a nod to King Frederick, who feigned ignorance again. "Handel is our king of the organ." The crowd of *Italiani,* ever loyal to their own, bellowed in protest. "*Pace, pace*—I am not finished!" said the cardinal. "And Scarlatti is our king of the harpsichord!"

Vivaldi, seeming indifferent to the outcome, held himself apart from the tumult. But I have no doubt that he was jealous of the tributes these other, younger musicians were receiving—and fearful, I'm sure, of losing the favor he'd so newly won from the king.

There was the joyful pop of a hundred bottles of champagne, and little shrieks from the ladies as the corks flew everywhere. I lost track of Vivaldi then. I was trying to pull Giulietta upright when an elegantly dressed young man appeared by my side. "May I be of help, Signorina?" he said in an accent I recognized as German. In defiance of custom, he raised his mask to let me see his face.

Such a lively, intelligent face with warm brown eyes that danced in the candlelight. He smiled at me a smile so genuine—so full of simple regard—that it felt suddenly as if I'd never been

smiled at before that moment, or been seen before those eyes
seemed to look right through my mask and into my soul.

Poor Giulietta! I nearly dropped her, so taken was I with the
feeling of standing close to this young man. I felt parched all of
a sudden. As if he could read my thoughts, he took two glasses
of champagne from a passing waiter and handed one to me. I
drank it down in one toss. "Will you dance with me, Signorina?"
he said, holding out his hand. It was only then that I noticed the
orchestra was playing again.

"A tiny moment," I said to him, coming rather closer to his
chest than I had intended. I pushed myself back and turned to
face the other girls.

"Dance, you goose!" said Claudia, laughing.

"But I haven't been introduced to him!" I whispered franti-
cally.

Claudia, looking so very pretty and buxom in her dress that
I instantly felt afraid he would prefer her over me, walked up to
the young man and spoke to him in Italian—I suppose so that I
would understand the content of their exchange.

"What's your name, *ragazzo?*" she said as if she were speaking
to someone selling vegetables.

He smiled good-naturedly. "Franz Horneck," he said, click-
ing his heels and bowing in the Prussian style. "Here to further
my studies in the violin and harpsichord and to procure musical scores for the Archbishop of Mainz." His eyes glittered then.
"And to disport myself in Venezia as much as may be possible!"

Claudia gave him a very proper nod. "Franz Horneck, may I
present to you Signorina Anna Maria della ..." She hesitated,
realizing, I think, how dangerous it would be to identify me as
a foundling of the Pietà. Giulietta, Bernardina, and I could all
receive fearsome punishments were it found out that we'd left
the premises without receiving written permission, and to attend

such a worldly entertainment as a ball! And Vivaldi—even then I think we realized that Vivaldi had put himself greatly at risk.

"Anna Maria della Foscarini!" Giulietta chimed in, having apparently recovered from her faint.

"Giulietta!" I cried in protest. But Master Horneck kissed my hand and in the next instant whispered in my ear, "Don't worry, Signorina, your secret is safe with me."

Claudia had meanwhile grabbed a glass of champagne for herself and was drinking it greedily. "Franz, Annina. Annina, Franz. Now you may dance!"

And we danced. It was even more wonderful than I had dreamed it would be. Despite the unaccustomed shoes and my lack of experience. Despite the glass of champagne or perhaps because of it, we danced as if we were leaves born aloft on a wind.

No, we danced as one being, one soul, one heart, so that for the first time in my life I did not feel alone.

We did not stop dancing, I think, except to stop briefly for more glasses of champagne. But even when we were not brought together by the pattern of the dance, it still felt as if we danced together.

I fear I drank too much. We all have our allotment of wine at the Pietà, but it is mixed with water until we come of age.

Franz guided me out to a balcony where we could cool ourselves in the night air. All around us there were others from the party in various states of dishevelment and intoxication, wrapped around each other like strands of seaweed. Claudia was there with Scarlatti, laughing and hiccupping as he nibbled at a bunch of grapes tucked into her décolletage. He had doffed his mask and was wearing an expression of intense concentration. He was the handsomest man I had ever seen.

I quickly looked away.

"Should we go inside again?" Franz asked me.

I was about to answer when the notes of the "Cum Sancto Spiritu" drifted up from the canal. I instantly recognized the sound as the voices of our own *figlie di coro*. Franz and I walked hand in hand to the edge of the railing, and there they were, ranged over the same gondola that had taken us to the palazzo. Each girl carried a candle. They wore the sprigs of holly in their hair.

It was such an odd sensation to watch and listen to them from the outside, as if I had died and my spirit were looking down upon the orphan musicians of the Pietà. The *serenata* was unspeakably lovely as it rose in the air. And the sensation of my hand held in Franz Horneck's seemed to make a liquid of all the solid parts of me.

As the last notes of the music died away, the night was rent by a series of whistles and explosions, immediately followed by fountains of colored lights cascading and purling through the darkness. When, clapping my hands and jumping up and down, I turned to Franz, he caught me in his arms.

He took off his mask. And then—slowly, carefully—he took off mine, and we stood there face to face. He did not gasp in horror at the sight of me, or laugh or run away. He smiled as his eyes traveled over every part of my face. With one of his hands he caressed my hair—and then, seeming to ask permission first with his eyes (and seeing that I granted it), he brought his face close in to the nape of my neck, just above my shoulder, and inhaled deeply, as if he were savoring the fragrance of some rare flower.

His eyes lingered on me before he spoke again. "I have two things to give you tonight, Anna Maria. This is the first."

And then he kissed me, mouth to mouth, so that our breaths were mingled. It was as if, in that moment, we had each opened a secret door and the other walked through into places where even I had never ventured in myself before—whole continents, oceans, and islands of Anna Maria unmapped and uncharted.

We stood there, looking into each other's eyes with a new knowledge of what lay beyond. Then Franz let me go for a moment, and I wanted to tell him to hold fast to me, as my knees felt in danger of buckling. But I said nothing, only swaying a little in the breeze that reached us, suddenly feeling the cold.

He found what he had been rummaging for in his pocket. "I don't want you to think this is the only reason why I sought you out. I have heard you perform every Saturday and Sunday since my arrival in Venezia. I would give my birthright to be able to play the violin as you do."

Then he placed something in my hands.

"What is it?" I asked him, peering down at the small object, metallic and cold. And then I saw that it was a locket on a gold chain. It was rather ugly, really, and of strange Levantine design, heavy and bejeweled. When I tried to open it, Franz turned it over to show me that it was fashioned with a tiny keyhole; it was locked.

I looked up at him. "Where is the key?" I almost forgot about the locket when I looked at his face again.

He shook his head. "I told him you would want to know."

"Who?"

"The Jewish banker who serves Herr von Regnazig, resident consul for the Archbishop of Mainz—the one from whom I have been procuring musical scores."

"But—I don't understand! What do these foreigners have to do with me?" I looked at the locket again. "And what does this have to do with me?"

"I'm sorry, darling girl—I don't know. He simply bade me give it to you—and I was thrilled by the chance of doing an errand that would bring me close to someone I so admire."

⤞ ⤞ ⤞

*H*ow many nights, over how many years, did I drift off
to sleep borne aloft on the memory of Franz Horneck's kisses?

Dawn was breaking as the maestro secreted us and all the
singers back over the threshold of the orphanage, the *portinara*
conspicuously absent from her post and the door unbarred. Off
with our finery and into our beds—but none of us slept. We lay
there retelling the evening's adventures, and we had nothing but
praise for Vivaldi in managing it all so well, as if it had been an
opera and he the impresario. The choir girls told us how he had
returned for them in the gondola and directed their midnight
serenade below the Foscarini balcony—but it was hard on them
to have been left on the outside in their orphans' robes while we
were at the ball.

I clasped the necklace tight in my fist all night long, puzzling
over what it could mean. Rather than an answer to my questions,
I'd been given yet another locked door.

My mind kept returning to the locket while the other girls and
I told what we wanted to tell and kept the rest to ourselves to
savor in private, like a sweet sucked gently to make it last as long
as possible. I would hazard that Marietta first formed her plans
that night, lying in the dark and listening to our tales of kings
and pearls, dueling musicians, and kisses given and taken.

Had I made my decision even then? No—I was still a child,
incapable of understanding that everything I loved and valued
was as unstable as the shimmering surface of the canals, and as
unpredictable as the winter rains.

CHAPTER 6

ANNO DOMINI 1709

Dearest Mother,

I am writing from one of the third-floor cells where miscreants are confined. The Prioress has meted out a jail sentence of three days for me. Sister Laura tells me that I might get out sooner if I write to you at length and with honesty about all my trespasses.

I have no doubt done much that I should not have in my life, but I have been unjustly punished this time. And even if I could have refused to cooperate with the plans of my elders and betters, I swear I would have done just what I did all over again. I have no remorse.

The maestro colluded with the portinara and one of the nuns here to secret Giulietta, Bernardina, Claudia, and me out to a ball at the Palazzo Foscarini. Our presence there was requested by no less a personage than the King of Denmark and Norway. The portinara has been demoted. The nun has been sent back to her convent. And it remains to be seen what will happen to Vivaldi.

I'm in this cell by myself on rations of bread and water. I can't be certain, but I'm fairly sure that Giulietta and Bernardina are in a similar pickle, somewhere on the premises. Claudia, I am praying, will not be sent back to her parents in Saxony. I don't know how the Prioress has chosen to punish her, but probably in more comfortable circumstances than these.

Sister Laura brought me ink and paper today, as well as an apple. I clutched at her sleeve as she was leaving, begging her to tell me if and how these letters reach you. I told her that I need to know—that I have something of utmost importance to ask you. When she removed my hand from her sleeve and made to move away, I stamped my foot. When she looked amused at my show of temper, I started to cry.

I told her that the time for games and fairytales was over—that I am not a child anymore.

She assured me then that she would not entrust me with this opportunity to write to you if I had been a child.

"But why can't you trust me enough to tell me who I am?" I demanded to know. "It is my right."

Sister Laura shook her head then, as if I had disappointed her. She told me, indeed as if speaking to a child, that none of the foundlings here has the right to know. Only if a parent comes to claim a figlia of the Pietà will the book of the scaffetta be opened and the girl's identity revealed.

Why is that book closed to those who most desperately need to know its secrets?

Our lives are arranged so that every piece of every day and night is fit together into an intricate mosaic of music and study and prayer. But it is only a counterfeit of real life. We have no more reality in the world than the trompe l'oeil floor tiles of the church have depth or height. Our faces might as well not be faces, for all that anyone ever sees of them. We are but voices and sound, the pipes through which the Republic sings for God and begs for His mercy.

We have no more substance than the wind. And if one of us dies or leaves, another comes to take her place. There is an endless supply, it would seem, of unwanted girl babies in and around la Serenissima. One more or less makes no difference. Who we are, one by one, has no importance or meaning.

And yet, don't my thoughts matter as much as those of any oth-er person born of woman in this world? Do my aspirations and my feelings count for less than those of girls growing up, by accident and good fortune, within a family? If I love, is it right and just that my love remain forever unheard and forever unanswered?

We orphans and foundlings of the Pietà have only each other to turn to for comfort and meaning—friendship must stand in for the families that abandoned us to our fate here. And yet we are told time and again, "Amicitia huius mundi inimica est Dei"—The friendship of this world is inimical to God. *We are denied the ties of blood that are rightfully ours, but we are discouraged from having ties of any other kind.*

We are told to turn to God. And perhaps it's blasphemy to say so, but God has never once shown me that He is listening or even knows that I'm alive. Is it my faith in God that Sister Laura is test-ing when she tells me to write to you? For you have never shown me either that you are listening or even know that I'm alive.

The ceiling of the church is painted to seem a sky above our heads and a passageway to God. But it is more like the lid on a sarcophagus than a doorway to Heaven, and we are each trapped inside this holy coffin. Whether or not we grow old, we all die young here.

Will I stay then and become like Sister Giovanna, with all the life and sweetness of her dreams as dry and shrunken as a pome-granate left over from last year?

No—I have no remorse. If for only one evening, I felt the heat of life in me. And if only for a few hours, I was seen. I was known. And I was loved.

In despair,
Anna Maria dal Violin,
Student of Maestro Vivaldi

➤◆ ➤◆ ➤◆

never did have a taste for remorse, despite the high favor in which it is held. It seems to me, by and large, to be a state of mind that causes more ill than good. It is said to be the doorway to Heaven—but that door is closed to me. And so what use do I have for a feeling that will only open the door to sadness and pain?

I felt elation, even from my jail cell—and, of course, far greater elation when I was released after three days. The usual order of things was disrupted by the excitement and punishments that resulted from our unsanctioned outing. And everyone was abuzz about whether the measures the Prioress had taken were sufficient to allay further sanctions from the governors.

Some of the more enterprising girls among us organized a little lottery. Bets were placed as to whether Vivaldi would keep his position, despite this latest and most dramatic act of defiance against the rules.

All the outside teachers are at risk every year, even now. Whether they are retained depends not only on their good service, but also on whether they are providing a service that can't be rendered by a resident of the Pietà.

Vivaldi was originally sought out because the governors wanted to strengthen the skills of the string players. Later, when he began composing for us, his position seemed assured: then, as now, he wrote an astonishing amount of music.

The governors know full well that the people of Venezia come to our concerts to be moved by the music they hear. High up in our choir lofts, our faces are hidden and the sounds we make seem to come from the heavens, leaving our audience in a state of mystic rapture. All of this adds up to larger audiences and larger donations to feed, clothe, and educate the *figlie* of the *coro* and the much larger group of foundling boys and girls of the *comun*. Thus there is an insatiable appetite for new and ever more beautiful music—which Vivaldi, for all his faults, has never failed to provide.

We couldn't imagine how they could even think about slaying this golden goose who came cheap at a hundred ducats a year.

All the string players and many of the singers were betting on the maestro. After all, King Frederick had been delighted with us. There was even talk of a large donation he intended to bestow upon the Pietà.

Of course, the dismissal of Sister Celestina and the demotion of the *portinara* were serious things. But rule-breaking and its consequences are ever a part of institutions such as this one, as woven into the fabric of daily life as prayers and bells and meals.

The organizers of the lottery—three singers and a trumpet player—used a small part of the pool to engage a spy from the *comun*, the buxom, rosy-cheeked girl who served refreshments to the governors during their meetings. This girl was to signal us the results of the ballot concerning the maestro: If he prevailed, she would stand in the center window in the group of three arched windows overlooking the courtyard. If he was voted out, she would stand in the side window closest to the *rio*.

I was among those in the courtyard awaiting Paolina's signal. Several teachers walking by—including Sister Laura—urged us to come in out of the cold. I protested that we were enjoying the sight of the clouds overhead (which we were, in truth, after our imprisonment, despite the frigid air).

I asked Bernardina if she was also given the opportunity to write letters during the time when she was confined. But she only looked at me—always a particularly striking experience, as she put all the expression of two eyes into her one—as if I'd gone a little queer.

"To whom would I write?" she asked me.

I shrugged and stole a glance at the windows again. We both stopped as Paolina's plump form seemed to hover at the side window. And then she moved—with deliberation and even a little backward glance into the courtyard—to the middle of the center window. Without another word to each other, Bernardina and I raced inside to spread the news.

The board voted that day—albeit by a slim margin of seven to six—to retain the services of Don Vivaldi as *maestro de' concerti*. I really didn't care much about the coins I'd wagered. But it was a huge relief to me to know that the maestro would stay with us. I think it was not until that twenty-fourth day of February, anno Domini 1709—pacing in suspense in the cold courtyard—that I realized how much his presence meant to me.

The winnings had not yet been distributed—we were waiting for the hour when we gathered for mealtime in the refectory and could pass coins under the table—when an out-of-breath Paolina pulled me aside in the passageway between the choir lofts and the practice rooms. "There was a second ballot!" she panted. "Signor Balerin demanded a recount. It was six for and seven against this time. Vivaldi is out!"

That night there were as many rumors fluttering from room to room and among the residents of the Pietà as there are pigeons in the Piazza. Some whispered that the Red Priest was seen at Ca' Foscarini kissing a *figlia* of the Pietà. This was, of course, utter confabulation. Yes, there were kisses at the palazzo that night—and there was that kiss he happened to give Claudia on the ice that day—but Vivaldi was entirely too taken up with making a good impression on King Frederick and his retinue to have allowed himself to engage in such folderol. He was far too immersed in his own ambitions than to risk his musical career on a girl.

Some said that the Grand Inquisitor himself was behind

the recount. Others said it was ultimately because of Vivaldi's refusal to say Mass, using the transparently thin excuse of ill health (which never kept him from far more strenuous activities, including frequent trips to Mantua and other cities, where he performed as a soloist, sought out further opportunities for patronage, and erred in ways that would forever change the course of his life). Still others—the most cynical and simpleminded among us—said it was all a natural consequence of his red hair.

I suppose Vivaldi had managed by then to earn a widespread reputation as a scofflaw. But it seemed terribly unfair to me that his six years of faithful service—years in which the *coro* had definitely maintained and perhaps even exceeded its prior fame—would not buy him the board's undying gratitude. Simply from an economic point of view, it made utter sense to keep him: the more the Pietà was able to earn through donations, the less money of their own the governors would have to contribute to keep the institution financially afloat.

Of course, I understood next to nothing of such matters then, beyond my own earnings. We were each paid a small salary, almost all of which went to the purchase of our food and candles and clothes. Whatever we could save we were allowed to invest at a particularly favorable rate of interest—a rate that rose (along with our salaries) as we ourselves rose in the ranks of the *coro*.

The governors thought—wisely, as I now realize—that a working knowledge of money was important for us, even though we were and might ever be cloistered from the rest of the world. And, in fact, those of us who chose to stay on here have far more to do with commerce than we ever would if we had chosen to marry. Among the women of Venezia, only the courtesans are as well-versed in matters of business as its cloistered virgins.

The Pietà is like a little country in its economy. We own and manage properties. We run the factories here—the lace-making, sail-making, and silk-washing businesses that have provided our population with work as well as income.

But I never thought about such things when I was young, being far too taken up with music and the longings of my own heart to care or even notice the inner workings of the *ospedale*.

Several of us wrote letters to the governors, begging them to reinstate our teacher without delay, praising his skills and attesting to the personal progress we'd made under his tutelage. But the governors were far less compelled by us than the audiences that filled the church every Saturday and Sunday to hear us perform.

Our letters not only failed to sway the governors, but they didn't even give Vivaldi the chance to bid us farewell. We watched as his personal effects were carried out of the sacristy and loaded onto a gondola. It was as if he had died.

A pall settled over all of us, but especially the string players. Vivaldi was the closest that any of us ever had to a father. It was like being made an orphan a second time.

The pain I felt only strengthened my resolve to find my mother and learn my father's identity, no matter what I had to do, no matter what rules of the cloister I had to break. I would put flowers on a dead parent's grave. I would throw myself upon the mercy of a parent who was alive. I was possessed with the thought that I was not a daughter of the choir, as we were so coyly named, but the flesh-and-blood progeny of two flesh-and-blood parents.

I didn't think about how making my presence known might affect my parents, if they lived, or might even endanger the life or livelihood of one or both of them. Nor did I think overmuch about how my own life might change. In what other place or in what other station could I spend all my waking hours playing, practicing, and listening to the best music of the age? I didn't considerer how those things that were most important to me might, in fact, be taken away.

Like any adolescent, I took for granted what was around me, and yearned instead for things beyond my reach. I was not driven either by logic or sensibility in my longing. It did not occur to me then to feel gratitude that I had not been dropped in the canal as an infant rather than placed in the *scaffetta* of the church on a moonlit night. Nor that any reason apart from a lack of love might keep a mother from claiming her child.

No one was found to take over the maestro's classes, to say nothing of the prodigious amount of composing he did for us. We were left in the hands of our *maestre*, the internal teachers, who were rehearsing us in a new oratorio by our ailing *maestro di coro*, Signor Gasparini.

Oratorios have ever been the governors' great compromise for our repertoire. Set to sacred text, Gasparini's work had all the stylistic elements—save costumes—of the operas we longed to perform. Perhaps the governors felt it wise to distract us with something as like an opera as possible, given the taste we'd lately shown for stepping outside our prescribed roles.

Our board did, in all fairness, do their very best then—as they do now—to balance our happiness against the needs of the institution, without ever letting one shipwreck the other.

Gasparini's work told the apocryphal tale of Susannah, held captive in Babylon, falsely accused of adultery, and finally rescued by Daniel. The names were from the Bible and the texts were sung in Latin, but the plot was just as operatic as one could wish for. The oratorio offered us the salve of abundant musi-

cal challenges, excitement, and even controversy, complete
with snare drums, kettledrums, and trumpets (all of which were
banned for sacred choirs, along with opera, by papal decree).

Bernardina and I—although still *initiziate* then—played in
among the rest of the *coro*. As the maestro's favorite up-and-
coming violinists of that era, she and I suffered equally in his
absence. This fact formed a sort of bond between us, at least for
the time.

Marietta, Apollonia, and a newly confirmed *maestra* named
Rosa sang the leads with a sound worthy of any opera house.
Looking in on one of our rehearsals, la Befana remarked with
her usual sourness that the music might make our listeners want
to dance the rigadoon or glide in the minuet, but was not likely
to make them want to pray.

The oratorio was to be performed on Palm Sunday for the
newly elected Doge, Giovanni Cornaro. In a fit of lavishness, the
governors decided to give us new robes for this special occasion.
And so we had an out-of-season visit from Rebekkah, the seamstress from the Ghetto who made and remade the clothing worn
by the *coro* in those years.

I always liked Rebekkah with her pockets and pins and bright
laughing eyes. When it was my turn to be measured, she turned
my face to the light and looked at me carefully, as if looking for
the shadow of someone else. The rhythm of my heart acceler-
ated as I thought of the locket and its Levantine design, wondering whether there might be a connection between Rebekkah and
me.

For the first time, I pondered her age. She was, without doubt,
of an age to bear children; but whether she was either too young
or too old to have been my mother, I found it impossible to determine. Her skin was smooth, but her dark hair was threaded with

gray. We were both of us brown-eyed and long-fingered. I had seen too few mothers and daughters to have gained any understanding of the ways in which they may and may not resemble each other.

When I looked upward from my own hands at Rebekkah, she seemed to be able to read the question in my eyes. "I was only noticing how you've changed, Anna Maria, since the last time." She spoke in a rich contralto that made me think that she was also musical.

If she were my mother, surely she would give me a further sign now. I stopped breathing in that moment, waiting for the squeeze of the hand or the upwelling of tears in Rebekkah's eyes or whatever token she would give me without letting anyone else see what she had done.

And so it was that I wondered if I was dreaming when she reached into one of her pockets and put something small in my hand, folding my fingers around it. "Save it for later!" she whispered.

Time itself seemed to freeze as, all around us, the other girls and women of the *coro* shivered in their underclothes, for the most part patiently waiting their turn. I swallowed hard and put the small object in the pocket of my chemise. Whatever it was, it seemed to be wrapped in paper. I longed to show her that I understood—and yet a shyness overcame me, and I couldn't even meet her eyes.

The tiny package was light, small, and round. It seemed far too insubstantial to be another piece of jewelry, although I reasoned that it could have been something very delicate suspended from a chain. Surreptitiously, I shook the thing in my pocket to see if it rattled.

I wanted to stay and glance sidelong at Rebekkah in this new light. I had sometimes wondered whether, with my dark eyes, I might be a Jewess or a Gypsy or a southerner. My mind raced. If Rebekkah was my mother, then who was my father? Did he also come from the Ghetto? It seemed unlikely for a pair of pious Jews to give up their child to a Catholic institution. Had Rebekkah borne me out of wedlock? What was her connection with the Pietà, anyway? Why, when we had our own tailors on staff, was she brought from the Ghetto to make and mend our robes?

I couldn't wait to get away to some private place where I could examine the contents of the gift she'd given me.

CHAPTER 7

$\mathcal{E}$VERY EFFORT has always been made in this place to discourage personal vanity. There is only one sanctioned full-length mirror in the whole of the *ospedale*, and that is kept under lock and key in a small practice room off one of the passageways connecting the church to the orphanage. Singers are taught there to look at themselves while they practice their art in order to ensure they are using the proper technique for producing the best sound. And yet it is a place where the prettier adolescent girls especially have become entranced over the years, standing before their own reflections.

Marietta, who was as pretty as they come, used every ruse she could think of to increase her time in front of the full-length mirror, although *maniera* is usually taught only once a week.

Girls and women of the Pietà have ever been resourceful in finding ways to gaze at themselves in objects other than the mirror in the practice room. They inspect their faces in the polished bowls of their porridge spoons. They find reason to gaze out of dark windows at night, even though all they gaze at is their own reflection. In my time, coins were exchanged for the privilege of looking at oneself in another girl's eyes—and the price was double if she'd managed to dilate her pupils with a dose of purloined belladonna.

When the *portinara's* keys are lost or stolen—as they are from time to time—it is as often to break into the practice room with the mirror as it is to get into or out of any other locked part of the orphanage.

The governors have always strived to make us into one self-less body of prayerful musicians, each working for the good of the Republic. And yet every one of us—or perhaps just the most imaginative among us—has led a double life. In this second life, we are each the heroine of a drama that has nothing to do with saving the collective soul of Venezia. We become celebrated courtesans, ballerinas, or opera stars. We are remembered and reclaimed by long-lost parents. We hatch a secret plot to run away. How can we envision ourselves in these dramas if we don't even know what we look like?

Not only do we not see ourselves, but no one else sees us, either, apart from the daily view we have of one another. When Franz Horneck looked at my face, and looked at it so slowly and carefully and with so much pleasure, it was as if in that moment I truly existed for the first time. I saw the possibility of a real rather than a fantasy life apart from my cloistered existence. And, suddenly, both lives seemed of equal potential.

Although mirrors are banned to those who most long to gaze in them, nearly every senior member of the *coro* keeps a mirror of some kind in her chamber. If she has primarily been an instrumentalist, she may decide to sing in the choir for a season. To that end—and, of course, for no other reason—she will petition the governors for a mirror to be affixed to the wall of her room. If she has been a singer all along, and she is confirmed as a *figlia privilegiata*, she will say that she needs her own mirror as a tool for instructing a private student in her care. And if neither of these excuses works for her, she will save her money and bribe one of the servants with access to the outside to buy a mirror for her so that she can hide it in her chamber.

Make no mistake about it: every girl here has memorized, by the time of her first blood, the locations of all the rooms with mirrors. It is only lately that I retired the small mirror, prettily housed in a silver frame, given to me as a gift from the Foscarini family and emblazoned with the family crest.

God knows why, but when the fitting session with Rebekkah was finally over and it was time to go to dinner, I made for one of the mirror rooms. Perhaps I wanted company when I made my discovery. Or perhaps I wanted to be caught and kept from knowing.

In those minutes of walking as quickly as I dared down the deserted hallway, a sense of dread was growing inside me. Finally knowing where I came from would cut off every other path, including the path that might lead me back into Franz Horneck's arms. Even though I knew nothing of his family, I was quite sure that they were not about to let him marry a Jewess.

How odd it was that I assumed, even then, that Franz would want to marry me, long before he'd made any declaration apart from that kiss on the balcony at the *palazzo*.

The room toward which I made my way had belonged to the banished Sister Celestina. I knew she'd kept a mirror there, hidden under the bed (it was Marietta, our resident expert in such matters, who had told me). I hoped that the mirror hadn't been found when the disgraced nun's other belongings were packed up and sent away with her.

Did I want to inspect myself, with Rebekkah's image so fresh in my mind's eye, to see if I resembled her? I don't know. Perhaps the Virgin took pity on my sorry state and led me to that room—because when I slipped through the door and my eyes grew accustomed to the darkness, I could smell the smoldering wick of a candle and I knew that I was not alone.

"Who's there?" I whispered.

No one answered. Emboldened by the knowledge that I had not yet done anything wrong, whereas whoever I found there in the room probably had, I spoke with brio. "Show yourself—or I will guard the door and call someone else to go and get the *settimaniera!*"

"So uncharitable of you, Annina!" It was Claudia's voice. She struck a flint, and I saw two of her faces in the light of the candle that burst into flame—her real one and her reflection in the mirror she'd propped against the headboard of Sister Celestina's deserted bed.

I closed the door behind me and sat down on the nun's hard bed beside my friend. We embraced and said each other's names, both greatly relieved, I have no doubt, that it was only the two of us who were involved. She pushed me away then and showed me something she held in her fist—what looked like a sweet wrapped in paper, twisted at each end. I reached into my pocket and took out what Rebekkah had given me. It was identical to the object Claudia held.

"I'm expecting a message from Scarlatti. Forgive me for saying nothing, Annina! I know the risk is greater for you than it is for me."

I had never thought of the possibility of Franz Horneck sending a note in such a way. How worldly Claudia was compared with almost all the rest of us! She carefully untwisted the delicate paper of her packet, flattened it on the bed and then held it up to the candle flame. And then she met my eyes. "There is nothing written here—*nichts!* There is only—"

"A chocolate," I said, unwrapping my own little packet.

The insides of my cheeks began watering even as the tears sprang into Claudia's eyes. Chocolate was a great delicacy for us in those days. Claudia's parents sometimes sent her chocolates, and I was always in awe of her willingness to share them.

Nothing, I am quite sure, can transport a living being closer to the delights of Heaven than the taste of chocolate. I am the fortunate recipient of chocolates from time to time, now that my name is better known. But in my girlhood, I would have eaten it even if I'd been assured that it would bar me from Heaven forever. Chocolate is the one earthly pleasure I would not exchange for the promise of infinite pleasures deferred.

I contemplated the confection just long enough to gauge its size. It could only have been poured around an object as small as the innermost doll that fit inside Rebekkah's fantastic Russian toy—the bean-size doll, I thought with sinking heart, that didn't open.

While Claudia's present was no doubt beginning to melt in her fist, I parted my lips and placed mine on my tongue with all the reverence of a communicant receiving the Host. I was determined to suck it slowly.

As the chocolate warmed up in my mouth and released its magic, my tongue poked at it, trying to find out whether it was chocolate through and through or hid something else inside. The shape and texture of that thing began to emerge as the chocolate disappeared. There were ridges on it and points at both ends. The size and shape indicated something my mouth soon recognized.

I carefully sucked off all the chocolate, and never did a sweet thing taste so bitter to me. Spitting the uncoated object out into my hand, I didn't want to believe that the thing I found was only an almond. I broke it with my teeth, just to make sure.

Claudia was by then crying over the instructions from her lover that had failed to arrive, and I was staring balefully over some half-chewed nutmeats in the palm of my hand.

Our eyes met, and we started to laugh. Once we started, it was hard to stop.

I gauge the closeness of my friends even now by how help-lessly they can make me laugh. Barely able to breathe from the effort to laugh silently, Claudia and I were both crossing our legs to keep from wetting ourselves. When Claudia coughed and made wind, we both fell off the bed, upsetting the candle.

I can only marvel now, looking back, that Sister Celestina's old room didn't go up in flames.

Everything was so overheated for me then. I saw signs and portents in the simplest events of daily life, imagining that they all referred to me. I felt barbs where none were meant, and I heard criticism ten times louder than any praise. I felt a sense of closeness to my friends so intense that I couldn't imagine that life would ever have the temerity to part me from them.

I understood almost nothing then.

*W*hen Rebekkah returned toward the end of our re-hearsals with the half-made new robes, she had an ap-prentice with her. There was a good deal of giggling all around, because the person she'd brought into our midst—although feminine in both gesture and manner—was clearly a boy.

He looked harmless enough, slight and delicate of build, with skin that would be the envy of many of us here. I knew that boys of the *ospedali* sometimes apprenticed to tailors, and all of us, in our schooldays—before the *figlie di coro* were winnowed out from the *figlie di comun*—learned sewing and spinning side by side with the youngest boys, along with arithmetic and reading. It wasn't until Rebekkah's assistant was at my feet with pins in his mouth that I recognized the comical gleam in those eyes of his, and I clapped my hand over my mouth to keep myself from laughing out loud.

"Silvio!" I whispered.

"Shh! Yes—I hoped I'd see you here! I heard you were in the *coro*. How pretty you are, Annina!"

"I'm not!"

"You are! Would that I had those eyes—and that beautiful ass!"

And then I couldn't help myself from laughing, so that la Befana—who was supervising the proceedings—glared at me and said in a loud, clear voice that there was to be no idle chatter.

Rebekkah turned my head and had me hold my arm out to my side, taking its measure. "Were you two playmates, then?" she said close to my ear.

I knew I should have felt grateful to her for the chocolate. But I was sulking over the promise she'd unwittingly held out to me and then taken away. I nodded without giving her the smile I knew she wanted from me.

Silvio and I had all our classes together until I was plucked out of the *comun* and made an *iniziata*—how long ago it now seemed! And then he was sent away altogether at the age of ten, as are all the boys who are taken in as foundlings here. We hadn't seen each other in four full years, a space of time that may count as nothing to an adult, but seemed a lifetime to me then.

Silvio had been our king of comedy, able to impersonate each of the teachers with such accuracy that I received many a punishment for laughing out loud at inopportune times.

I looked longingly after him when my hems were pinned and he'd moved down the line to the next girl. But he managed to steal a look back at me. Even with pins in his mouth, he made a face so utterly like la Befana in a froth of disapproval that I burst out laughing, just like in the old days, only just managing to cover it with a feigned groan.

"Are you ill, Anna Maria?" la Befana asked me—a little hopefully, it seemed.

I nodded, biting down hard on my lower lip as Silvio carried on his impersonation, unseen by any but me.

"Then report to the infirmary!"

Silvio blew a little kiss to me and, emboldened by the memories of all our past mischief, I pointed to my bottom as I swept past him.

Luckily—because I really wanted to see Silvio again—the gorgeous red taffeta robes were ready for us to try on the following week. I was prepared for him this time: As Silvio laced up my sleeves, I slipped a note into his hand. Accomplished actor that he was, my old playmate pocketed the missive without betraying its presence to anyone.

Or so I thought, until Claudia confronted me that night as we lay in my bed still whispering after the final Angelus had rung. "You know what he is, don't you, Annina?"

"He is the dearest, funniest boy I ever knew—and of course I know that he is not like other boys. He has always been neither boy nor girl but like something in between."

I turned so that I was whispering into her ear. "I asked him to find out, if he can, about the locket—to seek out the banker who serves von Regnazig, learn its history, and find out who has the key."

Claudia said nothing, but I could tell that she was taking in what I'd told her, thinking it over. "And if that history, once learned, is not to your liking?"

I felt annoyed with Claudia when she said this sort of thing. Her words were forever revealing the ways in which she was far wiser than I, even though she always said them kindly.

I knew that finding out my identity would open one door—even while it closed others. As an anonymous *figlia* of the *coro* with no grave physical defect, I had as good a chance as any of receiving a rich offer of marriage when I'd served my term and trained two musicians who could serve the *coro* in my stead. I would have a place, if I chose to take it, among the richest and most refined people of Venezia. What chance of this would there be if I unraveled my history to find out that I came from a whore or a beggar or a Gypsy? What rich merchant or nobleman would welcome me then as a wife?

But, then again, I did not want to be anyone's wife except perhaps Franz Horneck's, and what chance was there that his family would allow themselves to be allied with someone who might well be a child of the gutter? Without his family's blessing, there would be nothing to live on. And without the governors' permission—unlikely to be given for my marriage to a Protestant and a foreigner at that—there would be no dowry for me. And even if I was given the dowry due every *figlia* of the *coro* who serves her time here, I would not accept it—because it would mean that I would be barred by the laws of the Republic from ever performing again.

None of the paths or possibilities open to me was acceptable. I would never become a wife if it meant that I would have to stop playing music. I did not feel called to become a nun, and especially not unless I was of noble birth, for it is, as everyone knows, only the daughters of noble families who can become choir nuns, while all others are relegated to *converse*, who serve the convents as menials. And I did not want to grow old at the Pietà. I looked at la Befana and I swore I would not let such a fate befall me.

It was soon afterward, while I sat in church, that the idea first came to me—the first idea of mine that seemed to hold real promise for bringing about a resolution, even while it threatened to bring about my ruin if it failed.

I had been thinking once again—with the offended sense of justice peculiar to adolescence—that all of us in the *coro* were, in the manner of trompe l'oeil, only a simulation of dimensional things. Instead of life or blood in our veins, we were filled with music. We lived not for our own salvation, but were indentured as slaves to the salvation of others—of all those others who had real lives and passions, who were allowed to see stars every night and to cross vast expanses of land and water every day. They knew who they were and what they could expect of life, while we were condemned to having our real selves—both our histories and our destinies—locked away.

It was then that I lit on the idea I should have thought of before, if I had possessed a mind more disposed to scheming. What I longed so much to find out was inscribed in the *libri della scaffetta*—the well-guarded, locked books of the registry where every detail about every baby left here has been recorded through the centuries, since the founding of the Pietà. There are two *scrivane*, the scribes chosen anew every three years, who write in these books and keep their contents secret.

It dawned on me that if I could befriend or bribe a *scrivana*—or steal her keys—I could settle, once and for all, what I was sure was a matter of life and death, and worth any risk I had to take.

The identity of the two *scrivane* was itself a closely held secret. But I was sure that, with persistence and perhaps some help from my friends, I could find out which of our keepers stood between me and what I needed to know.

*A*s we stood trembling in our choir lofts that Palm Sunday, poised to perform the oratorio for the Doge, we heard what sounded like a dozen trumpeters announcing his arrival. Peeking through the grille, we watched the procession of grooms, ducal pageboys, and ensigns, all in their splendid uniforms, pouring through the church doors. This first wave was followed by the rest of his entourage, bearing with great solemnity and self-importance the Doge's chair, scepter, sword, and cushion.

Il Doge Giovanni Cornaro was the fourth man in his family to hold Venezia's highest office. From where I stood, peeking through the grille, he looked terribly unhappy beneath the heavy cloth of gold of his vestments and his ermine cape lined in scarlet silk. His weary expression bespoke a man who would have far preferred to be sitting in a cozy place somewhere with a book in his lap, rather than serving as the center of this noble storm. Neither he nor his family can venture anywhere outside his palace without just such a phalanx of guards, servants, and sycophants. It amazes me that men seek out these high offices that rob them of their freedom to come and go in anonymity in a city in which such anonymity is the very key to happiness.

We ourselves were resplendent in the fine new red taffeta robes made for us by Rebekkah. Such was the pomp and glory of the occasion that I felt convinced for the time it lasted that we were indeed angels with a fearful power to redeem and transform.

Much to the credit of Signor Gasparini, who had to work much harder to rehearse all of us in Vivaldi's absence, the oratorio was a great success. The next day, the editors of the *Palade Veneta* sang the praises of the *figlie di coro* of the Pietà. Marietta, Rosa, and Apollonia were all singled out for the celestial beauty of their voices—and Marietta especially. She had somehow got hold of the broadsheet and showed the sentence that featured her name to all of us over and over again, until someone threatened to throw the whole thing into the fire.

But none of us, in truth, has ever been immune to the surges of delight and hope that come with praise, especially when we are mentioned by name outside the walls of the *ospedale*.

We sucked all the sweetness and comfort we could out of our triumph, which was the result of weeks of practice and the culmination, for many of us, of a long-held dream.

But there followed, as there so often does after a victory of any sort, a period of doldrums. Marietta was cross with everyone for treating her as they always had, despite the fact that, in her own words, she was now, clearly, a soloist. In fact, she wasn't yet even officially a member of the *coro*. Marietta's promotions—like mine—were forever being postponed as a punishment for bad behavior.

Even sweet-tempered Giulietta snapped at me, saying that my tone was no longer what it used to be. It was worse because she was right: I desperately needed my bow rehaired, and yet couldn't trust anyone but Vivaldi to get it done properly and in good time.

Claudia—usually so serene—was also agitated and out of sorts. I watched her push her food around on her plate rather than put any of it in her mouth. Several of the chubbier girls took to paying for the privilege of sitting beside her at mealtimes and eating her leftovers. Increasingly thin, with a haunted look in her lovely blue eyes, she was forever hanging around windows, looking out—and she stopped sleeping with me. She said it was because the weather was changing, and it was too hot for her, in the middle of the night, with the two of us sharing the bedclothes.

She asked to start in on voice lessons—but I knew it was only because of that full-length mirror in the practice room. Every time a visitor was announced in the *parlatorio*, all the blood drained from her face. When a rumor circulated at supper that Scarlatti was quitting Venice to return to Rome, Claudia actually let out a shriek. The room fell silent. But no one—not even the nuns in attendance—said anything. We all went on eating—

all of us except Claudia—as if nothing out of the ordinary had happened.

I came up beside her at bedtime that night as she stood by the window brushing her hair. "Do you want me to do it?" I asked her. Claudia had thick honey-colored hair that fell below her waist when it was unpinned. She was allowed to keep it long, and it was the envy of the *coro*.

She closed her eyes while I brushed, and I could see tears popping out from under her lashes. "After all his pretty words!" was all she said. "I will never trust an *Italiano* again. A German would never say such words without meaning them."

"Oh, Claudia," I said, "you were the one to tell me that all men, from whatever country, speak in the service of their—what did you call it?"

"I never called it anything. But you're right—how much harder it is to heed one's own advice in these matters!" She turned me around and then brushed my hair, which was cut—according to the rules of the institution—just above my shoulders.

Having one's hair brushed by someone else is surely one of life's sweetest pleasures, and I emptied my mind of all other thoughts so that I could enjoy it completely.

"It's colder tonight, I think," Claudia said when she was done.

I nodded my agreement and smiled—because it was the first time in a long while that she had spoken to me as a friend.

We climbed into the same bed that night without saying anything at all about the matter. I fell asleep, I think, as soon as she curled herself up against my back, her hand held in mine.

I thought I was dreaming at first as the music came drifting in through the window, poking at my sleep. But then Claudia stirred, and I could sense that she heard it as well.

I cracked my eyes open. The sky was that pale shade of green streaked with pink one sees sometimes at sunrise in early spring. I could hear three *flauti dolci*—a tenor, an alto, and a soprano—and a single man's voice, surprisingly rich and strong as it rose above the *rio*.

We all dragged ourselves from our beds and looked out the window, rubbing our eyes, at the gondola bedecked with pink roses. Scarlatti stood in the prow, his hands stretched wide, his face tipped upward, singing a barcarole.

When the *matinade* was finished, he kissed his fingertips and threw his hands up toward our window, where we had all shoved aside to give Claudia the best spot at the center.

"I don't imagine a German would do *that*," I ventured as the gondola turned and grew smaller, silhouetted in the rising sun.

Claudia started eating again after that morning serenade, and didn't even argue with her parents when they wrote to say they'd picked out a bridegroom for her and made a down payment on her dowry. "Because he needs to wait for me," was her only comment. "He needs to wait until I turn seventeen."

*O*n the first warm day after that memorable winter, the Prioress rose from the head table at dinner to announce that the *figlie di coro* were to have a special holiday. His Excellency Andrea Foscarini, head of that noble house and on our own board of governors, had granted a dispensation to pay for an outing to the island of Torcello.

We threw our napkins into the air to signal our joy, knowing that any great noise might cause our treat to be taken away.

Donna Emanuela warned us to sing our prayers with special sweetness as we made our preparations for bed—because if there was the slightest threat of rain, the outing would be postponed.

The sound that night must have warmed the heart of any

Veneziano who passed beneath our windows. Marietta especially
sang with such strength and clarity as she brushed her hair that
I expected to hear applause when the last "amen" shimmered
with all the brilliance of rain caught by sunlight.

I lay in my bed and thought—as I so often did at night—of
Franz Horneck. It had been one full month since I'd felt his
lips on mine. I reached under the bedclothes to find that place
again—for the merest touch of it would waken the memory of his
kisses.

The day dawned fair. One by one we propped ourselves up in
our beds. Giulietta, who was usually the most difficult among us
to waken, was first at the window looking east over the Rio della
Pietà. The rising sun shone through her chestnut-colored curls.

Marietta woke up as if someone had shouted "Fire!" into her
ears. "Oh, *Dio!*" she cried out. Then she threw on her clothes
and ran barefoot out the door.

"Where's she off to?" Bernardina asked me. I was able to say
with perfect honesty that I didn't know. But I guessed—though I
kept it to myself—that she was sending a message through Matteo. A message to whom or to what purpose, I had no idea. But
when she returned—daring us with her baleful looks to tell on
her—I noticed that she paid special attention to her toilette, and
even washed, much to our amusement, between her legs when
everyone else was done with the water.

Our old red robes had been newly laundered. We pinched our
cheeks and bit our lips to bring the blood to them and chase away
our winter pallor. More than one of us arranged her veil so that
wisps of curls showed through. We knew full well that the eyes of
Venezia would be upon us as we were rowed through the canals
in the stately gondola of the Foscarini, northward to Torcello.
Each of us thought of the one we hoped would be watching.

ANNO DOMINI 1709

Dearest Mother,

You must think that I spend all my time in jail. But it is not true. It is just that these are the only times when I am given the opportunity—indeed, compelled—to write to you.

But compelled or not, I do so gladly. If it is only an illusion that I speak to you, the illusion brings me gladness nonetheless. I can tell you things that I could not say to anyone else—and perhaps more so than if you were a flesh-and-blood mother at my side. Writing to you brings a relief even greater than that of prayer, a cleansing as sweet as Confession.

Two days ago, one of the huge gondolas of the Ca' Foscarini came to take us away for the entire day and much of the night, as it turned out, to the island of Torcello. Wearing our colors, we wound like a red ribbon first along the Grand Canal and then northward, wending our way between palazzi and under bridges, where people gathered to hear us sing as we passed by. I am quite sure that for many of the boys and men who gathered, the goal was also to catch a glimpse of our faces. They cheered. They called more than one of us by name. They threw flowers, and some threw gold and silver coins. A boatload of bare-breasted courtesans drew up alongside us somewhere along the way, waving and calling gaily. "I was at the Pietà!" said one, and another, smiling sweetly, said, "I have a daughter there!" They made no special sign to any one of us, though I searched their faces.

When we passed by the Iron Bridge, there was the seamstress Rebekkah waving at us. I looked in vain for her apprentice, Silvio, who was my classmate and a favorite friend of mine before I was chosen for the coro. Many Jews of the Ghetto gathered to see the sight of us and hear our singing.

As we passed the Mendicanti, just before we headed out into open waters, the *coro* there joined in our song, so that their notes floated down on us as our notes floated up to meet them, and they mingled in the air.

And then the fresh wind was full in our faces and the whole watery world opened up before us. I could feel how much harder the men rowing had to work suddenly.

I wish I could find the words to describe what I felt as la Serenissima began to grow smaller and smaller behind us, and the vastness of the lagoon made the sound of our voices so small that we were stunned into silence. Without a word, we reached for one another's hands and held tight. The teachers who accompanied us—even la Befana—seemed just as awed.

I expected to see a whale rise from the deep at any moment to swallow us. Yes, the sun poured over our sides, warming our faces even as the breeze blew fresh upon us. But although Venezia is upon the water, she is anchored there by the thousands of tree trunks driven down into the mud of the canals to hold up the stones of our palaces and churches, our bridges and every manner of building. Though made of water, Venezia is also, secretly, of the earth—a celestial nest perched at the top of hidden trees.

But now there was no vestige of earthliness to separate and save us from the waters, which were ever a darkening and deepening blue. For the first time in my life, I felt a sense of the smallness and weakness of this body in which my soul, for the moment, resides. The blueness called to me, the blueness of Heaven and all eternity—and I felt the smallness of the things we care about. In that moment, the sea seemed a mother to me, sang out and called to me, and I cried softly because I longed to be held by her, lost in her arms.

We were carried along by the oarsmen on a journey that brought us neither farther away nor closer to any shore. We were in a middle place without any way to mark the passage of time except the sun—no bells, no chores, no lessons, no prayers. Some dainties were brought out for us to eat. Some of us could eat without remorse. But others hung like wilted plants, with faces just as green, over the sides, and retched so piteously that we were all soon left without an appetite.

And then the island came into view. What a welcome sight, the Basilica with its church and bell tower after the sick-making journey across the lagoon! And the trees—trees such as I've never seen before, whole forests and fields of green and windswept gold. The sun was high in the heavens by then, and as soon as our feet touched the ground we were hungry.

But first we sang for the fishermen and farmers who met our boat and greeted us with baskets of food and flowers. The servants of the Foscarini set about making fires to cook the fish that seemed to be jumping out of the waters to hear the music we made.

I stood by watching as a magnificent picnic was spread upon a green meadow where the first violets had been teased into blossom by the weak winter sunshine. Two twin girls who have lately joined the coro—Flavia and Alicia dal Basso—sat upon the grass and began weaving garlands of violets and buttercups while chattering in the secret language they share.

The maestro made a great fuss over these two when they were brought in as iniziate. They look like any other girls of twelve (although they look exactly like each other). But through some trick in the way they are made, they can sing in the low baritone range. The maestro, sighing over them, said that it's only once in a decade that such a voice comes along—and then to have two, identically rich and mellow! Now that the maestro is gone, la Befana makes them sing their parts an octave above, insisting they'll do themselves an injury otherwise—and perhaps even grow male parts! She says it is a sin against nature for a girl to sing like a man.

I hear footsteps approaching, which gives me hope that my time here is done. I will tell the rest of the tale to you later, when Sister Laura lets me.

Claudia always signs her letters to her mother with kisses. And so I will also sign this to you with baci—*thousands of kisses, from your loving daughter,*

Anna Maria dal Violin

I CAN FIND NO CONTINUATION of the tale in my box of letters. But I have only to close my eyes to see Torcello again, that island that seemed like a paradise to me—a paradise that held within it a tiny corner of Hell.

I remember that I was enjoying the warmth of the sun on my face when one of the Foscarini's serving maids brought me a prettily arranged trencher of food. Deep in thought as I was, I didn't really look at her face, but merely thanked her. And then I was rudely woken from my reverie by a sharp little kick from the toe of her shoe.

Fortunately I did not have time to cry out in protest before I looked full in her face and saw, peeking out from her starched little cap and row of curls, my old friend Silvio.

"Signorina," he said, his voice disguised and bowing apologies. "My errant foot kicked out all on its own at your juicy little ass!"

He managed to say this so that it sounded like normal speech, and to maintain a beautifully servile expression, so that no one would have taken note of the interaction even if anyone had been watching.

"I wondered why I didn't see you with Rebekkah!"

"Shh!"

"Come eat with me!"

"Don't be daft—I can't! And please ignore me properly, as fits my station."

I pretended to eat while he hovered over me.

"I spoke with von Regnazig's man about your bijoux—look down, for God's sake, Annina!"

"Please, Silvio—tell me quickly!"

"I can't now. But when you've done eating, go off into the woods—there, to the left, away from the Basilica—as if to have a pee. I'll find you there—and I'll tell you everything I know."

He went off to serve the others, and I was left with a trencher of food I no longer felt in the slightest bit capable of eating.

Now that I was about to find out who had sent the locket to me, I felt, once again, more dread than relief. I was convinced it had something to do with the secret of my identity—what else could it be? I was far too young—and too unknown—to be receiving tributes from a suitor. But all the possibilities I could think of filled me with fear. What if I learned that my mother was some low whore, or a criminal imprisoned beneath the Doge's Palace? What if, once found, she wanted to claim me again, to use me, as Marietta's mother used the children in her keeping? Or—far more likely, given the locket's strange appearance and my own strange looks—what if one or both my parents came from another place, perhaps a savage place, where I'd be put out in some desolate field to herd goats? Or tasked day and night with spinning? Or married, against my will, to some rude merchant who would make me play jigs for his drunken friends?

My fantasies ran in other directions, too. There was the young noblewoman who had borne me out of wedlock—who read my letters and was using whatever influence she had to better my position in the *coro*. Who had been watching over me and was just waiting for the right moment to make herself known to me. Who would visit me in the *parlatorio*. I would tell her all my secrets, all my fears, and she would give me her counsel in whispered words meant only for me. We would resemble each other in some odd way that would make both of us laugh—and I would know that I was not alone in the world.

How ardently I wanted to believe in answers! I never allowed myself to linger more than a terrified moment on the consideration that even the best outcome could open a Pandora's box of complications and contradictions. I could not let go of my quest—I was like a dog that, sniffing something buried in the ground, will not give up digging for it, no matter that the bone he hopes to find turns out to be something infested with maggots and rot, something that should have remained forever buried.

I was pushing the food around on my plate, wondering how I'd break away from the group to go into the forest. Giulietta and Claudia came up from behind me, one after the other, each demanding that I walk with her on the outing to the Basilica. I said yes to both, just to buy myself more time. And then Marietta knelt down beside me, kissed my cheek, and whispered a plea for me to follow her into the woods.

Knowing that Marietta had some kind of mischief afoot—and having so lately got out of jail—I had little desire to do anything she suggested. But her proposal happened to coincide this time with my own purposes. I laid the trencher in the grass and chased Marietta across the field. We made out that we were playing a game of tag, laughing and squealing, and straying all the while farther and farther from the picnic.

And then, suddenly, she was running in earnest away from me, toward the dark line of trees.

I had never run such a long way before, and never with the yielding earth beneath my shoes rather than dead cobblestones. I was panting several paces behind Marietta—who was ever fleeter than I—as she reached and then penetrated the edge of the woods, so extravagant in the growth and greenness of the trees that grew there, like a living wall.

It took several moments for my eyes to adjust to the gloom. Following the direction of Marietta's footfalls, I thought I saw some people hidden among the trees. When I got over my surprise and could see clearly again, I made out a gentleman, with two servants in attendance. As Marietta ran full-tilt toward him, her arms outstretched, he stepped out into a beam of sunlight that fell through the canopy of the trees. I could see his black hair and ruddy cheeks, his fierce eyes and full mouth. He could have served as a model for one of Sebastiano Ricci's paintings of the ancient gods.

He embraced Marietta—and then she gazed back at me with a look that begged my complicity.

I shook my head in envy and disbelief. "Do what you want, Marietta!" I shouted at her. "I wash my hands of you!" And with that, I turned my back and ran farther into the forest.

It was my first time ever being in a forest (unless, I reasoned, I had been born on the mainland and carried through a forest as a babe in arms). It was at once frightening and beautiful—and the sight of Marietta in the arms of that nobleman, as handsome as she was lovely, stirred up my senses to a ridiculous degree.

I felt that I could smell and see with an unaccustomed keenness. I could hear the very leaves breathing, and the tiny movements of birds and insects among their branches. Although I had read of the forests and oases of the Bible—and had spent as much time as any other girl of the Pietà beneath the two twisted pomegranate trees and the palm in our courtyard—I had no idea that trees, when massed together, had such a beautiful smell. The leaves, the bark, and their exhalations filled the air with a fragrance fit for angels.

I really did need to relieve myself by then, but didn't want to for fear that Silvio would happen upon me. I reached a clearing and decided to wait there for him. I remember wondering if there were lions there on Torcello, or other creatures who might wish to make a meal of me. I prayed to the Virgin for protection. Meanwhile, because Silvio was such a long time in finding me, I chose a sheltered place and made a tent of my skirts to release my water, being careful not to wet my shoes. And then I laughed, because it was the first time that making water had seemed to me a lovely thing, there among the trees and the low-growing brush and the dew and the flowers.

I had barely pulled up my knickers when I heard someone running, and turned to see Silvio, pink in the face and a little wild-eyed. "I thought you'd been eaten by a lion!"

I ran to him laughing and, in truth, a little frightened. I put my arms around him—of course, "he" was still dressed as a "she"—and laid my head on his shoulder. "I'm so glad you found me!" And then I whispered, "Are there lions here?"

"I grew up in the same pile of stones as you did, little sister, and heard the same stories. There were lions in Ancient Rome, I think."

"Bugger Ancient Rome!" I said—or something equally vulgar. "Tell me what you know about the locket, Silvio! Tell me quickly, before anyone finds us!"

"Or eats us!"

"This is not a time for jokes!" I took both his hands in mine and wondered at the length and slenderness of his fingers. It seemed suddenly unjust to me that boys of the Pietà are not allowed to study music.

"I thought you liked my jokes!" He pulled me down so that we were sitting on the grass, knees to knees. "This is what I know, Annina."

I closed my eyes, praying to the Virgin that what he knew would be something I wanted to hear.

"The locket was left in the keeping of a pawnbroker in the Ghetto, the Banco Giallo."

"Is that the bank used by von Regnazig?"

Silvio nodded. "There are three different pawnshops in the Ghetto, each known for the color of the receipts they give: red, green, or yellow—*rosso, verde,* or *giallo*. All the nobles use them."

"Hurry!"

"I'm hurrying. The locket was originally given as a pledge for a loan—the usual thing. It was a young nobleman, in some desperate need, and not very long ago. He was masked and didn't give his name. And then someone else came to pay back the loan and reclaim the pledge—a relative of his. A *zentildonna*."

"For the love of God, *who?*"

Silvio shook his head. "She was also masked. The only thing the pawnbroker could tell me was that she seemed, from her voice, to be rather young—although not so very young. She repaid the pledge and then paid something extra to have the locket delivered to you, specifying that it had to be done in secret. The pawnbroker promised her that he would find a way."

This news filled me with a sense of excitement at its significance: a noblewoman. But then I realized that I was no closer than I had been to being able to find this lady. "Couldn't he tell you anything more?" Poor Silvio, after all his trouble! I probably sounded more annoyed than grateful.

He shook his head. "There was only one small thing."

"Tell me!"

He took both my hands in his and kissed them. "This is where we must tread carefully, my sweet Annina, because not only your future but mine, too, may rest upon how we proceed." He looked in my eyes as he spoke. "The lady told the pawnbroker that he'd been recommended to her for his honesty and probity."

"And what good does that do me?"

"Well, you see, the person who recommended him was Rebekkah."

*W*e didn't linger long after that. Silvio promised to find out everything he could from Rebekkah. And then he ran back, before he was missed, to join the group of servants the Foscarini had allotted to the outing.

I ran in the direction of the tower, and then through an entrance to the ancient church, where I could hear the echoing voice of a guide as well as the echoed whispers of my restless friends, who no doubt would have far preferred to stay out of doors.

Wedging myself between some girls at the back, I tried to calm my breathing and look attentive as the voice droned on about the mosaic depicting the Last Judgment on the back wall, the Harrowing of Hell at the top, the Elect at the bottom left, and the Damned at the bottom right. The scene seemed particularly appropriate to my situation.

"Where have you been?" Bernardina hissed at me. "And where is that trollop, Marietta? La Befana has been asking about you both!"

"I went to relieve my bowels."

"And you needed her to wipe you?"

"Bernardina, that is disgusting!"

"Well, you are disgusting, the two of you, with your intrigues and assignations!"

"I've had no assignations!"

Bernardina snorted in a way most unbefitting a well-brought-up girl. "Which is more than can be said of your best friend—washing between her legs, indeed!"

The guide was droning on: "The Basilica was remodeled in the first years of the eleventh century by Bishop Orso Orseolo, later Patriarch of Aquileia."

"She's not my best friend."

"If she's not, who is, then? I suppose that title belongs to your Saxon bedmate."

"Silenzio!" Maestra Meneghina's voice boomed from the front of the group. Magically, and much to my horror, the group parted like the Red Sea at the sound of it. The parting formed a straight pathway to where I had placed myself at the back, hoping to look inconspicuous.

After surveying the effect her voice had upon us, la Befana walked slowly toward me. She didn't stop until I could see the mole on her chin and the two black hairs growing out of it like beheaded flowers.

I could hear everyone holding her breath. La Befana looked at me for what seemed a very long time before she spoke, as if her eyes were special instruments that could see beneath the surface of things to the most compromising truths inside. Then she smiled—but it was not a friendly smile. It never was with her, not in all the years she cast her shadow here.

"We are honored to have you join us, Anna Maria." She waved behind her. "Please, *Signore*, carry on!" And then, to me, "Follow me, young lady!"

I followed her through a doorway that opened onto a winding staircase; I realized it must be the tower. As we passed one of the arched windows, I looked out through the grille at the pale green and yellow leaves of the forest—and suffered a pang of guilt that I hadn't even tried to stop Marietta from whatever folly she was about to engage in. An image passed before my eyes of Marietta transformed into a woman in the manner of her mother—ruined, corrupt, and ill.

Distracted as I was, I stumbled. La Befana turned to look at me; there was no sympathy in those eyes. "Be quick! And watch your footing!"

She seemed to me uncannily fit for one who was so old. I was breathing hard by the time we reached the top of the staircase, which ended in the small, round, unadorned room that housed the bell. There were bars on the window. Again I looked out and thought of Marietta. And I thought about how different a landscape looks from far above.

We cannot really see things when we are in the middle of them. I did not know that then, but I know it now. I couldn't imagine why la Befana had brought me up into the tower, unless it was to hurt me.

I was, of course, afraid. La Befana was famous among the foundlings for knowing how to hurt while leaving us unblemished, with no bruises for us to show the Prioress. I think she must have made a study of the places she could press and squeeze and twist and poke without leaving any trace behind her, apart from the hatred for her she burned onto our souls. The governors have always been unforgiving when it comes to physical maltreatment of their wards. But we knew that our words alone weighed nothing in the scales of justice.

"And now . . ."

"And now, Signora?" I tried to keep my voice from shaking, but I doubt I succeeded.

"And now perhaps you'd like to tell me where you were—and what has become of Marietta."

I looked steadily at her. I know I did, because I can still see the way her face looked to me in that moment. I can remember the hardness I saw in her eyes, and even a glint of humor there. She was enjoying this. It was, for her, a treat. "I felt sick after the journey. My bowels threatened to loosen as soon as I had my first taste of food. I pleaded with Marietta to come with me, because I was afraid—well, I was afraid of meeting a lion."

It astonished me how prolifically the falsehoods were breeding, and how easily they tumbled from my mouth into the world.

"And did a lion eat Marietta, then?"

"I told her to leave because—because I didn't want her, or anyone else, to bear witness to my misery. I asked her to stand well away from me."

"And then?"

"And then, when I was finished finally, I looked for her everywhere. I called and called her name. I thought she must have grown impatient waiting for me, and hastened to join the others here for the tour of the Basilica of Santa Maria Assunta."

"And the tower, Anna Maria. Let us not forget the tower, so far away from everyone—as far away as if we were alone on a mountaintop, you and I."

"A mountaintop," I echoed, looking around the room in the weak light that filtered in from the waning day outside. I wondered if she hated me enough to kill me. Girls died often enough—and it would be easy, in such a place as this, to make it seem an accident.

"Sit down—there." She motioned to a rough bench against the wall. And then she sat down beside me, very close. Too close. I could smell her—a smell of sweat and spittle and rot.

I know now that ill luck was as much a part of la Befana's evil mien as the bitterness she harbored in her soul. Tooth decay, smallpox, and time itself had long ago robbed her of the sweet looks that excuse the small cruelties of the fair.

Is there such a thing as evil, plain as simple? She was the closest to it I have ever known. But, even in her, evil was a complicated thing, made of many layers and wearing many masks.

Beneath it all there was a wounded thing, more animal than human. The crime was that such a person was allowed to be a teacher here—to have so many tender young souls in her power.

Even her hatred of me—her very particular hatred—was somewhat impersonal. She was trying to hurt someone else by hurting me. I was a pawn in the game she played. But, no mistake about it, she wanted my downfall. She was bent on causing it, and bent, too, on making it seem that I had brought it upon myself.

"Are you aware," she said to me, moving even closer, "that one in twenty people in Venezia is either a priest or a nun."

"I didn't know the number was so high. But the call to God is, no doubt, a call of great power."

"No doubt. And yet a true religious calling is relatively rare. Far more often it is the Republic's inheritance laws that make nuns and priests of so many whose families have a claim to a title or lands. And it is simple hunger that makes priests and nuns of the others."

I only realized that I had been holding my breath when I began to breathe again. She was going to lecture, not beat me—at least not for the moment.

She smiled again. Her smile, I swear, was more frightening than anything else about her. "Have you ever thought that you had a calling to God, Anna Maria?"

It was some game she was playing. I knew I had to be very careful about what I said. "My calling is to music."

"Yes," said la Befana. The smile was gone. "It is just as I thought. Have your eyes adjusted to the lack of light here? I want to show you something."

I quickly looked about her person, but didn't see anything she could use to hit me, apart from her hands. Her hands were frightful things, though. She sat unmoving, seeming to take note of my fear. Then she bent down and pulled the skirts of her robe up over her knees.

My eyes had adjusted well. The skin of her thighs was as lumpy and mottled-looking as loaves of bread left out in the damp air.

I couldn't tell if the sick feeling in my stomach had more to do with the sight of her exposed flesh or the fact that I hadn't eaten anything since the bit of bread I'd had at breakfast.

La Befana spoke in little more than a whisper, and yet the smallness of the room pressed her voice against my ears. "I was the maestro's *favorita,* in my time. I was just as talented as you are—and I was pious, too. I loved God with all my heart, and tried with all my heart to be good, even when the Devil tempted me." It was a different voice than she'd ever used with me before, as if she spoke to a friend. As if she loved me. "I would have become a choir nun, had I been able. Yes, I wanted with all my heart to take vows."

As she spoke, she began unwinding the bandages that were wrapped around her legs from her knees to her ankles. "But only the daughters of Venezia's noble houses are considered fit to be choir nuns. No matter what the talents of a base-born girl, nor how supreme her efforts to serve God well, she is not considered good enough to sing God's praises for the Republic's salvation. If she takes vows, she can be no more than a serving wench to the choir nuns of Venezia." She unfastened her shoes. There were more bandages beneath, stained with sweat and time—and underneath those, her naked feet.

I had never seen an old person's naked feet before. Each misshapen toe had what looked like a hard little lump of flesh set upon it like the hat of an organ grinder's monkey but drained of all its color. The toenails were thick and yellow where the flesh beneath them wasn't stained a brownish-looking purple. Her lower legs were likewise covered in bruises, and the veins stood out upon them blue and swollen.

Apart from torturing me with the sight of all this ugliness, I couldn't imagine why she was showing this to me.

She grimaced and pressed both of her naked feet onto the dusty floor.

I remember wondering if she really *was* a witch, who could read people's thoughts. Could she do it only when her feet were bare? I made myself pray, although no doubt it was a particularly great sin to do so on the heels of a lie. *Deus in adjutorium meum intende. Domine ad adiuvandum*, I repeated as hard as I could inside my head until she began speaking again, so softly that I wondered at first if I was hearing her words inside my head as well. But I saw her lips moving.

"I was *la favorita*, in my time, just like you. A prodigy. 'A gift from God,' the maestro told me often enough. We had special lessons together, just he and I." She wrapped her fingers around my collar and pulled me even closer, so that I could see the coating of spittle on her teeth. "Do you know the meaning of sacrifice, Anna Maria?"

I closed my eyes. I'm sure I was wincing. I thought before I spoke, wanting to give the right answer—and to avoid whatever special torture she'd devised for me this time, high in the tower, where no one would be able to hear my cries. "Jesus sacrificed himself so that the rest of us can rise on Judgment Day and live again."

She suddenly let go of me. "You answer like a child." Her friendly tone, like her smile, was gone. "I am speaking of the sacrifices made by a woman."

I didn't consider either of us to be a woman then—neither myself nor la Befana. I watched in horrified fascination as she lifted up her right foot and held it in both her hands, turning it sideways to expose the inside of her ankle, just above her heel. The skin was as cracked and rutted as a dirt pathway after a time of drought. I saw the brand there, burned into her skin: the letter P, with a cross at its base, boxed in by four flourishes, the top right one ending in a hook.

I knew the secret history, even then. The Senate passed a law at the turn of the century prohibiting the branding of children. But branding was still in practice when I was brought to the Pietà, as near as I can calculate, in anno Domini 1695. Because our facilities have ever been cramped, most of the babies who enter the system are sent out to board with wet-nurses, as far away from Venezia as possible. Ever mindful of the expense of raising us, the governors count on at least some of these foster mothers growing attached to their wards and wanting to keep them.

But poverty on the mainland is such that a foster mother would sometimes murder the foundling in her keeping, using her pay to feed and clothe her own child, whom she would return to the Pietà at the age of ten to complete her education at the continued expense of the State.

The governors, in their wisdom, lit upon the solution of having the surgeon brand us, on the arm or the foot, so that no other child could be raised and returned in our stead.

I didn't know that la Befana had been a foundling. I should have, because nearly all the grown women of the Pietà begin their lives here. And yet, like all children, I had trouble thinking of the adults around me as having ever been other than what I saw and felt them to be: alien beings with their own language and code of conduct. Unlike the Prioress and Sister Laura, and even Sister Giovanna, la Befana was not around when I began my musical studies.

I cast my mind back. I remembered her from the time when I was nine or ten. She entered as a member of the *coro*. And then, some years later, she'd been promoted to *maestra*. Where had she gone, then, in the time between? And how long had she been away?

She wiggled her toes and began to wind the bandages around her feet and legs again.

I tried to keep my voice steady as I looked her in those cruel eyes of hers. "Were you at the Pietà, Signora, when I was brought in?"

My question seemed to give her pleasure. She looked at me a long time, reached out her hand, and touched my face. She touched me softly, and yet I flinched. "Yes," she said. "I was one of the first who ever laid eyes on you."

How could that be? I knew that she could not have been one of the *cariche* then. She was not even a *maestra* yet, so she could not have been one of their trustees.

"You were a very small baby, so delicate and small and sickly that the priest was sent for straight away."

I mouthed more than said my next two words: "Tell me."

"Whether you were dressed in silk or rags? Whether there was any special token about your person—or perhaps a letter? Half a letter, or half a drawing, or half an ancient coin?"

She sat back, smiling again—more like the rictus of a corpse, it seems to me in retrospect, than an expression of pleasure or mirth. Truly, when I look back, I can almost feel sorry for her. "Alas, I can't remember." Her smile vanished. She looked straight at me, her eyes filled with hatred.

"No doubt, I can't remember because I was too distracted by the sense that everything I'd ever strived to build had just fallen in a heap of rubble at my feet. That everyone I'd believed in had lied to me. And that all the sacrifices I made were for nothing!"

I caught a glimpse, in that moment, of the wounded, suffering thing she carried around inside her—the part of her that was indeed dead or dying. She saw me see this and I could tell that she regretted having spoken so unguardedly.

She seemed on fire when she spoke again. "Do you know the special fate reserved in Hell for liars, Anna Maria? How their flesh, no matter how smooth and pretty, is perpetually rent from their faces, torn away, over and over again, for all eternity, by the Devil's birds of prey?" She reached out to touch my face again, but I shrank away from her. Crows were cawing as they flew past the tiny window of the tower.

"Yes, I was there when you came into the world." Truly she seemed like a monster to me. A whispering, lying abomination. "How could I not have been?"

Everything began to swirl then, so that I thought the tower must be about to fall. A hand fell hard across my face. "Don't you dare faint, you foolish girl!"

I whimpered like a puling infant. It was the first time I had ever cried in front of her.

What had she always wanted but to hurt me? Why would she not do everything in her power to hurt me now—and surely now, more than ever before, I was in her power.

I told myself that la Befana was a devil and a liar who only wanted to make me pay for every wrong she'd ever suffered. I reasoned that she would have said something about the locket if she had not been merely trying to convince me of her power. She knew nothing of the locket. We were marked by the same brand— and perhaps she had been at the Pietà when I was brought in. But that meant nothing. I was well on my way to finding out what I wanted to know—and I wouldn't let her bar my path, nor put false answers in my way.

I stopped sniveling, crossed myself, and stared straight

ahead of me, even though I felt like hanging my head and weeping some more.

"You are a fine one, with your religious airs, Anna Maria."

The tears filled my eyes and, like a child, I held my hands over my ears.

She regarded me coldly. "You have yet to learn the meaning of duty or sacrifice. You pretend to be an *inserviente della musica*, but you are servant only to your own desires. And your own ambition. You are selfish and self-indulgent and, yes, remarkably like your mother."

I wept harder then, so relieved to hear her phrase it thus, removing herself from any possibility of filling that position. She got up and stood looking at me from the top of the stairs. "You are very little like your father, though. Yes, sometimes I wonder if it wasn't perhaps someone else who sired you."

She turned to walk down the stairs, then stopped and looked back at me one more time. "Bear in mind, Signorina, that if anything befalls Marietta, you will be held responsible—with the full weight of the punishment that would entail. Think hard upon it."

I sat there in my own silence for a long time, and then I think I must have fallen asleep. The sky outside the window, when I became aware of it again, was the color of a freshly bitten ripe plum. I could hear voices calling below me—"Marietta! Marietta! *Dove sei?* Where are you?"

I ran down the spiraling stairs, pausing to curtsey and cross myself at the sacred basin beneath the gilded statue of the Virgin.

The purple sky was quickly giving way to a bruised twilight. I was truly afraid of lions now, as well as God's judgment, and ran harder than I had ever run before, until my sides were aching. I feared the boat would leave without me.

But at the water's edge the gondola, and the servants, were waiting. Many of the girls were already aboard and, what with shattered nerves, many of them were weeping. I looked for Silvio and found his face, which looked chastened and silly now in his woman's garb. He gestured for me to ignore him.

Giulietta came up and stood close to me. "They found her. They were about to go searching for you, but la Befana said she knew where you were and that you would come by yourself before daylight ended."

"I nearly didn't! I fell asleep there in the tower."

"Marietta also says that she fell asleep, but in the woods."

The twins, Flavia and Alicia, drew near and held on to our robes. "My grandmother says that this island is enchanted," said one of them—I still hadn't learned to tell them apart. "The spirits of the ancient ones still roam here."

"Look at that sky!" the other one chimed in.

The sky was now the color of the skin of a plum that has been bitten through in places, leaking out the brighter color of its juices.

"There was blood on her skirts!" Giulietta whispered.

"It was mud," said one of the twins.

"It was blood—but, hush! You're too young to hear of such things."

Scowling, the twins said something to each other we couldn't understand.

And then I saw Marietta walking toward the water's edge from the forest, flanked on each side by a nun. I crossed myself because, as everyone knows, it is bad luck to see two nuns walking together. I could tell by the way she walked and, then—when she was closer—from the look on her face, that Marietta had done or gotten what she wanted.

La Befana spoke before any of us could speak, and in a tone

of voice that would brook no dissent. "There is to be silence on the trip back! Any girl who speaks will be confined for three days with only bread and water. And that is on top of the punishments some of you have already earned! And now, *andiamo!*"

Both Marietta and I were locked up, though separately, for three days. On the second day, Sister Laura managed to bring me my violin, as well as some extra food beyond the bread and water that were my allotment.

I begged her to stay with me awhile.

"For a little while, Annina. But not long enough so that I will be missed."

She sat beside me on the little pallet that served as both bed and chair. A bit of daylight came through a small window near the ceiling, but mostly it was twilight in the cell—and after the sun went down, it was completely dark.

Sister Laura put her hand into her pocket and fished something out of it. "I brought you these as well," she said, placing a candle and two flints on the floor.

"You are very good to me!"

She brushed the hair out of my eyes with her hand. "I'm glad you think so. I was once a girl here—and though it was long ago, I can remember it well."

I searched her eyes. "Do you wear the brand of the Pietà, as Maestra Meneghina does?"

"I must go!"

"Forgive me, Sister! You have been so kind. It was just that, on Torcello, la Befana—" I put my hand over my mouth.

She smiled at my blunder. "We know the names you call us. We served our teachers in just the same way."

"I have never heard any girl speak ill of you!"

"Ah, but you should hear what the other teachers say. I am not well liked among them."

Even though I did not dare ask again, my question was still in my eyes as she got up to leave. But often I did not even need to speak for Sister Laura to understand me, so attuned was she to what I was thinking.

She sighed. "I wear no brand—at least, not on my flesh. Goodnight, Anna Maria."

"Goodnight, Sister. And God bless you!"

She did something then that she had never done before. She bent down and kissed my forehead.

I held my fingers over the place for a long time after I heard the door close and the key turn in the lock.

CHAPTER 9

*M*Y PUNISHMENT, for a week following my release from jail, was to spend all my free time copying scores into the *libri musicali*. With all the musicians here, and all the use our music gets, there is a perpetual need for new copies of old music and fair copies of new music to be made. Girls who are good with ink and a quill are made to specialize in this work. Many end their lives with weakened eyesight from the strain of writing for so many hours every day. They're given an extra allotment of oil for their lamps. But the work always takes its toll, and it is work I have never done gladly. The thought of going blind has always been particularly fearful to me.

I was passing by one of the practice rooms, carrying a pile of freshly penned scores to the Prioress, when I heard the maestro's voice. "Signorina, *prego!*"

Vivaldi looked as delighted to find me passing by as I was astonished to see him there, standing at the *clavicembalo*. Seated at a small table near him, half hidden behind a heap of music paper and quills, was a man I didn't recognize but who nonetheless seemed vaguely familiar to me. I curtseyed. Both were without wigs and had the heated, unbuttoned look of men engaged in a lively discussion.

"Don Vivaldi!" I said. Then, more softly, "Maestro!"

"Yes, yes, Annina—you're just the girl I want to see. Here, take this quill and write for me! My hand aches from all the composing I have been doing today."

"Vivaldi, leave off trying to impress me!" the other man said in lightly accented Italian. When he smiled, I suddenly recognized him from the Foscarini's ball: it was Handel.

"How could I possibly hope to impress you, after the triumph of your oratorio? It seems that I hear of nothing else these days."

Handel bowed. "As many came to hear the violin soloist as to hear the singing."

Because I'd first seen Handel wearing a mask, it felt to me now as if the face I saw covered his true face, the Harlequin he wore that night when Giulietta—and, no doubt, countless others—fell in love with him. It was a broad face, rather fleshy, with eyebrows like two caterpillars perched upon his brow. His eyes shone, though, and he had an almost pretty, boyish smile.

"You shouldn't tell lies to a priest, young pup. But, anyway, that was well spoken and quite gracious of you. You are well bred, you Saxon nobles."

Handel chuckled. "I am no more noble than you are, Padre. In fact—" He bowed to me again, in that single gesture acknowledging my presence and including me in his confidence, "My father was a sort of barber, just like yours."

"And a musician, too, was he not?"

"Not a bit of it! He had no interest in music and, in fact, wanted me to become a lawyer."

The maestro wasn't looking at me, but I could feel his attention shift away from Handel. "Yes—parents can be very inconvenient people to have around."

"Perhaps so. But it was only the intercession of my mother that allowed me to pursue the gift God gave me."

Vivaldi nodded thoughtfully. "It gives one pause to consider the good or the harm a parent can do. For instance, most of the girls here would have perished if left with the mothers who brought them into the world. Most, but not all, of course. But they are well taken care of in this place, wouldn't you say so, Signorina? But please," he added, noticing my discomfort in standing there with the books stacked in my arms. "Lay down your burden, child!"

Setting the stack of scores down on a corner of the table, I looked hard and long into the maestro's eyes, wondering what he was after and whether there were deeper meanings hidden beneath his flippant words. He looked somehow older to me; his eyes were troubled. But now I wonder if it is only hindsight that has made me remember him in this light on that particular day.

I hadn't yet learned that we all wear masks, whether or not it's Carnival. Though he wore no mask that day, Vivaldi was hiding—perhaps even from himself—the single event that would have the greatest consequences for him of any event in his lifetime.

Of course, I knew nothing of this and suspected even less. All I knew—and that through rumor—was that he was recently returned from Mantua. "Excuse me, Maestro," I couldn't keep from asking, "but is it possible that our letters to the Board of Governors—?"

"No, no. No, no, no, no," he said, making it sound like a rhythm he was marking. "They rest with their decision. Although, for your efforts to reinstate me—you and the other *putte*—"

I bowed, then looked into his eyes—his light-colored eyes that range between gold and green, depending on his mood. I couldn't find a trace of the despondency I'd just seen there, not a moment before. Vivaldi was, once again, his usual, lively self. He is, and has ever been, a person of changeable humors.

"Based on my most prolific career, the governors wish me to continue composing for the *coro*: at least two motets per month, two new Mass and Vespers settings—one for Easter, and one for the Feast of the Visitation of the Blessed Virgin—to whom this venerable institution is dedicated, for your information, Handel."

"I didn't know." Handel smiled at me, as if the maestro's speechifying were all part of some jest that was bound to end in a delightful surprise.

"And so, in consideration of these works and others for funerals and the Offices of Holy Week, and the requirements for interpreting all of them correctly—"

My eyes opened wider as I took this in. "You'll be teaching us still?"

"Occasionally. As required. Or more, perhaps." The maestro, rather to my surprise, winked at me. "But enough of this idle chatter, strictly against the rules! Take up your pen, Signorina!"

After copying scores for hours and hours on end all week, writing some more was surely the last thing I wanted to do. But I shook out my ink-stained hand and picked up the quill for the maestro. What wouldn't I do for him, even now? He gave me his chair and pushed a clean sheet of parchment in front of me. "To your Excellencies, distinguished Governors of the Pietà. In consideration of the great success and enormous popularity of *La Resurrezione* last year—"

"Please, Maestro, you're not giving me time to dip the pen."

Vivaldi carried on, ignoring me, "—testaments to the talent of Signor Giorgio Federico Handel, the young but undoubtedly distinguished composer visiting *la Serenissima* from the court of Saxe-Weissenfels"—he nodded at Handel, and Handel nodded back at him, while I wrote as fast as I could—"who, with the guidance and advice of our own dear *maestro di coro*, Signor Gasparini, is composing an opera to be mounted at the now gloriously reopened Teatro San Giovanni Grisostomo, pride of Venezia . . ."

He went on in this mode, and I wrote as fast as I could.

"... and thus we are proposing that certain *putte* of the *coro* of the Ospedale della Pietà be allowed to participate in these performances, thereby bringing the attention of a wider public to the celestial music, which will, without doubt, be followed by bequests and benefices to the greater glory of this institution ..."

I laid down my pen. "Maestro, do you think they will let us?"

He shook his head, smiling. "We will see, Annina. It is at least worth a few strokes of the pen to try. Especially if I am not the one who has to do the writing."

An opera! It pleases me to remember that the first thought that came into my head was how happy Marietta would be—for once I was thinking of someone other than myself. This was the very chance Marietta had been waiting for.

She had not been the same since that day on Torcello. I felt guilty every time I thought about how I'd failed to even try to talk her out of her folly. Now, of course, I know she would not have listened to me—and that she should not have, either.

But at the time I saw this as a second chance for both of us—a chance to wash out whatever harm was done that day. A chance to earn the title Marietta had given me of best friend.

ANNO DOMINI 1709

Dearest Mother,

Sister Laura will be surprised when I hand her this letter to post for me, because it is the first I will write on my own initiative, without her complicity.

You see, I have been set to copying scores—a job that is sometimes a privilege and sometimes a punishment here. The putte *who are given this task are naturally given a supply of paper, ink, and candles. I've been writing the notes in so compact a style that*

I can save one in every five sheets of music paper. I hope it doesn't bother you to read my words within the staves.

But I have two bits of great news—or, at least, it seems tremendous news to us, a veritable revolution of opportunity. There are plans afoot to mount an opera, either by Maestro Gasparini or Signor Handel of Saxony, based on the tale of the ancient Roman queen Agrippina, and set to a libretto by Viceroy Grimani of Napoli. This would not be great news in itself were it not for the fact that Maestro Vivaldi has made a request to allow certain putte of the Pietà to be part of the performance. An opera, Mother, in a real theater!

I have no idea whether the governors will listen to Vivaldi, especially now that he is no longer employed as a teacher here. But he has made a good argument—and I know this because I took the letter down myself from his own dictation. At the end he made me promise that I wouldn't tell anyone else about it, lest it all come to nothing. But I can't see the harm in confiding the project to you—and my heart will burst if I don't tell someone.

The other piece of news is even more amazing than the first one. King Frederick—still traveling here as the Duke of Olemberg—commissioned Venezia's own Rosalba Carriera to paint a life-size portrait of the goddess Diana. And—imagine this! The king instructed her to choose a figlia of the Pietà as her model.

I can't begin to describe the excitement spawned by this news. Rosalba is best known for her exquisite little pictures on snuff boxes and spot boxes and the like, painted in oil pastels. The grander ladies who come to visit us in the parlatorio have shown us examples of these, and we have always marveled at their wondrous detail. Lately Rosalba has come much into vogue among the nobility both here and abroad, who are commissioning her to paint full-size portraits for their collections.

There was endless speculation about which member of the coro had so caught the fancy of the duke (as we are still instructed to call him) that he wanted to have her face hanging on his wall. Girls, teachers, and even servants here placed bets on which of us would be chosen.

The Prioress addressed us at dinner the night before the inspection to tell us to wash our faces and brush our hair with special care, and to be sure that our fingernails were clean and tidy.

But, really, we didn't need reminding to attend to our looks. For days before, ever since the announcement, we'd been brushing our hair till our scalps hurt, and putting stolen honey on our faces. Marietta was discovered with a vial of belladonna, which all of us insisted that she share with us. Even I, without any hope of being chosen, prayed to the Virgin to clear my complexion for the big day.

Aside from our own hopes of glory, we were all of us thrilled that Rosalba—the humble daughter of a lace maker and a clerk—has won this commission from among all the brilliant artists of Venezia. As a woman—and a woman of the people, at that—her success can only bode well for us. She has no husband, and yet she has recently bought her own palazzo, where she lives with her sister and their servants. If Rosalba, without high family connections, has accomplished so much through the perfection of her craft, why can't we aspire to similar accomplishments in our turn?

I have always believed there to be only three possible paths for me, barring an early grave: the profession of Holy Vows; a cloistered life here, playing and teaching music; or a marriage that would bar me from ever performing again. And yet it seems that there is a fourth path, the path carved out for all the women of Venezia by Rosalba. My God, she should be made a saint!

One can't see the movement of the sundial's shadow, and yet it moves. Why couldn't one of us become a world-famous performer in the manner of Albinoni or Corelli? Why couldn't our compositions be played not only here, within these walls, but in the theaters of Venezia and beyond? What do Handel and Scarlatti have, beyond the world's permission, that allows them to go where they choose, from city to city, attending every ball and courting every patron? Surely that extra lump of flesh between a man's legs has nothing to do with making music!

Believe me, Mother, when I tell you that my knowledge of such things comes only from hearsay and looking at paintings. I am virtuous—but I am no fool. If girls were not as good at making music as boys, then the governors would surely have chosen boys to be Venezia's choristers.

The maestro is not as happy about Rosalba's commission as we are. But I am sure that jealousy has also played a role in his pique. After all, Don Vivaldi won no such commission from the king of Denmark and Norway, despite his schemes and all they cost him.

All anyone can talk about is Rosalba and the king. There's certainly no practicing going on. If only I could tell the others of the marvelous possibilities presented by the upcoming production of "Agrippina"—they would all ensconce themselves in the practice rooms!

After Matins on the great day, the Prioress inspected us, paying special attention to our fingernails. (She is obsessed with fingernails.) She exhorted us to be on our best behavior, and then led the flock of us behind her down the grand staircase to the parlatorio, where a crowd of visitors sat waiting.

The painter—as a mark of respect, I'm quite sure—rose from her chair when we entered. She is short of stature, but quite a delightful, cheerful-looking person, with a dimpled chin, a strong face, and white hair swept up onto her head and fixed there with ornaments in the shape of dragonflies and flowers. We recognized her sister at once from among the others sitting there: her fine brown *eyes are a mirror image of Rosalba's (even though the sister, who serves as the painter's assistant, is prettier, younger, and taller). The king—masked, of course—sat behind the grille with his entourage of attendants.*

Rosalba's sister took notes and made sketches as the painter went from girl to girl, turning our heads this way and that to catch the light, all the time saying kind things, even to the plainest among us. She had us bare our arms and lifted the cloth draped over our throats to better see our bosoms. And even as she did this, she looked into each girl's eyes and seemed to greet the person inside, so that each of us, I'm quite sure, felt a surge of love for her, and hoped we would be chosen.

"Such beautiful girls, each of you worthy of a goddess," she said in a clear voice so that everyone could hear her.

After conferring with her sister, and then conferring with the king, Rosalba held her hand out to Giulietta—Giulietta with her fair skin and full breasts and her cascade of chestnut-colored hair and pale green eyes, dilated now, as all of ours were, by the belladonna.

"Perhaps," said the artist, leading Giulietta closer to the grille, "perhaps this is our Diana."

Of course I felt a pang of envy—how could I not? But there was also a part of me that was very happy for Giulietta, and I vowed to ask her to question the artist in my stead—to find out how she had managed to climb to a place of such prominence and independence in a world in which an unmarried woman so rarely has either.

And then there was a thump, and we all of us turned and gasped to see Marietta fallen in a faint.

Her face was too deathly pale for her to have merely been making a last-minute bid for the artist's attention. I dropped to my knees to aid her, helping to lift her head and shoulders and loosening her clothes. Opening her eyes, Marietta looked at us with an expression of horror. And then she vomited all over herself and several of us as well.

You can imagine, I am certain, the embarrassment and disorder that ensued.

I was asked to take Marietta to the infirmary. Walking with my arm around her waist to help support her, I expressed my concern and asked her how she felt, but she only shook her head, and I let her be. On our way, we met Sister Laura, who went ahead of us to make sure the doctor was on hand.

In the examination room, Marietta begged me to wait with her, and Sister Laura said I might. A nurse fetched a basin of water and fresh robes for both of us.

"Your color is better now," Sister Laura told her. But Marietta, her green eyes full of tears, merely turned her head away.

"It is not a comment on your beauty," I said, stroking her hand. "You're just as pretty as Giulietta—but no doubt the painter has a scheme of color in mind that is better fit by Giulietta."

Marietta only shook her head and murmured, "You know nothing of the world, Anna Maria." I felt unjustly hurt by her words, and pulled my hand away.

The doctor's assistant came in and I was told to leave while the doctor examined Marietta—but Sister Laura and I both stayed nearby, outside the door. The assistant emerged and told me to fetch the Prioress.

The Prioress dismissed me as soon as I'd delivered my message.

Our rehearsal had been canceled for the artist's inspection, and there was another hour before our lesson. And so I took my violin off to my window and turned to my music for help in hearing my feelings. As always, the music was large enough to hold everything I poured into it—all my questions, all my uncertainty, all my fears.

Oh, Mother, we fool not only the world but also ourselves with the masks we wear!

Giulietta came to call me to the lesson, and we held hands as we walked down the hall.

"Marietta is to be married!" she whispered to me.

"But why?" Even at this late hour, I hoped to make it untrue.

"Because she's pregnant, of course!"

As soon as she said the words, I recognized the veil I had put up inside myself. With shame and self-loathing, I realized that I had known without letting the knowledge through. And I felt the burden of guilt again—for abandoning Marietta to her foolish impulse. And for failing to see what was before my eyes.

Mother, I beg you to pray for Marietta and for the child she will bear. Pray that she will find a wealth of love and strength and kindness such that she has never known before. And pray for me, that I might in future have the clarity of mind to recognize the Truth and live by its light.

With love and humility,
Anna Maria

*P*erhaps someday a woman composer of surpassing skill will be able to achieve the equivalent of what Rosalba has done—to live as an independent woman in *la Serenissima*, without either a husband or an institution to protect her. But for those of us who live in relationship to our instruments, rather than directly in relationship with God—who interpret rather than create—no such path will ever be possible. How can it be, when only cloistered women are allowed to perform? It is one of the great injustices of this fair city. And it has made me dream sometimes of other cities—of London and Paris and Vienna, where, I've heard, female instrumentalists have actually been welcomed, from time to time, on the performance stage.

And yet how could I ever leave Venezia? When I think such thoughts, I think of Giulietta, who wasn't even alone and yet perished in poverty and pain.

I was called to the Prioress's office the very next afternoon after writing that letter. Marietta was seated there. La Befana, her face nearly purple, hovered over her. Sister Laura sat at a side desk, taking notes.

"Anna Maria," said the Prioress in not an unkind tone of voice, "Maestra Meneghina has told us that you may be able to help us sort out a mystery here."

I stole a look at Marietta. She hadn't slept in the dormitory that night—none of us had seen her since the gossip about her had begun its rounds.

She looked much as she had the day before, of a greenish cast, and I wondered if she was going to vomit again.

"I am at your service, Reverend Mother."

La Befana broke in, "Did Marietta or did she not meet a man in the woods on the day of our outing to Torcello?"

I looked at Marietta again. But she looked as if she cared not a whit what I said.

"Anna Maria, please," said the Prioress. "Answer Maestra Meneghina's question."

I said a quick prayer. "Marietta and I went into the woods together," I began, trying to remember the exact wording of the tale I had told la Befana that day in the tower. "I was ill—and I asked her to leave me."

"Yes, we've heard that version of the story already, *figlia mia*." The Prioress folded her hands, waiting for me to say more.

Marietta had begun to weep silently. They were real tears—but there was something in her voice I distrusted when she spoke to me. "Tell them!" she whimpered. "I am undone unless they believe me."

"There was a man," said the Prioress. "Would you recognize him, Anna Maria, if you saw him again?"

"Yes," I answered—and I was sure I would. "The gentleman's looks were very striking."

La Befana pounced on this. "So you admit you lied!"

The Prioress motioned for her silence. "We will deal with that later," she said. Then she turned her gaze to Marietta. "Be careful what you say, child. Your future, as well as the future of many others, will rest upon your answer."

All eyes were on Marietta—and I thought how, even in the depths of her difficulties, she looked happy now, here at the center of everyone's breathless attention. "Who is the baby's father, child?"

Marietta raised her eyes to Heaven, and I wished the painter could have seen her face in that moment, because it was a worthy model for the Holy Virgin herself. She took a deep breath and then looked at each one of us in turn before speaking. "He is the second son of Andrea Foscarini." The words were no sooner out of her mouth than Sister Laura let out a little cry and slumped to the floor.

"Such a plague of fainting!" said the Prioress. "Anna Maria, fetch the doctor!"

Marietta and la Befana were both gone by the time I came back with the doctor. Through the half-open door, I saw Sister Laura, paler than usual, sitting in her chair again, sipping a glass of wine. I heard the Prioress say, "We shall see!" before the doctor knocked on the door and betrayed our presence.

That night I was called down to the *parlatorio* by Maestra Evelina, who put her arm through mine on the stairway. "Such a lot of excitement, Anna Maria!" she whispered in a manner just as companionable as if she were not a teacher but one of us—which she was until she was confirmed as a *maestra* the year before. "Giulietta has permission from the governors to pose half naked for the painter. And Marietta is either to be married or sent away in shame, depending on what you say."

Her words stopped me dead. I turned to her. "But I can't—I won't be the one to decide poor Marietta's fate!"

"Oh, Annina!" she said, "Marietta's fate was decided long ago. All you have to do is tell the truth."

"But what if . . ." I stammered, "what if the fate she's meant to have rests on the necessity of a falsehood?"

"You mustn't lie, *cara*, or else you'll put your immortal soul in peril!"

My head ached suddenly. "I must go to Confession."

"But then again," said Evelina musingly, "if we tarry—if, for instance, for the good of your immortal soul, we were to sit on the stairs here a while and I were to catechize you—" She took my hand and pulled me down beside her, and put her arm around me.

We were sitting thus, talking of this and that, when la Befana came storming to the base of the stairs. "Hurry up! What are you doing? They are there already. They have seen her!"

She hustled us into the *parlatorio*, where Marietta stood unveiled and looking well pleased with herself and uncannily pretty.

I was given into the hands of the Prioress, who walked me up close to the grille.

Andrea Foscarini stood there. As one of our greatest patrons and a distinguished member of the Board of Governors for as long as I had been at the Pietà, his face was well known to me.

A younger man—although still not a very young man, nor even

one as handsome as his father—stood beside him, grinning in an unbecoming way. I heard him say the word *bella*.

The Prioress let me have a long look, even though I knew at first glance that the man was not the one I had seen waiting in the woods for Marietta. There was no mistake about it. And yet he looked delighted with her. Would he be pleased enough or foolish enough to lend his name and fortune to another man's bastard? And I realized that, of course, this was what Marietta had planned all along, step by step, and I was in awe of her cunning and cleverness, and frightened of her utter lack of fear.

"Well?" the Prioress asked me, in a voice barely above a whisper. "Is that the man you saw in the woods?"

CHAPTER 10

I AM QUITE SURE that San Pietro will shake his head and turn me away when my immortal soul asks for entry at the gates of Heaven. There is too much stacked against me. I could have done everything I've done and still gained entrance if I had the will or even the opportunistic turn of mind that would groom me for repentance. But there is only one act of mine for which I truly feel remorse—and that was an act of ignorance rather than intention.

No—when I think of who my companions will be in Hell, I feel rather glad that I will be going there. It will be filled with those I most well and truly loved.

In the moment that I understood Marietta's plan, I was determined to help see it fulfilled. I looked a long time at Tomasso Foscarini. I looked into his foolish blue eyes and I knew that he would make an excellent husband for her. He was the second son of one of Venezia's premier families. He did not look very smart. But Marietta, I felt quite sure, would be smart enough for both of them.

I spoke slowly, as if after careful deliberation. "Yes, Signora. That is the man."

I felt the gentle touch of a hand laid upon my arm and turned to see Sister Laura. "This is an important matter," she said in hushed but urgent tones, "of consequence to more than just Marietta."

I met her eyes, and I felt an upwelling of love for her. She was far too pretty to be buried here in her nun's habit, and far too kind not to have had the chance to have children of her own. I remember wondering if she had been a younger sister, too—someone for whom her family could afford the bequest required by a convent for a bride of Christ, but not the forever-inflating dowry required by the nobility of Venezia. Only the very wealth-iest families—or the most foolishly romantic men—will make an offer of marriage to a girl or woman who comes without money.

These days, more than ever, a girl's dowry is the most impor-tant thing about her. Families who lose their fortunes gambling at the Ridotto can establish themselves once more through a well-dowered daughter-in-law. First-born sons are auctioned off to the highest bidders among the fathers of such girls.

Lately the price has soared so high that hardly anyone at all among the gentry can afford to get married. The noble houses of *la Serenissima* are stuffed full with the aging bachelor sons of greedy, profligate, and desperate fathers, and the convents are filled with girls who have been placed there against their will.

Not for the first time, I wondered what it was that allowed Sister Laura to avoid the bitterness that poisoned the lives of Sister Giovanna and la Befana.

Sister Laura's eyes, when she looked at me, were filled with all the tenderness of a teacher for her favorite protégée.

I placed my hand on hers. "I know," I said—although I knew nothing then except that Marietta would be honor-bound to help me if I helped her now. And that she would be able to help me more if she lived outside the walls of the Pietà.

La Befana stepped between us. "Think carefully, my girl. Think long and hard about what happens to liars!"

I wish I could remember the look, if any, that passed between la Befana and Sister Laura in that moment. I know their eyes must have met—and I would give a lot now to have seen the look in them. But my mind was fully occupied in turning over and over again the decision I felt could gain me so much and yet would cost me so much, too. I remember thinking that I would rather go to Hell than betray my friend and please my greatest enemy all in one fell swoop.

I turned to the Prioress. "That is the man, Signora, the same man I saw with Marietta on the island."

I saw Marietta only once more before she found a way to end her pregnancy and became a bride.

It was a season for brides. Our thirty-six-year-old *figlia privilegiata*, Madalena Rosso, finally succeeded in getting permission from the governors to marry the oboe teacher, Lodovico Erdmann, late of the Pietà. He was some nine years her junior, and not even a Catholic till he converted for her. Duke Cosimo III interceded with the Doge to grant a dispensation. The unlikelihood of such a marriage—and the fact that it had actually taken place in the church of Santa Maria della Salute, and we'd seen Madalena in her bridal gown beneath our windows—filled all of us with a weird restlessness, a sudden belief that perhaps anything was possible.

It was also the season of my first blood. I was prepared for it; I had even been impatient for it. But I hated the mess of it when it finally came. I stripped the sheets, too embarrassed to leave them for the *conversa*, and unwilling, anyway, to sleep on the soiled bedclothes until the day arrived when she came to clean our dormitory. Sister Laura, who was the *settimaniera* that week, gave me permission readily enough to go down to the linen room to get a clean set of bedclothes.

I had been there only rarely since becoming an *iniziata* in the *coro* so many years before. The linen room is next to the laundry, which is peopled by the *figlie* of the *comun*. Walking past the great bubbling vat of lye where the soap is made, and through the steam from the washtubs where a hundred red-faced girls stood scrubbing and bleaching, I remembered how the girls of the *coro* looked to me when I was a girl of the *comun*.

One takes the twists and turns of one's own pathway pretty much for granted until confronted with the paths one might have taken if Fate and Fortune had been less kind. What was it that kept me from such a life of drudgery but a certain accidental affinity for music?

I shielded my eyes as I walked past the furnaces where the irons were heated. And then I saw Paolina, our spy for the lottery, puffing and sweating over a stack of smartly creased linens.

"Signorina Anna Maria!" she said to me, then cried out as she burned her finger.

"Signorina Paolina," I answered, not wanting her to be more courtly to me than I was to her. "Forgive me if I startled you."

"I never see you here."

"I've come for clean sheets for my bed."

She looked at me slyly. "*Congratulazioni, cara!* You are a woman now."

"A woman with a belly that feels as if it's made of lead."

"*Poverina!* Here—" She passed her iron over the towel again. "Put this under your chemise! Apart from time, heat is the only thing that ever helps."

I looked around, lifted up my skirts and placed the warm towel inside my clothes. "You are the best of girls, Paolina."

She looked over her shoulder. "I'd best get back to work." And then she added, as I turned to walk away, "The oratorio was so beautiful, Signorina. And your playing! It was like being in the presence of angels."

It was my turn to blush and duck my head. When I looked up again, I saw Marietta through a swirling mist of steam.

She was flanked by two *cariche*, the *dispensiera* and the assistant prioress. With a languid air, she was indicating with either a nod or a shake of her head which linens she wanted. All the ones she nodded at were stacked in a large chest at her feet. Our eyes met.

The *cariche* had their backs to me. Marietta suddenly fanned herself, and I could see her miming that she wanted to sit down. They left her there, presumably while they went off to fetch water or a doctor.

The moment she was alone, Marietta beckoned me. "Faster, Annina! *Più veloce!*" Then, jumping up and clasping me in her arms, she wept real tears. "I thought I would never have the chance to thank you."

I did not return her embrace. Did she think that a few tears and a thank-you were compensation for the peril in which I'd placed my immortal soul by lying for her?

"You will have the chance to thank me soon."

"Yes, when I am married—"

"No—before then!" I think my tone surprised her. "Send word to me when you know where you'll be confined."

"I know already—San Francesco della Vigna."

"Good—listen carefully. A young nobleman pawned a golden locket not too long ago at the Banco Giallo. Find out his name!"

"*Cara*, I'll be in a convent!"

"A convent filled with the aunts and sisters of such men, who have nothing better to do than keep abreast of their news."

Marietta looked thoughtful. "I'll make friends among the nuns and find out what I can."

The *cariche* were coming back. "Only use a messenger who can be trusted. And, Marietta—" I squeezed her hand. "Stay safe! I can't wait to see your baby!"

When I turned away from her, she had tears in her eyes.

People say terrible things about Marietta Foscarini, but only some of them are true. She will do—and has done—anything to get what she wants. But she will do the same for those few she counts as her closest friends. And it's untrue that she doesn't feel pain for the pain she causes. She does—she's just very good at keeping it hidden.

I walked straight up to the *dispensiera*, curtseyed, and told her that I'd been sent by Sister Laura to fetch clean linens for my bed.

ANNO DOMINI 1710

Dearest Mother,

I write to you today not on stolen music paper or from one of the jail cells, but rather from my own room. Sister Laura has given me my own supply of paper, ink, and quills. On my birthday—or, rather, on the day we've always called my birthday—she gave me sealing wax and a seal stamped with my initials: AMV.

I pretended that it was you who gave me the seal and sealing wax and kissed me on my forehead.

Do you not think that it is odd for a young woman to have the name of an instrument in place of a family name? Was I made, then, in the workshop of a violin maker? (Even if I had been, I would still have been given his family name.)

I have been left much to myself lately. Claudia is still away in Saxony. Giulietta, accompanied by Sister Giovanna, goes every day to sit for la Rosalba. *A gondola comes to call for them in the morning. From my window, I watch them float out from the* rio *toward the Grand Canal.*

Every night Giulietta slips into my bed and tells me all about her day. She says she hopes the painting of Diana will never be finished.

Rosalba's house is in the Calle di Ca' Centanni. She is attended there by her old mother, who has a lapis lazuli box she keeps filled with fresh-baked gingerbread for everyone who crosses the painter's threshold.

There are only females in the palazzo: Rosalba's sister, Signorina Angela, who is engaged to be married to the painter Antonio Pellegrini (whom she calls her burattino). And the other sister we saw on the day Rosalba came here, Giovanini, whom everyone calls Neneta.

They are all short of stature, so that Giulietta says that she feels like an Amazon among them. Rosalba's family calls the painter la putela—for she is the very shortest of them all. She starts the day in high-heeled shoes that make her taller, but always kicks them off after an hour or two of standing at her easel.

Everything is beautiful there, and the place is filled with sunlight. There's a landscape on one wall that shows the countryside of France—a gift of his own work by the painter Watteau. The studio has a spinet, where Rosalba sits sometimes and plays while Giulietta—who gets pins and needles from sitting so long—walks around the room.

They talk then, just as naturally as if they had known each other for years instead of days. It turns out that Rosalba worked as a lace maker, plying her mother's trade, until the age of eighteen. And then she met a French artist, Monsù Jean, who taught her to paint miniatures on ivory and vellum. He broke her heart when he left Venezia to return to France with a trunkful of lace for his bride-to-be.

For her first portrait, painted for a friend, Rosalba was paid in two pairs of gloves and two perfumed sachets. For the head of Diana, it is widely rumored, she will receive a king's ransom of twenty-five Luigi!

Every day, Neneta dresses Giulietta's hair. She sits her on a *wrought metal stool with a striped damask cushion at Rosalba's dressing table, where, among the paints and perfume bottles, the artist keeps a brace of pistols.*

Rosalba also has a violin, the gift of Francesco Gobetti from the workshops of Matteo Goffriller. How I would love the chance to play it!

The king has twice looked in on these proceedings, each time in a different disguise—once dressed up as a ladies' maid, and then the second time as a Hussar. Giulietta says that he's wonderfully vain, spending as much time admiring himself in the mirror as checking on the progress of the painting. Sometimes an apprentice comes to help mix the colors, a young Veneziano named Giambattista Tiepolo. But he is not allowed in the studio while Giulietta is posing, although she has caught glimpses of him looking at her through a half-open door.

Rosalba has instructed Giulietta to dream the daydreams of a goddess and thus infuse her features with the right expression for Diana.

Giulietta says that she sits there and thinks of love and the terrible price it exacts of those who fall under its spell. She thinks of Actaeon, happening upon her as she bathes naked in the sacred pools of Arcady. In the moments before Actaeon is turned into a stag and devoured by his own hunting dogs, Giulietta imagines a kiss between the goddess and the hunter—a single kiss so divine that Actaeon will gladly pay for it with his life.

Sometimes the hunter's lips stray to Diana's naked shoulders, and his hands, smelling of the forest, fall upon the goddess's jasmine-scented breasts.

When Giulietta ends these stories, we both lie awake, though wordless, in the night that is still but for the lapping of the water outside, the sound of our breathing, and the occasional song of a gondolier.

She has talked much to Rosalba of my playing, in hopes that I may be invited one day to make more of the artist's violin than just a bibelot. But I'm sure that I will not be allowed—not as long as Sister Giovanna is the chaperone for these expeditions.

I am due for my lesson.

A thousand baci, Mother dear, wherever you are. May this letter reach not only your hands and eyes, but also your heart.

Anna Maria dal Violin

I cannot but wonder, reading over these letters now, that I had not the slightest inkling of Giulietta's plans. Were they plans—or did she sign her fate in a single impulsive moment, carried away by the strength of her feelings? We were, after all, best friends. If she had planned this, she would have told me, surely.

I was like King Shahryar and she was Scheherazade, with her tales spun out, night after night, in the bed we shared.

If I heard such tales today, I would know precisely what they portended. But I was far too caught up in my own dreams of love to do anything more than listen raptly while Giulietta gave me glimpses of hers. And she would not have let me stop her, even if I had possessed the wisdom and will to try. Love burns ever hotter in the presence of obstructions. Who knows this better than I?

While I waited for diligence from Marietta, I busied myself in trying to find out which two of the nine senior members of the *coro* and *comun* were currently serving the Pietà as scribes.

The various duties and privileges of the nine *cariche* rotate every three years, but on a changing schedule—so it was not an easy thing to determine at any given time who was responsible for what (beyond the more obvious roles of *dispensiera* or assistant prioress).

It was a period of particularly gloomy weather that winter. The rain poured down unceasingly, and those few people who came to see us at the grille of the *parlatorio* looked half drowned. On many visiting days, no one came at all.

The cooks endeavored to lift our spirits (and also dry out the walls of the *ospedale*) by baking more than usual. We were all at breakfast one day, exulting over the unwonted array of pastries set before us, when we heard—all of us heard it, except Signora Geltruda, who was stone deaf—the tolling of the single bell that hangs hard by the *scaffetta*.

"A baby!" someone murmured. And then the word was taken up by a dozen other voices in the room, pronouncing it with varying degrees of tenderness and delight.

There are some years, and some seasons, more plentiful than others for babies. Sometimes two will arrive in a day. And then sometimes three months will go by without the arrival of a single one. When the bell of the *scaffetta* sounds, it is always the role of the Prioress, wherever she may be at the time (unless she is ill), to go into the Church, to the place in the east wall where a compartment opens on the outside and is pushed through to the inside—not a *ruota*, or wheel, as at the convents, but a kind of drawer, cleverly wrought of stone. She is always accompanied by one of the two *scrivane*, who takes careful and detailed notes in the special books of the *scaffetta* kept in an annex of the Prioress's office—books that have been kept and hidden there over hundreds of years, since written records were first kept at the Pietà. If the baby appears to be diseased or deformed, the doctor is also called in.

The Prioress was with us at breakfast that morning, I think in tribute to the cook's offering of pastries. I saw her look straight at Sister Laura, who nodded so subtly that anyone who knew her less well than I did would have missed the gesture. The Prioress slipped a sugared *cornetto* into her pocket, daubed her lips with a napkin, and told us all to play with special care today, because a new set of ears would be listening. Not two minutes after she quitted the room, Sister Laura also got up to leave.

"So soon?" I asked, looking hard at her as she walked by. "The cook has baked an almond cake."

My eyes, I'm quite sure, spoke of more than almond cake, and my heart was beating fast. Sister Laura, a *scrivana!* Was this new? Would she be as kind to me in this regard as she had been in other matters? Would she search through the books, then, and tell me what I needed to know?

"Save me a piece, *figlia mia,*" she said, pausing long enough to push a stray lock of my hair under my wimple.

I knew I would need an accomplice to save her a piece of the cake that had not yet been served, and also follow her. But Giulietta had already gone to *la Rosalba*'s, Claudia was still away visiting her parents, and Marietta was gone from us forever. I turned to Bernardina, who sat at my left. I touched her first because I knew it was her blind side. "Would you do something for me, *cara?*"

Bernardina never asked me for anything, and I never asked anything of her. We were sworn enemies in those days. If there were two solo violins in a new piece that was written for the junior members of the *coro,* we did battle with each other every time to determine who would get the bigger part.

Once, before an audition, she managed to insert a dry grain of rice through one of the F-holes of my violin. It was after I had tuned the instrument, and the horrible buzzing sound it made took me completely by surprise. La Befana dismissed me as insufficiently rehearsed when I asked if I could start my piece over again, and I ended up leaving the audition in tears.

A month or so later, Giulietta played avenging angel by pouring a large measure of *olio di baccala*—the horrible-tasting fish oil the pharmacist uses to dose girls who get rickets—into Bernardina's soup on a night when she had a cold and couldn't taste anything. She spent the entire next day—which also, as it happened, was an audition day—on the privy.

Bernardina was the one who had told the Prioress of my escape with Marietta to the theater, landing me in jail. She always seemed to be watching me, waiting for my next mistake so that she could profit from it. At times, I really thought she wished me dead.

She turned at the touch of my hand.

What did Bernardina see when she saw me then? With her one eye, it always seemed that she could see much more than other people could normally see with two. We looked at each other for a good long moment—I with an expression of supplication, and she with suspicion. I hated having to humble myself before her that day, but I really felt I had no choice. There was no one else there I could ask to help me.

She glanced at the doorway through which Sister Laura had just slipped away. Then she smiled—and it seemed like a real smile to me. It seemed to me suddenly as if Bernardina wanted to be my friend—as if she'd wanted this all along. "Go after her!" she whispered. "I'll snag two extra pieces of cake, if I'm able."

When I got up, Signora Geltruda called out in the overly loud voice she used, even when talking to herself, "Why is everyone leaving? The cook has made an almond cake for us. She will be very cross!"

I hid myself behind a pillar in the hallway. After a long wait there, I saw the assistant prioress come out with a swaddled infant in her arms. The baby—a tiny thing with a face like an old man—was squalling pitifully. It's odd because the very sound of it made tears come to my eyes. Did I also squall in just the same way? At least this baby wouldn't be branded, as I was, and there would be a wet nurse waiting for it in the nursery, poor little motherless thing.

I had to wait quite a while longer for Sister Laura to emerge, wiping the ink from her fingers.

I stepped out from my hiding place and we looked at each other in silence before she spoke to me. "Shouldn't you be in class now?"

"I didn't know that you were a *scrivana*, Zietta." I sometimes called her *zietta*—auntie. Such is the custom for girls taken under the wing of a particular teacher.

"I was only recently given the job. As you can see," she said wiping her hands, "I'm not very good at it."

"You seem to be very good at everything you do."

"That is where you're mistaken, Annina. There are many things at which I'm exceedingly bad."

"It is your modesty speaking."

"Oh, speak to Maestra Meneghina, if you don't believe me."

I snorted. La Befana? She spoke ill of everyone. Sister Laura looked at me reprovingly. "She was my teacher, you know, for many years. I would not have my place here were it not for her."

My tone of voice was not as nice as it might have been. "Forgive me, Zietta, but I find Maestra Meneghina to be an odious person, as well as an odious teacher."

"Really? You do her an injustice, then. She is one of the finest musicians we've ever had here."

I remembered what la Befana had told me in the tower—how she had been a *favorita*. "Perhaps she was not so sour, in the old days, when Maestro Gasparini taught here on his own."

"And there you're misinformed again, my dear. There was a string teacher here then, just as now—the brother of Don Giacomo Spada, who was predecessor to Maestro Gasparini." She looked away from me. And then she finished her little speech by saying the brother's name, "Don Bonaventura Spada."

Giacomo or Bonaventura—these names meant nothing and mattered even less to me. What did I care about the priests who taught here long ago? Sister Laura was the one who could help me now. We were there, and perhaps alone, just outside the secret room. It would be but the work of an instant for her to let me inside. All she would have to do would be to look the other way. She had on countless other occasions shown her willingness to break the rules for me.

I was trying to find the right words to persuade her to let me in—or to look in the books on my behalf. I could stand guard at the door.

And then I realized that the silence between us had gone unbroken too long. She'd mentioned the old maestro, the one who'd come before Vivaldi. I said to her, "I suppose that only a priest—or a eunuch—is considered safe enough to teach in a place such as this one."

Sister Laura looked away from me again, out toward the window where tepid sunlight was filtering in from the day outside. It was the first sunlight I'd seen in a long time. "Bonaventura Spada was no eunuch, child. And although a priest, he was in love with Meneghina. Everyone knew it then. Everyone but I."

She looked back at me from the window and could see readily enough that I found the idea completely ludicrous that someone had actually been in love with la Befana. "She was quite good-looking when she was younger, before she almost died—along with so many others that winter—from the smallpox. And she played like an angel. You will see, *figlia*—time leaves its mark on everyone. The marks we can see and the marks we can't see. But no one goes unscathed."

"Please, Sister—" I burst out. "I beg you to look in the *libro della scaffetta* for me. Find my name and whatever is written about my state when I was found. And whether there is any hint about who I am."

My heart was beating so hard that I could hardly breathe.

Sister Laura reached out her hand and touched me, softly, raising my face up so that I had to meet her gaze.

"There is nothing about you in the book of the *scaffetta*. I have looked there."

My whole heart told me that she was lying. I hated her in that moment. I hated her for being so selfish and smug and unfair. It was worse because she pretended to love me. I pushed her hand away. "How can that be? Information on every child is recorded."

"And yet there is no record for you, Anna Maria."

The anguish I felt then welled up in my eyes. "You know who my mother is—you give my letters to her. Or else you've made me live a lie!"

She looked as if I had struck her. "I am not the courier for your letters. You must trust me, Anna Maria."

"You speak of trust—and yet you won't trust me! How can you know what you know and not tell me? Even la Befana seems to know who my parents are! How can it be right that everyone knows but me?"

She held me by both shoulders and looked straight at me with her clear blue eyes. "You should stop asking and stop seeking. There are some things that are better left unknown."

I stared right back at her. "Are they murderers, then, my parents? Is my mother a whore?"

She winced and yet she hung on tight to me—so tight, in fact, that she was hurting me. When she spoke, she spoke with difficulty. "Trust me—you have to stop looking for them!"

I wriggled out of her grasp. "I will never trust you again!"

"How you try my patience, child! There is nothing written about you in the book of the *scaffetta!*" She took a deep breath then and smoothed the fabric of her robes. I heard the whisper of the silken petticoat beneath them. It sounded like the hiss of a snake to me.

When she looked at me again, her face was once again composed. "You ought not to assume that you know the truth based solely on what you see before your eyes. I suggest that you get to your class, Anna Maria, before you earn yourself a bigger punishment than you have already."

*N*ot long afterward, the Prioress called me into her office.

"Anna Maria," she said, looking up from a stack of papers on her desk and removing the spectacles that had been made for her in Switzerland, a gift from the Grand Inquisitor. She looked at me for a long time after I had curtseyed. "Sit down, child."

As a general rule, the Prioress only meted out bad news. I braced myself for whatever she was about to say, reviewing in my mind all the rules I had broken lately.

"Are you aware, Signorina, that every one of your teachers has nominated you for promotion to the *coro?*"

I shook my head.

"Then you are no doubt equally ignorant of the fact that each time a vote was about to be taken about whether to confirm you, you committed some gross infringement of the rules that made it impossible for us to do so?"

"No, Signora. That is, yes, Signora. I was ignorant of this as

well." I kept my eyes focused on the painting by Antonio Balestra hanging on the wall behind her, all the while praying to
the Virgin to keep me from showing how distressed I was by the
priora's news.

"*Figlia mia,*" she said, sighing and rubbing her eyes. "You
have a considerable gift. Several *iniziate* who are less talented
than you have already been confirmed in the *coro*. It pains me. I
feel it as a pain here"—she put her hand over her heart—"every
time a vote is taken and I have to deny your promotion."

I could see that she meant what she said. I noticed a resemblance in the painting between Saint Elizabeth and the Prioress,
and realized that the painter must have been commissioned to
paint it thus.

"It pains me—it embarrasses me, Anna Maria. We have always
had great hopes for you."

I bowed my head, furiously angry with her and all the adults
who had me in their power. Talent is what should have mattered,
not whether one was able to follow all their stupid, petty rules.
When I looked up, she'd put her spectacles back on and was
searching through her papers again.

"It is my sad duty to inform you, Signorina, that you will not
be among the *figlie* whose confirmation in the *coro* will be celebrated this Sunday with cakes and wine. Giulietta dal Violin-
cello is to be confirmed that day." She looked at me, I suppose to
gauge my reaction. But I felt glad enough for Giulietta. "And so
is Bernardina dal Violin."

Well, then. Bernardina. Had she known of the upcoming
confirmation when she made the bid for my friendship—when
she made it possible for me to miss class yet another time? Perhaps it was Bernardina herself who had pointed out to Sister
Giovanna that I wasn't there. Did she exult when the black mark
was made beside my name?

I bit down hard on my lower lip, staring at the feet of the Angel Gabriel. When the Prioress said nothing more but continued to look through her papers, I got up to leave.

"One moment, Signorina." She took several sheets of music out from the pile on her desk, rolling them up and then tying them together with a blue ribbon. "This has been sent to you by Don Vivaldi. It is a concerto in D minor, which he has written for the three of you—you, Bernardina, and Giulietta. You were all three to have played it at the confirmation party. I have yet to decide what to do about this . . ." She paused. "Awkwardness."

She handed the scroll to me. "Don Vivaldi particularly wants you to try out the first violin solo. He says he is quite sure that you are the only one—save himself—who has the skill."

Dear Maestro!

"And one last thing, before you leave."

I looked at her, wondering what further piece of bad news she had saved up for the end of our interview.

"I've already told Bernardina—you are to begin giving her lessons, twice a week. Close your mouth, Anna Maria. The expression is most unbecoming."

I may have been mistaken, but I thought I saw her smile—and, at first, I thought she might be mocking me. Bernardina would rather die than accept me as her teacher—and she a full-fledged member of the *coro* now! And yet she would have to if she hoped to keep her place.

"What are you waiting for, child? Go!"

I curtseyed and left, the scroll tight in my hand and the other news coursing through my veins.

*T*he solo was, just as the maestro had implied, fiendishly difficult to play, much of the fingering so close to the bridge so as to make it nearly impossible. I was hard at it, trying my best to make the thing work, when I felt a sudden draft and felt sure that I was no longer alone in the practice room. Turning around, I saw Giulietta in the doorway.

"Did you write that?"

"Of course not! What are you doing here, *cara?* Is the portrait finished already?"

"No one else *knows* I'm here, Annina. I'm here to get my things."

"What are you talking about?"

"I heard you playing—it could have been no one but you . . . or maybe the maestro."

"What do you mean, you're here to get your things?"

"The only part of the whole plan that bothered me was not being able to say goodbye. And now I can."

"Giulietta!" The words caught in my throat. "Are you running away?"

Giulietta took my hands in hers but couldn't meet my eyes. "Rosalba says that it sometimes happens two or even three times in a lifetime. But for others, there's only ever once. And if you allow that one time to pass you by—"

"You can't leave now!"

"If you don't take seriously what he says when he says it—"

"Listen to me!"

"If you act overly modest and girlish and shy—if you try to do what's proper instead of what your heart tells you to do—"

"Giulietta, you're about to be confirmed in the *coro!*"

"I don't care, *cara.* I'm in love."

"At least let it happen first! The maestro has written a concerto for you, me, and Bernardina." I showed her the music. "*This* concerto."

"Kiss me, Annina. Kiss me and say *addio!*"

"And now there'll be no one to play it—no one but that Cyclops!"

"I will send word somehow, when we've found a place where we can settle. But he says we may be on the road—living like Gypsies—for a long while."

"You'll be gone, and Claudia is nearly seventeen, and I can't seem to stay out of trouble long enough to be confirmed ..."

"I'll be able to play my cello, and he'll look for commissions wherever we go. Venetian painters are much in demand all over Europe now."

"Please don't leave me here alone, Giulietta!"

She embraced me, and I held on to her as I would have held on to my mother when she left me here, had I been old enough and strong enough instead of a helpless newborn baby.

I couldn't speak. I didn't want to let go.

She finally peeled my hands away and dried my tears with the corner of her apron. "If I have a daughter," she promised gaily, "I will name her Anna Maria."

*M*any years ago, I received a present from Rosalba—a miniature copy of the portrait of Diana she painted for King Frederick. She sits here on my table, dreaming of Actaeon.

The gossips of Venezia speak of Christina, the daughter of a gondolier, who serves as the model for so many of the saints and Madonnas in Tiepolo's frescoes. Only those of us who remember Giulietta know that the gondolier's daughter was given this job because she looks like Tiepolo's first love, the girl he loved when he himself was nothing more than a boy and powerless to save her. Pretty Giulietta, who died giving birth to Tiepolo's baby, the two of them friendless and penniless, somewhere in a field in Slovenia.

No one was ever able to tell me if the child was a girl.

There is another Anna Maria here who is my pupil now, a violinist with chestnut curls. She was born too soon to have been Giulietta's, but only by a couple of years. I have told her all about Giulietta, every wonderful story, so that the two of us have laughed long and hard together, and I know that Giulietta will not be forgotten as long as this other Anna Maria is alive. When she calls me *zietta*—as, of course, she does—I love her just as much as I would if she were truly the daughter of my dear, departed friend and had been named for me. She is very gifted. I am quite sure she will be a *maestra* one day.

$\mathscr{W}$E WERE AT OUR EMBROIDERY LESSON when Maestra Evelina slipped through the door and waited, as was fitting, until Maestra Rosa looked up from the sacred text she was reading out loud. There were some whispered words between them while all of us pretended to continue working, all the while listening just as hard as we could.

It's strange to realize that the piece of work in my embroidery frame that day was a spray of pomegranate blossoms that became the cushion for a chair—the same chair I sit in now. The flowers are faded and the fabric is worn—but it is my favorite chair and always will be. I remember, while I worked on it, how I pictured the finished cushion on a chair in the house where I imagined living one day with Franz Horneck. In my picture, there was a fire in the grate and there were two or three tousle-haired children on the rug at my feet while I read to them from Ovid or Ghiliermo Shakespeare but never the solemn words of God.

When the bells rang to send us to our rest time, Maestra Rosa asked me to stay behind. I sat there waiting until all the other girls had filed out, one or two with a sympathetic backward glance at me.

Maestra Rosa waited a long time before speaking, so that I was surprised when all she had to tell me was that I had a visitor. I thought I saw her look at me searchingly—but then I thought I may have been imagining any special look from her. She smiled at me before gathering her things and quitting the room.

I knew that it was visiting day, but, usually, there was no one who visited me.

Loneliness has nothing to do with being alone. I was surrounded day and night by others who shared so much with me. And yet, without Giulietta, Claudia, or Marietta, I felt unanchored from what little sense I had of who I was or how it was possible to find any happiness at all. In their absence, I traded the world of daily life for a world inhabited by people—alive or dead, real or imagined—who loved me. I walked through one life while I dwelt in another.

A sense of excitement dawned in me as I made my way down to the *parlatorio*, stair by marble stair. Who could my visitor be, but a messenger from Marietta? How quickly she'd worked! I hadn't expected to receive word from her so soon.

Maestra Evelina greeted me with a barely suppressed expression of glee. "There's your visitor, *cara*," she said, turning backward toward the grille.

I saw a black-cloaked noblewoman sitting there, masked and so well covered that it would have been impossible to recognize her even if she had been someone I knew well. Had Marietta herself come in this disguise—a costume she would soon enough be wearing in her new life—to tell me what she'd found out about the locket? And then I wondered in a wild, improbable moment if this masked *zentildonna* could be my lodestar and the recipient of my letters. Had she finally come to me?

Would she love me? I touched my cheeks and hair. Would she be disappointed in me? I wished fervently that I were taller and plumper, that I had arresting green eyes like Marietta and lustrous auburn curls like Giulietta or a fine bosom like Claudia.

But I had none of these.

Maestra Evelina winked at me. "You won't mind, will you, *cara,* if I slip away for a moment or two?"

I watched her go and then approached the grille slowly, filled with fear.

The lady gestured for me to sit down. I sat. And then she inclined her head very close to the grille. Her voice was barely a whisper. "Let me touch you, child. Give me your hand."

It wasn't Marietta—of that much I was certain. I poked two of my fingers through the grille. The masked woman grasped them. Her grip was terribly strong. She bent her face over my hand, and I felt my hand grow wet with her tears.

And then I heard the voice that I had heard so often in my daydreams. I felt the scratch of whiskers as he kissed my fingers and I felt a charge course through me, as if I'd been struck by lightning.

"Franz!"

"My angel."

"You haven't forgotten me."

"How could I?"

He lifted his mask so that I could see his eyes. Franz Horneck's eyes! I touched his face through the grille. "Why do you weep?"

"Because life is so unfair."

"I know—I know!" I loved him looking at me. Not because I thought he admired me, but because I felt he saw me. "Do you remember Giulietta, from the ball?"

"It's the talk of all Venezia, how she has run away with the young Giambattista Tiepolo."

I wondered if Franz had come to ask me to run away with him. I've wondered much over the years what I would have said.

"Anna Maria, I have to leave Venezia. I am called home."

"Is there bad news from your family?"

Franz sat back so that his face moved away from mine. "They think it's good news," he said bitterly.

I said nothing. What could I say? What right did I have to ask anything of him?

He moved close to me again and, although there was no one else in the room, he spoke to me in a whisper. "Please believe me. If I could choose a bride, I would choose you. I would live with you and love you for the rest of my life."

Tears came into my eyes, but still I said nothing.

"But I am not free to choose. These travels of mine—as well as a bad investment my father made—have left my family close to ruin. They have found a girl with a fortune, whose family would like to link itself to ours. And so I am to be married, against my every inclination, when my whole heart belongs to another. Oh, sweet Signorina, my heart belongs to you."

I placed my hand against the grille, and he placed his hand against mine, so that there was only the thinnest filigree of metal between us, and I could feel the heat of him and the floral pattern—a design of pomegranate blossoms—press itself into the flesh of my palm. "I will keep it safe, then, Franz Horneck."

I heard Maestra Evelina clear her throat, signaling that she had come back, and that the time for the visit was over.

Franz lowered his mask. "Forever," he whispered.

It surprises me now, looking back, how hard I thought in that moment about myself and Franz and the years that would stretch on without him. I think, as in a vision, I saw my entire life. People who have almost died say that one experiences just such a vision—one's entire life in a flash of light—in the moment one sees the face of the Angel of Death approaching.

The words came unbidden, against my better judgment. After all, Franz Horneck was about to be married, and I was but fourteen and a virgin. And yet the words would come—the words would be spoken. "Forever," I whispered. *"Per sempre."*

ANNO DOMINI 1710

Madre mia carissima,

Dearest Mother, I write to you in desperation! I think sometimes that God must hate me to leave me here cut off from those I love. And yet haven't I served God well, dedicating my very youth to singing His praises? What have I done to deserve to be abandoned here—again and again abandoned here? How I wish that you could send word to me somehow and tell me that I do not write to you in vain!

There are ways. The girls who work in the laundry seem to have the greatest access to contact from the outside. I have an ally there—a girl of the comun *who has shown herself quite happy to carry out commissions for those of us who need her services. Only recently she slipped a letter into my hand while she passed me in the hallway with a pile of clean linens. This letter was from Marietta, who knew full well that it would have been burned without ever reaching me if she'd sent it in the normal way.*

Poor Marietta has had a miscarriage. She wrote to say that she was carefully tended by the good nuns of San Francesco della Vigna, who massaged her and gave her herbs at night to help her sleep. And yet her baby broke free of its moorings well before it ever had a chance to grow. It was just a mess of clotted blood that came out of her more awfully and painfully than the worst period she'd ever had.

She is still engaged to be married to Tomasso Foscarini, who loves her à la folie. At least now, writes Marietta, his family will not tax her with the shame that would have been brought upon them by a pregnant bride in the wedding processional.

Because the Foscarini are so rich, Marietta's father-in-law is willing to forego her dowry—which means, of course, that no contract will have to be signed, apart from the marriage contract, and Marietta will be free to pursue her singing career outside the Pietà.

It would not have happened this way if I hadn't lied for her.

No one was injured by my falsehood, and both Marietta and her bridegroom have been made very happy as a result of it. Why is my lie, then, a mortal sin?

I hope I live a very long time, because I have a terror of facing Judgment Day. And yet I have played only a small part in the great web of events that have conspired in Marietta's favor.

I told you of Handel's plans for an opera. The libretto is by Cardinal Grimani, whose family owns three of our greatest theaters: the Santi Giovanni e Paolo, the San Samuele, and—the very best of them—the newly reopened San Giovanni Grisostomo, which the composer dearly wanted for his opera debut in la Serenissima. I am well informed for a cloistered girl, am I not? Maestro Vivaldi always spoke freely with us about such things while he taught here.

The libretto for Handel's opera, naturally, had to be passed first by the censor. But, in this case, the censor was the Grand Inquisitor himself, Raimondo Pasquali—a great friend, as it happens, of the Foscarini. Influence is everything, and everyone, it would seem, has his price, whether it's paid in influence or gold.

Everything was in place. But Handel could find no one who pleased him for the role of Poppea—Poppea, who must be beautiful enough to be loved and desired by every male character in the opera, and yet must sing with the sweetness of an angel and the range and power of a whole host of angels over many hours.

Someone, it seems, whispered three words in the ear of our dear young Saxon composer, il caro Sassone, as everyone calls Handel now: Marietta della Pietà.

Oh, tell me, Mother, that it was you who told Handel about how perfect Marietta would be for his opera! It would be proof that you have been reading my letters, even though you have never answered them, not a single one.

I am hoping against hope that the figlie di coro *will be allowed to go see Marietta perform. She writes that so many flowers have already been sent to her that the* parlatorio *of the convent of San Francesco della Vigna looks like a garden.*

I feel sorry for those nuns who need to minister to Marietta's needs every day—Marietta the newly minted diva. Marietta risen up from the gutter to have her name written into the Golden Book, joined in marriage with Tomasso Foscarini. Marietta who promises to visit the Pietà in her wedding procession along the Grand Canal, who says she will stop here and give us enough chocolates to make us all sick for a week.

Thank you for helping my friend, if it was you who helped her, dear Mother. I wish there were some such magic you could work for me. But there will be no procession of gondolas for the wedding of Anna Maria dal Violin.

I received another letter this week, handed over to me by the Prioress herself. Claudia wrote to tell me of her bridegroom. He is not old and ugly as she had feared, but someone of a neighboring noble family who was her playmate during childhood—a great favorite of hers—before she was sent here to hone her musical skills (and stay out of trouble until she came of age). His family is noble and poor, while Claudia's has had its fortune and lands for only a couple of centuries. And so the match benefits both houses. She will actually have the title of princess now. Can you imagine that? La principessa *Claudia.*

She, too, has promised to bring us chocolates.

I have not one single friend left here in this place. Bernardina hates me more than ever, now that she has to take lessons from me. And Maestra Meneghina—la Befana—is the only one deemed skilled enough to be my teacher. She never has anything good to say about my playing. When she is silent at the end of one of our lessons, I feel that I have triumphed—because at least she has not been able to find any reason to fault me.

I can't remember the last time I laughed. I'm sure it was before Giulietta ran away, because she and I were always the ones who laughed most tremendously together—she and I, and Claudia, too, sometimes. When I lie in bed and pore over what we said and did, I can make myself smile and even, sometimes, laugh a tiny bit. But that kind of laugh—a remembered laughter—only makes me cry, in the end, because my friends are gone now, and I know how alone I really am.

I would probably be crying myself to sleep every night were it not for the music that Maestro Vivaldi continues to send me.

It seems that he is composing more and more. I'm sure it's what he cares about most, even though, of course, he's very vain about his skill as a performer. Half the time, I think, he composes simply as a means to show this virtuosity to the world. But then, at other times, he writes something so tender, and so filled with invention and sweetness and passion. What can this be but Divine Grace? I wonder mightily why some people in the world—even though they may not really seem to be more righteous or deserving than any others—are thus singled out. Sometimes I think that God makes artists quite by accident.

The Prioress handed me another of the maestro's compositions along with Claudia's letter—a sonata in B-flat. There at the top—just as he had that very first time—he'd scrawled the words, "per Signorina Anna Maria." Like the last solo he wrote for me, it's very hard to play. I suspect, in fact, that he gives them to me only to see if it's possible for anyone other than himself to play the music as he's written it. Please don't think me too vain—but everyone says this about the music the maestro dedicates to me.

I've come to believe that music is the one companion, the one teacher, the one parent, the one friend who will never abandon me. Every effort I give to it is rewarded. It never spurns my love, it never leaves my questions unanswered. I give, and it gives back to me. I drink, and—like the fountain in the Persian fairytale—it never runs dry. I play, and it tells me my feelings, and it always speaks the truth.

We are placed here to pray for Venezia and the grace of the Republic in God's eyes. But I have found the secret treasure in this task of ours, and it has nothing to do with any higher good but only my own satisfaction.

There—you see how self-serving I am. And perhaps I am, in truth, my mother's daughter. No doubt it serves you best to keep yourself hidden from me.

The priest and the Prioress and everyone else here would have us believe that nothing in this life is important at all, when compared with what comes later. And yet the afterlife holds no attractions for me, as I know it will be my lot to suffer when I am sent there. I will burn in Hell for these bad thoughts of mine. And pray God that no one in la Serenissima but you is ever party to them!

Dante Alighieri wrote letters to his beloved Beatrice from the time they met as children until long after she died. Letters that he never sent and she never read. When I wake at night and cannot sleep, I am possessed by the thought that my letters to you are like Dante's letters to Beatrice—like music played in an empty room.

I will give this letter to Sister Laura after I seal it. I like to think of you breaking the seal on my letters. I reach out to you across the void that has separated us and will perhaps separate us forever. I write and write even though I am afraid that you never read these letters—that no one reads these letters, nor ever will. That Sister

Laura simply throws them in the fire, satisfied that I have been given the illusion of being someone's daughter.

Across that void, nonetheless, I send my kisses to you. I send my love.

Anna Maria dal Violin

There was much I left out of my report of Marietta's letter. I may have been fearless in my writing when it came to betraying my own blasphemous thoughts, yet I was determined never to reveal information that might betray my friends.

But Marietta wrote without censoring a single thought or deed. Each time I receive one of her letters, I've contemplated burning it. More than one in the pile I have here has singe marks on it from the initial impulse that made me throw it into the fire after my first reading.

Marietta's letters were and have been a secret indulgence for me. I read them whenever I am feeling dull or bored, and I've hidden them—along with all my other secret things—so carefully that they will not be found.

All my letters—and my one little book, if not the other—must be hidden, at least until I am dead. But, for now, they are a companion to me such that I have never had in my lifetime, there for me whenever I want them. They are like a passageway into my youth again, and a window onto the sort of life I know I will never have.

Annina,

What a foul place this is! All but a few of the nuns are vile creatures who get their jollies by making life as miserable as possible for the novices and other young people—like me—thrown into their midst.

You can imagine what hay they made of my pregnancy. It's only the fact that my darling dolt has two aunts here that kept the most self-righteous of the old biddies from throwing me down a well! I told them that I didn't want to be pregnant, and would be quite obliged to them if they could give me some herb or push me down the stairs or something to make it go away. But then all I got was more sermons about how I'm more wicked than the Grand Caliph and Genghis Khan put together for wanting to do away with To-masso's precious baby. I thought if I could get hold of a couple of those aunties and drop a hint or two that Tomasso had nothing to do with the state I was in, I might get a bit of help.

And then I heard from one of the choir nun's private maids that my name was being bruited around for the role of Poppea in Handel's opera. She's the one who's loved by every one of the male characters—and so she has to be beautiful as well as a brilliant vocalist, and able to sustain her role for a full five hours or so.

That was the last straw for me. I sent for my future mother-in-law and told her that if I didn't get her help, I'd be giving birth to someone else's bastard. Of course, I was a bit more refined in the way I said it, but clear enough not to leave her in any doubt about what to do.

She's a whirlwind, that future mother-in-law of mine. No sooner had she left than one of the nuns came in from the apoth-ecary with what she said was a sleeping draught for me.

I drank it down with a prayer that Mamma Foscarini hadn't decided to go the easy route and just poison me. She's quite fond of Tomasso, though, and I was banking on her not wanting to tell him that his fiancée just happened to drop dead after a visit from her.

The bleeding started after Vespers and went on and on through the night and well into the morning, great clotted masses of it, and all the while the nun—who stank!—stood by and kneaded my belly as if I'd been a lump of dough. It hurt, too, worse than any period you can imagine. But the nun told me that she had no particular need to please the Foscarini, and that if I screamed she'd kill me.

When everything had all come out and I realized I wasn't going to die, the nun put a powder of dragon's blood in my opening, and gave me another foul-smelling potion to make me sleep. And it was as if, in sleep, I became a virgin again.

Oh, Annina, you cannot imagine the relief of waking up and knowing that I was no longer with child! I'll bear children—because I'll need to. And I'll probably even love the little blighters. But it's far too early now, and, really, it wouldn't be fair to give Tomasso a child that wasn't his own.

When did a sense of fairness ever enter into my plans? Don't be too quick to judge me. I have as much a sense of right and wrong as the most pious-seeming nun in this place. It is just that my sense of justice is mingled with the practicalities of living in the world. And I do not hide my evil, unlike the rest of them.

A message came from Handel, just as I knew it would. He'd found everyone for his opera—the great fat soprano Margarita Durastanti to play the title role of Agrippina; the bass Antonio Francesco Carli to sing the role of Claudio; two castrati who get treated like gods, Giuliano Albertini and Valeriano Pellegrini, for Narciso and Nerone; the contralto Francesca Maria Vanini-Boschi, wearing breeches for the role of Ottone; and her husband, Beppe, a bass, to sing Pallante.

But Handel couldn't find his Poppea, he wrote, because his Poppea was hidden away in the convent of San Francesco della Vigna.

The mother-in-law again intervened—and I can see why, too.

If I become an opera star, no one will remember the gossip about how I snagged her son. The more famous I become, the happier she'll be—as long as I behave myself from now on. And believe me, she extracted just such a promise from me, promising in turn that she wouldn't hesitate the next time to have me poisoned if I dared ever cross her. And yet she as much as told me that I'd have my cicisbeo, *providing he was from a noble family and we comported ourselves with discretion.*

I think I'm going to like this mother-in-law of mine.

All right. I know you're reading this and asking, yes, that's all very well, but what about the thing Marietta promised to do for me?

I haven't forgotten, cara. *I was just saving the best news for last.*

Just as I said I would, I asked around about who might have a brother or uncle who's been in financial trouble lately. It seems that just about everyone does—so that led nowhere. But then my mother-in-law let something slip about Tomasso—how she hopes I'll take a strong hand with him and straighten him out, as he's really been going to Hell in a handbasket lately.

I played as dumb as I dared, expressing the opinion that nobles have it all over the common people when it comes to moral behavior. Mamma Foscarini gave a great big snort and advised me to keep a close eye on my jewels (as if I had any!), as Tomasso had lately stooped so low as to steal something out of his own sister's room and pawn it in the Ghetto.

So maybe every duke and duchess in Venezia steals one from the other, as far as I know. But the situation seems to bear a passing resemblance to the one you described. Wouldn't that just be something if the man you're looking for turned out to be Tomasso!

Trust me, Annina, I'll find a way to worm out the rest of the tale and whether this path will lead you anywhere or suddenly end. I think it's a big mistake for you to try to find out in the first place.

There's a reason we're stuck in these holes. Don't imagine that your mother, if she lives, is going to thank you for throwing back the curtain and showing the whole of Venezia what she has probably gone to a great deal of effort to hide. But I'm bound to help you, and help you I will.

I don't know yet which sister had her property purloined, as Tomasso has a handful of them, and each one—married, cloistered, or dead—still has a bedroom at the Ca' Foscarini.

As soon as my mamma-to-be noticed how interested I was in her story, she clammed right up. But I'll figure her out and find out more—don't worry. This zentildonna nobile is more like my own sainted mother than I would ever have thought possible before I started to move among the gentry.

I've told Handel that he must speak to Vivaldi—or speak to someone—who can arrange for all of you to come hear me sing. How I long to have everyone see the flowers and poems my fans will throw to me, and hear the ovations! I've already won all sorts of praise from among the cast and their servants and all those others who hang about during our rehearsals. The parlatorio looks like a garden, it is so filled with flowers my admirers have sent to me.

The wedding is to be in March—and, believe me, the relief is great in this family that the bride will not be pregnant! I will make sure that the procession stops beneath your window so that you can get a really good look at me in my wedding dress, which is sure to be ten times more beautiful and costly than old Madalena's. And I'll have one gondola filled with enough chocolates to make all of you sick for a week.

Mille baci, *Annina! I will look for a husband for you.*

Marietta

❧ ❧ ❧

*I*t was suddenly a season of letters arriving one after the other, after a lifetime of almost no contact from the outside.

I've wondered a lot about this lately. Why is it that one thing seems to make way for another similar thing that follows? Are the passageways of communication like the passageways that water cuts through the land? The first trickle marks the rivulet's pathway, making it possible. And a dry place, over time, is turned into one that is wet and lush, a place where things can grow.

Soon after I received and devoured Marietta's letter, I found a very different sort of note stuck beneath my pillow. My life was transformed, in that moment of finding it, from a friendless desert to a fertile plain. Whole vistas opened up before my eyes when I unfolded the scrap of thin paper, the type that is used in making patterns.

Signorina Anna Maria,

I have information that will be of interest to you—but you will have to pay for it. Go to the water gate tomorrow night. Silvio will come for you. Bring your violin.

Rebekkah

*T*he day she named was a Friday. I remember that it was October 17, because we drank the health of Sister Laura that evening, to mark her birthday. At the celebration, I told Bernardina that I had a headache and gave her my measure of wine.

At least leaving the *dormitorio* without being detected would be easier, now that my friends were gone. Of course, Bernardina would be watching, awake or asleep, drunk or sober, and I had to be clever if I hoped to escape right out from under her nose. Ever since our lessons had begun, she reminded me at every opportunity of her membership in the *coro*, and I knew she took careful note of everything I did, hoping yet again to catch me doing something wrong.

I waited until I heard her snoring. And then I tiptoed over to her bed and placed my pillow up against the side of her head and slipped her own pillow out a little, so that her head fell into the trough between them and both her ears were covered.

She stirred a little and moaned, but her eyes stayed closed. Then I dressed myself, grabbed my violin and peeked out into the hallway.

La Befana was the *settimaniera* that week, which was bad news for me. I waited behind the door until I heard her footsteps.

She paused at our doorway, listening, I suppose, to see if anyone stirred. I could hear her breathing. She'd drunk her fair share of wine at the celebration—I was praying she didn't slump to the floor right there on the other side of the door.

I held my breath, my cheek to her loathsome cheek, with only the door between us. I thought about what Sister Laura had told me about la Befana—and it made me reach up to touch my own cheek, making sure that the skin was still smooth, instead of pitted and scarred and horrid and old. I remember how afraid I felt that la Befana would open the door and find me there, fully dressed and poised to leave.

Finally, I heard her sigh and walk away, continuing her rounds.

I said a prayer and then slipped out, holding my shoes in one hand and my violin in the other. The marble of the stairway felt cold beneath my stockinged feet, but I scampered so fast that I was warm enough by the time I'd run down the three stairways and reached the water gate, triumphant because I hadn't met so much as a mouse along the way. Thus it startled me to see that the lowest reaches of the orphanage were lit by candles.

I ducked behind the balustrade. Judging by the sounds of laughter and crockery, there seemed to be a little party going on. There were some girls from the *comun* I didn't recognize, as well as some of the teachers from the lower school—foundlings, orphans, and bastards, all of them. And in their midst I saw Silvio, passing around little cakes and bottles of wine.

I stepped out from my hiding place. "Oh Signorina," gasped one of the girls. "Please don't tell on us!"

Silvio had grown taller. There was something odd about his costume, and then I noticed that he was wearing a yellow cap.

He didn't say a word to me but simply took the violin from my hands, kissed several of the girls in a most familiar way, and led me to the gondola he had waiting.

I felt all at once so happy to see him and so nervous and excited about whatever mystery awaited me at the end of this gondola ride.

Every time I started to speak—to ask him what was going on—he took my hand and hushed me.

I looked at the gondolier and then back at Silvio. "He won't tell. He's honor-bound not to. Isn't that right, Signor?" The gondolier, a tall and slender man with pale blue eyes, smiled and nodded at me.

"You see, Silvio?"

"Hush!" was all he would say, though once he opened my fingers and kissed the palm of my hand.

It must be one of the most beautiful things in the whole world to sit in a gondola with someone you love in the nighttime of Venezia, hearing nothing but the dip of the oar and the whisper of bubbles, and gliding along the black, star-studded water with the grace and stateliness of a swan.

After a while, I had no more desire to speak. As if in a dream, I wished that I could sit forever side by side in that gondola with my sweet, funny friend, and that neither of us would ever have to grow older than we were just at that moment—that beautiful moment—poised between the childhood we'd already left behind and the rest of our lives, all clothed in darkness, all unknowable.

CHAPTER 12

*W*E PASSED THROUGH THE GATES of the Ghetto without a word from the guard, who looked down at us and simply waved us through.

"I thought these gates were locked at night," I said to Silvio.

"They are," he answered me, "on every other night but this one."

We pulled up to a mooring, and the gondolier gave us each his hand as we stepped from his boat. Silvio paid him. I clutched tight to my violin. There was a distant sound of laughter and singing, hands clapping, and feet stamping.

"What is this?" I asked Silvio.

"A festival."

"I know of no festival today."

Silvio gave me his usual ironic smile. "That's because you don't know a thing about the Jewish calendar—despite your superior education."

"If you have something important to tell me, you exasperating boy, tell me quickly."

"It's not what you think, Annina. At least, I think it's not what you think. You've been brought to the Ghetto as a hired musician tonight."

He pulled me along a dark alleyway toward the noise.

"What's that horrible smell?"

"The smell of old cloth and used clothes—the smell of rags

and bones and too many people living in a small space. Here, go up these stairs."

We walked up one crooked stairway and down another to a *campo* softly lit by oil lamps and filled with a crowd of people singing and dancing, drinking and babbling in several different languages. A bearded man wearing brightly embroidered garments was dancing with a scroll that was itself richly clothed, ornamented and bejeweled. Men, women, and children stood around him, clapping and stamping their feet.

"Behold the bridegroom!" laughed Silvio.

And then Rebekkah walked up to us. I'd never seen her look so beautiful. She was always well covered up in the capacious black cloth of a *zendaletta* or a domino when she came to call on us at the Pietà, topped by the yellow or sometimes a red *baretta* marking her as a Jew. But now her head was uncovered and she wore a well-cut gown that showed her curves, lace sleeves and a mantle of pale blue silk. She took my hands and kissed me on both cheeks. "I'm afraid the party is already well under way," she said. And then she pulled me into the very center of the *campo*.

At the sight of me, everyone stopped singing and dancing, so that Rebekkah and I were left standing there in the silence of the night.

"Signori e signore," she said in Italian. "The present I promised to you, in memory of my sister Rachel and in tribute to her dream of reviving Rabbi Modena's plans for a musical conservatory in the Ghetto, the Accademia degli Impediti."

The people gathered round listened attentively and, it seemed to me, a bit skeptically to Rebekkah as she continued. "It is a dream of long standing that we who live here in exile can once again make music as beautiful as the music made by our ancestors. Do not forget, dear friends and neighbors, that the music now performed with such beauty and subtlety and to such great renown in the Christian churches of Venezia"—here she nodded her head to me—"was patterned on the music of the Second Temple, music composed and performed by Jews. Do not forget—even in the conditions of squalor in which we live here, even in the daily struggle to survive—that such music is our heritage and our birthright."

She lowered her voice, and yet everyone could have heard her even if she had whispered. "It is my honor and pleasure to present to you one of the finest young violinists in all of *la Serenissima*"— at this, she drew aside so that I stood alone in the center of the circle, clutching my violin, "Anna Maria della Pietà."

I stood there alone, unable to tell whether the crowd was sympathetic or not to Rebekkah's words. I saw a fierce-looking bearded man spit on the ground before turning his back and walking away. Faces followed him, and people murmured, but no one else left the circle. They stood there, looking at me as if I might suddenly grow horns or wings.

The silence lasted so long that I feared they might start throwing stones at me. All the grown men were bearded. Some of the women were richly garbed, but most of the people standing round—even the children—had careworn eyes and garments as plain and poor as my own.

One young mother, standing with her two children at the inner edge of the circle, started clapping her hands, slowly but encouragingly. A few others joined her. Someone else—another woman—let out a fainthearted cheer. And then—after an excruciating interval—lots of the people standing around started clapping and cheering.

"Play, Anna Maria!" Rebekkah shouted above the sudden noise.

I had never played before, in such a manner, standing alone at the center of a throng of strangers. I turned, looking for Silvio.

"Play, Annina!" he shouted, laughing.

"Play, Annina!" echoed a toothless old woman standing near him. And then a man's voice from the opposite side of the circle bellowed, "Play, Annina!"

The entire crowd took up the chant, clapping in time to the words. "Play, Annina! Play, Annina!"

How could Marietta, I wondered, actually wish to find herself in just such a situation? With all my heart I longed for the blessed anonymity of the choir lofts and the grille. "What should I play?" I murmured to no one in particular, scanning the sea of faces around me until my eyes saw a shock of red hair and a pair of laughing eyes beneath them.

"Maestro?"

There he was, standing elbow to elbow with the Jews of Venezia, who grew quiet again, so that it was just as if he and I were the only ones who stood there in that moment.

I hadn't seen him since that day I saw him with Handel. "Why not play your solo from the eleventh concerto of *L'Estro*?"

It was the latest piece he had given to me, and I'd practiced it so much in the past weeks that I knew it quite by heart.

I've learned since then that the way to do one's best in such a situation, uncompromised by all the attendant fears, is to pretend that one is playing for one beloved and trusted person who knows better than anyone else in the world how to hear the music. Only then will one give every note the proper measure of sweetness and feeling. Only then will one touch the bow to the strings with the open heart and certainty and commitment required to make the music sing as if this were the first and last time that a composition fit for the ears of God would ever be played.

Vivaldi has ever been that person for me, but I only knew it for the first time that October night in the Ghetto, that night of Simchat Torah, as I later learned, which celebrates a year of reading the first five books of the word of God in the original Hebrew, week by week, verse by verse.

I played for my teacher, just as skillfully, just as beautifully, as I was able. I closed my eyes while I played, but I saw his face before me. I saw those eyes that looked into mine when I was eight years old and discovered the musician hidden inside me, the musician I would become.

I was so focused on this vision that I was surprised, when I was done, to see the crowd of strangers gathered round me and hear their adulation, so loud that it made my ears ring.

Vivaldi walked up to me and shook my hand. "Well done, Signorina! It's uncommonly good, don't you think?"

The crowd was shouting for an encore. Vivaldi whipped his violin out from under his mantle. "Shall we play the largo from the first concerto?"

And thus it went for an hour or more, till Rebekkah took our hands and pulled us away through the protesting crowd to the door of a brightly lit café. "I would invite you into my own house, *Professore*, but it is against the law, and doubly so"—she nodded at me—"for the young one."

Vivaldi took out his *gnaga*, the same model of grotesque white mask that Marietta and I had worn to the opera that night that now seemed a hundred years ago. "I must excuse myself, Signora," he said to Rebekkah, bowing low. "I have an important meeting I must attend early tomorrow. But I cannot tell you heartily enough what a pleasure this has been for me. And, please—I hope you'll let me help in any way I can. It is a noble enterprise to revive the tradition of *ars musica* in this place. Surely the Creator is gladdened by the sounds of beautiful music wherever it comes from."

Rebekkah's eyes were shining. "Thank you, Padre! Believe

me, the humble students of our own Compagnia dei Musici will forever aspire to the musical heights that were scaled here tonight."

Looking quite happy with himself, Vivaldi turned to me. "I will see you safely to the Pietà, Signorina. But I suggest you travel *mascherata*, as I know for a fact that the Cattaveri are out in force tonight."

Silvio pinched me. "Ouch!" I said. "No thank you, Maestro. I'm sure that Signora Rebekkah and Silvio will see that I return unharmed."

"I will clothe her in a *zendaletta* over a domino," Rebekkah said, "masked in a *moreta* and a *bauta*, with a three-cornered hat on her head. She will be indistinguishable from the Grand Inquisitor himself."

"Perhaps a little shorter," said Vivaldi. "Very well."

"You'll send another piece to me, Maestro?"

"Without fail, Signorina!" He put on his mask and pulled the hood of his cloak over his head so that not even the faintest part of his red hair was showing as he ducked into the shadows of the *sottoportego* and disappeared.

*W*e sat down with Rebekkah in a quiet corner of the café. It was my first time in such an establishment, either within or outside the Ghetto. I looked around at the other people there, trying to find out the appropriate way to comport myself.

But it seemed a place with few rules. I was surprised to see both Jews and non-Jews there, all engaged in lively discussion. I could hear at least five different languages being spoken, besides our own. The words danced around the room like the call and response of a choir of Babylon, accompanied by an orchestra of glassware and crockery and hissing steam.

There were women there among the men, from every walk of life—and I thought then that I would give a lot to be able to move so freely in the world. I realized, too, that rules are only made in a desperate bid to prevent what is happening already and what, perhaps, is impossible to prevent entirely: there are no walls or guards or gates that can keep the people of Venezia separated from one another. After all, everyone moves together beneath their masks during the six months, all told, of Carnival.

I was but a girl of fourteen, but I realized in that hour, my first hour in a café, that the separation throughout the rest of the year is but the overture to the grander pageant of Venezia. We act out our separate parts in those months of repentance—black-clad aristocrat and yellow-hatted denizen of the Ghetto, swaggering gondolier and simpering virgin, priest and prostitute, clois-tered orphan and cherished daughter of a wealthy family, man and woman of any stripe. But the months of Carnival show the truest picture of *la Serenissima*, when we can be anything we dream of and do anything we dare.

I understood that night, sitting in that cheerful cacophony, occupying three corners of a table with Rebekkah and Silvio, that this freedom was also mine: I had but to take it. It seemed at that moment to be the biggest revelation of my lifetime.

Rebekkah ordered food for us from a swarthy waiter who took not the slightest note of who I was or whether I belonged there. It was only after an exchange of pleasantries and some time spent, on my part, happily looking around me, that I remembered why I'd been brought to the Ghetto.

"*Scusi*, Signora Rebekkah," I said, taking my first delighted sip of a frothy, fragrant drink. "You said in your note that you had information for me."

"And she has earned her payment, wouldn't you say so, Zietta?"

I was surprised to hear Silvio call her by this pet name—
auntie—and to use the *tu* with her. But, then, he worked at her
side every day, and she had, no doubt, become very fond of
him.

"I only hope," Rebekkah answered with a pensive smile, "that
my tidings will seem a worthy payment for her extraordinary
performance tonight, alongside *il Prete Rosso.*"

Silvio took my hand. "It's about the locket, Annina."

I looked at him quizzically. "I thought you said it wasn't."

"It's not what you thought it might be—not in the slightest."
Silvio was smiling. He had—and still has—the most beautiful
smile.

I waited without any of the old feeling of dread. Maybe it
was the calm that came after the courage demanded by the
impromptu concert with Vivaldi in the *campo*. Maybe it was my
sudden sense of there being many more choices open to me than
ever seemed possible before. I was still madly curious about
the locket, and why Franz had been asked to give it to me. But
the door I'd thought to unlock with it seemed to have suddenly
swung open of its own accord.

I took another sip of the wonderful drink, savoring its smell,
and then faced Rebekkah, ready for whatever she had to tell
me.

*Y*ou heard me speak tonight of my sister, Rachel," she
began, "may God rest her soul! She was, like you are, a
musical prodigy. My mother named her for another Rachel,
who sang with such beauty and became so famous that she was
given free rein to go from *palazzo* to *palazzo* in her gondola, as
free as any Christian, to perform for the nobles. Our Rachel, like
you, was a violinist.

"By the time she was fourteen, she had learned all she could from every music teacher in the Ghetto. Our father, who is a man of some influence, was able to use his connections to engage a priest-musician who taught violin at the Ospedale della Pietà, Don Bonaventura Spada."

The maestro's predecessor—I remembered the name from Sister Laura's speech to me. He was the one who had been in love with la Befana.

"Over the years this priest became a favorite with my family. He nurtured Rachel's talent. He listened attentively to my mother when she spoke of the Jewish mysticism she'd learned at the feet of my grandmother, who was a protégée of the great and learned Sara Copio Sullam. He earned not only his wages but also my father's friendship. He ate at our table on the days he came to teach Rachel, and he drank our wine.

"And then, when the War for Candia was lost, and the fortunes of the Republic waned, greater and greater taxes were levied against the Jews. All of us in the Ghetto—even such men as my father—found it increasingly hard to provide the basic necessities of life for their families, to say nothing of the luxury of music lessons.

"We met as a family—because my father knew that his decision would affect all of us equally. We met and decided to use Mother's jewelry to pay for Rachel's music lessons. She had a few fine pieces, and Father told us that—one piece at a time, if Don Spada would accept them—they would allow Rachel to continue her studies, and we would get a better rate of exchange this way than if we pawned them.

"None of us had even a moment's hesitation. What is a bauble compared with a gift such as Rachel's? She had greatness, Signorina, just as you do. And she lived for music."

Are all lives such a complicated puzzle? Maybe it's only in

Venezia—in this place where everyone's role is so strictly and precisely defined—that the cracks between the puzzle pieces tell as much a story as the pieces themselves. Each piece, seen in isolation, makes no sense at all—a corner of this, a limb of that; a leaf, a shadow, a section of water or sky. The meaning only becomes clear when all the pieces are fitted together.

Rebekkah held one piece of the puzzle, and I held another—two small pieces in a large, complex picture as richly detailed as any canvas by Canaletto. I had been sifting through all the pieces for a match to mine—and now she was holding it up before me, and it glittered. It was the coin in which she'd pay me for playing that night in the *campo*. But I knew that it was also her gift to me.

"Silvio asked me if I knew anything of a certain locket that had come into your possession. I could hardly believe my ears when he described it to me. There is no other piece precisely like it, as far as I know. It was made by a master goldsmith in Poland, over two hundred years ago. Yes, I know the provenance of your locket, Anna Maria. But I don't understand how or why it found its way to you."

I begged her to tell me whatever she knew.

"This same locket was given by my father to Bonaventura Spada as payment for Rachel's violin lessons."

I took this in, and yet it made no sense to me. "Do you think Don Spada sold it?"

"Perhaps. He was a very peculiar kind of man, Don Spada, although he was a priest. He won everyone's trust with his soft voice and soulful brown eyes that seemed to look deep inside one's heart. Both men and women loved him. And he loved them back. He won my parents' trust even as he stole my sister's virtue—and gave us Silvio!"

Silvio! There it was, the secret of his parentage, without any searching on his part—no combing through the books of the *scaffetta*. No hunt for clues or friends sent out to spy for him. And yet it was rather awful news.

I looked with renewed tenderness and sympathy at Silvio, my darling friend—that betwixt and between—the child of a priest and a Jewess, and a sodomite besides! How much more of an outcast could anyone possibly be?

Rebekkah had also turned to gaze at Silvio, who sat there looking perfectly comfortable with himself and not a tiny bit distressed. "When I look at him," said Rebekkah, "I see the eyes and smile and hands of the sister who was the sun and moon to me."

"But how," I said, when I'd recovered enough to pose a question, "how was your sister's child ever brought to be raised at the Pietà?"

"Yes, tell her, *Zietta!*"

Rebekkah sighed. "My father, in his grief and anger, disowned Rachel, who was no child but a woman of twenty-eight at the time—a woman, my father raved, who should have known better. He wanted to bring a lawsuit against Spada. But the only result of his inquiries was to bring the baby to the attention of the Council of Ten. When our Silvio was only a month old, and Rachel was already ill, the Cattaveri came and took him away to be baptized, raised as a Christian at the foundling home.

"Some of our neighbors, and even some of our family, agreed with them. Why leave a half-Christian baby to be raised in the direst conditions of poverty and hopelessness, here in the Ghetto, when the Ospedale della Pietà could provide food and shelter, a good education, and a future?

"After Rachel died, my father was inconsolable. He wanted to get his grandson back. But the most he could negotiate was a contract that gave me the right to mend and make the choir robes for the Pietà. I would be able to look in on Silvio and make sure he was faring well. My father's friends had their own friends, in turn, on the Board of Governors, who allowed that Silvio could become my apprentice when he came of age—although he would retain the rights and privileges of an ordinary citizen of *la Serenissima*. It was, in short, a Jewish conspiracy."

I turned to Silvio. "So you *knew* all this time?"

"I only knew that I had someone from the outside who seemed to care for me, who brought me sweets from time to time, and told me I was a good boy. I counted myself lucky."

Rebekkah leaned over and kissed him on the cheek.

"So you knew that day on the island!"

"I didn't know yet. The story only came out when I asked Rebekkah—and with great trepidation, I might add—if she knew anything about your locket. And, as you've heard, she knew everything about it."

"I know nothing about it after it ceased to be the property of Don Spada. I had always believed that my sister's teacher loved her just as much as she, to her eternal misfortune, loved him. And so it pained me to think that he would have gambled or given away the one token he had of her, apart from the son he couldn't claim without losing both his honor and his livelihood.

"But priests must also earn their bread, and a priest such as Bonaventura Spada probably had greater need of ready cash than most others. And the locket is worth a great deal."

Rebekkah turned her gaze on me. "Silvio told me how the locket was given to you, and by whom. But I still don't know why."

"You're as much in the dark about it, Signora, as I am. I was hoping you could tell me something about the proprietor of the Banco Giallo. He was the one who sent the locket to me via Herr von Regnazig, resident consul for the Archbishop of Mainz."

"I can only tell you that the Banco Giallo is owned by a good, reliable man. I've had many dealings with him."

"Did you, Signora—" I hesitated. "Did you perhaps recommend his services to a noblewoman recently?"

"I've recommended his services to half a dozen noblewomen recently. I have readier access to the city than most women of the Ghetto, because of my special relationship with the Pietà, and I have many clients among the nobility."

"Do you ever have dealings with the Foscarini?" I held my breath.

"Yes—the mother. She's had a great deal of trouble with her children. Too much money, I think, can be nearly as bad as too little. Only the eldest one, Marco, has done her proud. People say he will be Doge one day, if he lives that long. The others have only brought her sorrow."

She took my hand in both of hers, which were soft and stained from the cloth she handled. "It's late—it's nearly dawn. You'd best get back before you're missed."

"I'll come back again if you want me to, and if I can get out as easily as I did tonight. I'd be glad to give lessons—in memory of your sister and Silvio's mother. I envy both of you, even though you've lost her. It would mean much to me to have known someone who shares my blood."

I looked from one to the other of them, looking for some resemblance, but I saw none. "Signora Rebekkah, did the locket ever have a key?"

"Yes, of course—a tiny key with sapphires on it, I believe. It was a pretty thing. Has that been lost along the way? What a shame!"

I couldn't wait to get back to my room and look at the locket again in light of what I now knew about it. Where had it been since that wicked priest sold it—or perhaps he'd been forced to give it away to buy someone's silence. I worried that Rebekkah would resent me for possessing something so valuable—with no apparent right or reason—that had once belonged to her family.

She and Silvio covered me up, just as she'd promised the maestro, until no one—not even my mother herself—could ever have guessed my identity. Silvio also traveled *in maschera*.

Not all of the canals of Venezia go somewhere. Some simply run up against a building or an alleyway and end there. I knew so much more now than I had when I'd entered the Ghetto, only hours before. But, like a boatman who's lost his way, I had paddled hard only to arrive at a place with no passageway to where I wanted to go.

If my mother had wanted to send some sign by giving me a token, she would surely have sent something from her own family's treasure trove—not the family treasure of a family completely unconnected to her by kinship or tradition.

How could Rebekkah not have told Silvio in all that time that she was his aunt? I couldn't see then why anyone would keep secret a thing that could give such joy. I didn't yet understand how complex a thing happiness can be—nor the companionability of a well-kept secret, savored and nurtured till the time is right for its unmasking.

"You're so quiet," said Silvio.

"Does it not bother you?" I asked him.

"That I'm the offspring of a renegade priest and a musical Jewess? It came as no great surprise to me. I accept this heritage—I embrace it. It gives me license never to choose but to remain a traveler between the two horizons of my existence. And I have, besides, a family now—my good Rebekkah, who loves me, errant bastard that I am. She sees everything that is good in me, and forgives everything that is bad."

The night was very still. "I wish I had a Rebekkah."

"You have me, Annina. I will be your *zietta!*"

Silvio made such a funny face, and so like a kindly older woman, that I was laughing again when the gondolier pulled up to the steps of the water gate and I realized that we'd arrived.

I threw my arms around my sweet friend and hugged him hard. "Come again to see me soon!" I whispered. "And, Silvio—"

"What is it, little sister?"

"I want you to have the locket. It's yours, not mine."

"What a wealthy foundling you are, to be giving priceless jewels away!"

"I mean it. Next time we see each other, I want to give it to you."

"If you give it to me, I'll give it to Rebekkah."

"Good, then—it's settled. But if the key ever comes to you, you must promise to let me be there when you use it."

"I promise!" He kissed me right on the lips then, just before I jumped out of the boat and picked my way carefully up the steps and into the building, which was quiet and dark. I waited in a shadowy corner till my eyes had adjusted.

The entire place was quiet with that particular stillness of the hour just before dawn. I could hear the lapping of water in the canal outside, and an almost imperceptible scurrying—but there are always rats in the basement. And yet the sound of them made me bound with unwonted speed up the stairs, to the first landing, where I ran nearly headlong into la Befana.

CHAPTER 13

SHE GRABBED ME by the neck. "I have her!" she shouted. Others came scurrying toward us out of the darkness, carrying lamps. I saw Sister Laura.

"Please, *Zietta!*" I tried to say more, but la Befana had my throat in the crook of her arm and I could hardly breathe.

I will never forget the look that Sister Laura gave me then—never had she looked at me in such a way before, with an expression of rage I'd only ever seen in la Befana's eyes.

I struggled to loosen the arm that held me, so that I could speak. "Please, *Zietta*—help me!"

Her eyes were filled with the flames from her torch. She took my violin away from me. "I am not your *zietta!*" She hissed rather than said the words. I knew the world had gone mad then, and that Sister Laura had joined the ranks of Satan.

La Befana tightened her hold on my neck. "Out whoring, were you? Did he pay you well?"

This was too much for me to bear. I stamped down hard on her foot with the heel of my boot. And then things transpired in such a way that I would not have believed anyone had they foretold them to me even the day before. While Sister Laura turned to la Befana, who was howling in pain, I ran. I reached the landing and had begun to fly down the first stair when I was suddenly pulled up short.

It was like one of those dreams one has sometimes, of beginning to walk downstairs and then suddenly the stair isn't there anymore and one awakens with a start, suffused with the memory of falling. I was reeled around, the back of my robe held tight in la Befana's fist and pulled against my throat, cutting off my air. I saw her furious eyes in the torchlight, and I heard the jangling of her keys.

I recall these events with a mixture of awe at my boldness and shame at my utter lack of self-control. The very young never think of consequences when their passions are aroused. They feel everything with the conviction that their feelings—both good and bad—will last forever. Perhaps that is why we are all so much more indelibly marked by what happens to us in childhood than we are by countless events and impressions in the years that follow.

In a panic, I struggled to break free from la Befana's grasp. And then I pulled my own fist back, held my fingers tight inside my knuckles, and punched her. I punched her with all my strength.

She didn't cry—at least, I didn't hear her cry, although I saw the trickle of blood from her nostrils.

Someone caught my arms from behind and I was covered in angry voices from all sides. I found myself looking straight into Sister Laura's eyes as she loomed above me from where I lay pinned to the floor—her blue eyes now crazed with red and filled with fury. Eyes I'd loved and trusted throughout my childhood.

I thought the usual thoughts I thought in my moments of greatest distress. I conjured an image of the Virgin appearing there before me in all her glory. I heard the sound of wings and closed my eyes. But now I pictured both Sister Laura and la Befana falling to their knees in fear and pain. The Virgin would hold out her hand to me, saying in a voice as soothing and low as the bells of San Marco, "Come, Anna Maria." I pictured my mother, although I couldn't see her face. "Come, Anna Maria," she would say to me. "It is time to go home."

When I opened my eyes again, Sister Laura was still looming there above me. I felt overcome with the hollowness of the feelings she'd always shown me. What had she been but a mask, a traitor, and a false friend? It was worse—far worse—than if she'd never singled me out for her favor, never believed in me, never made me feel that she cared for me. Without taking my eyes off of hers, I spat out the words that were burning in my throat, "How I hate you! How I hate all of you!"

The torchlight loomed, and then the Prioress was there, high above me. "Enough—for shame! Release her!" As Sister Laura got up from where she was kneeling on me, the Prioress put her foot on my shoulder, so I stayed lying there on the cold marble floor. I saw her move her torch from face to face. "I see." She crossed herself and then said again, "I see."

Sister Laura said in a furious whisper, "She was in a gondola on the canal."

La Befana added, as if the words tasted of bile, "Kissing her lover!"

"He's not my lover!" I said, but no one was listening to me, and everyone was speaking at once.

The Prioress commanded silence.

By then people were leaning down over the balustrades from the floors above, some with lighted candles. Sister Laura, la Befana, and I were all trembling and breathing hard in a small knot of light.

"You have behaved disgracefully. You have dishonored this institution!" The Prioress included all of the *ospedale* in the sweep of her hand. "Leave us!" she said to Sister Laura.

Sister Laura tried to protest, but the Prioress said to her,

"Now—immediately!" and then held her lamp up close to la Befana's face. "Are you in need of medical attention?"

La Befana wiped her nose, looked at the streak of blood and mucus on the back of her hand, and shook her head slowly. Perhaps it was a trick of the light, but it seemed to me that she was smiling.

"Come with me, then." She took her foot off my chest. "Both of you."

As I walked between them, the torch lit up the stones of the walls enclosing us, and the stones of the floor entombing us. I had never before felt such a sense of anger and loathing. The Prioress cried out to the girls and women lined up in their nightclothes and looking down upon us, "Go back to bed—all of you!" But they stayed there, anyway, and I felt their eyes bore into me and I heard their whispers.

The last hallway leading to the Prioress's office seemed to have been stretched out so that it felt as if we would have to walk along it forever, the jeering eyes of all the *ospedale* watching, enjoying the show.

When we finally reached her door, the Prioress asked la Befana to wait outside. Then she closed the door behind us, set the torch into its place on the wall, and sat down with a sigh of exhaustion at her desk.

She spoke with utter calm. "I won't ask you to sit, Signorina," she said, "because I have very little to say to you. Please listen carefully."

I listened, although I know I trembled in every part of me.

"As of today, you are demoted from the *coro* to the *comun*. Your new job will be in the soap works, which is an appropriate place for one who has covered herself in the filth of dishonor. The instrument that was formerly your violin will be henceforth the property of Bernardina."

I was unable to keep my feelings from flowing over—I felt my face crumple, and tears fell from my eyes.

"Maestra Meneghina!" she called. La Befana walked in, her blood-streaked face suffused with a sour look of satisfaction. "Please take her directly to the laundry and see that she's assigned to a bed there."

Then she turned to me a final time. "I will pray for you, Anna Maria. I will pray for you to find your way again."

While the Prioress looked on, la Befana tied my wrists together with a length of rope and then nudged me to begin walking ahead of her. I tried to stay as far away from her as I could on that journey down through the bowels of the *ospedale* to the *comun*, but it was a short length of rope and I could feel her breath and hear her muttering behind me. The rope chafed at my wrists, and I felt a sense of dread in the small of my back, where I feared she'd kick me.

She didn't kick me, though, but handed me over to Signora Zuana, the head of the laundry, who was mightily cross at being woken. La Befana merely shook her head and smiled her horrible smile as she left me there, first whispering to no one, "Like mother, like daughter."

*M*aking soap is a backbreaking and loathsome process that requires great care, to be sure, and yet it leaves the mind disengaged to think all the hopeless thoughts it will.

My mind was free to agonize over my every painful memory. I thought how I'd wished for a new life, and how this wish had been granted me. My new life was so different from my old one that I hardly recognized myself as I went through the motions of living it.

My first job in the soap works was to make the lye water, pouring in and stirring the white ashes gathered from the stoves and fireplaces throughout the *ospedale*.

An extra *corbetta* of wood bestowed by the governors has always been a coveted mark of distinction among members of the *coro*. Play well and you will stay warmer over the damp cold nights of winter and spring. The ghosts of all those cheerful, comforting, status-laden fires are carried away in buckets by the menials of the Pietà, down to the workrooms of the laundry. There the ashes are mixed with rainwater and beef fat, and made into soap.

At the end of my first day I was powdered as white as the barber's assistant who carries his rack of newly dressed wigs to the gentry every Sunday morning. My fingers—those same fingers that so lately coaxed music from my violin—looked like the fingers of a dead person.

And yet I willed myself to keep the music alive in me. I would choose a composition first, listening to the whole of it in my memory, as many times as I needed to hear it in its entirety. And then, beginning with my own part, I would try to both see and hear the notes on the page, and the sounds made by each of them with my violin—or the violin that once was mine and was now being played by Bernardina.

I didn't dwell on thoughts of Bernardina, because they only made me sick with envy that she was still playing while I was being told by everything around me that I would never play again. As soon as I'd seen and heard my own parts, I went back and saw and heard each of the other instruments in turn. This was very hard for me: sometimes reconstructing even a few bars would take me hours.

I sifted through the buckets of ash, removing all the pieces of charcoal that had not yet burned. And then I had to stand on a ladder to ladle the sifted ashes into the wooden barrel with its noxious cargo. The ashes floated up and into my eyes and hair. At the bottom, where the spigot was, I had to strain the sodden ashes from the brown lye water, trying never to let it touch my skin.

Just so, I sifted through the sounds in my memory, finding the notes that now I wished I'd heeded with more care. Every forgotten note seared me with regret as caustic as the lye.

I had never thought in so focused a way about the different parts played by each member of the orchestra. It made me realize something more of the skill it takes to put them all together—and how all of them together create something far greater than each of them separately.

I felt as close as I ever had to the maestro at these times. I remembered how Giulietta and I had hidden ourselves in the sacristy and watched him compose. In silence, we'd imitated the terrible faces he made. Later, in our dormitory, we'd laughed so hard that we'd fallen onto the floor.

Now I wished I could see him and tell him that I understood: *Christus* really had stood before him, and angels had whispered the notes in his ears.

One could think of music while sifting and ladling ash. But utter concentration was required for tending to the great vat of lye and grease perched above the fire. When I had the job of stirring it, all I could think about was trying not to let any of it well up and burst in the air. A half-mad girl named Maria-Bianca, charged with teaching me my job, told me that the bubbles "speak" when the soap is ready to be tried. They come to the surface, linger there for a moment, and then explode. It took only one drop of lye searing my skin to make me turn every particle of my attention upon the work at hand, as if God himself and not the bubbles had been about to speak to me.

I could not think of anything then but trying to keep as much distance as I could between the exposed parts of my flesh and the boiling contents of the iron pot I had to stir with a wooden spoon that was taller, from bowl to tip, than I am. My back ached with the strain of it. Ninetta, a lame girl who stoked the fire beneath the three iron pots—two small and one large— had already been blinded in one eye. Her face and arms were streaked with white scars where someone careless, stirring the mixture, had dripped it down upon her. She was the one who showed me the trick of dropping a chicken feather on top of the mixture: if the feather began to smoke and dissolve, the soap was ready for salting.

Hell, I'm quite sure, is filled with vats of lye and poor sinners ever stirring it and stoking the fires beneath it, afraid of being dissolved by it to a smoking pile of bones.

I only thought of my friends when I lay down at night in the bed I shared with three others. As tired as I was, it sometimes took me a long time to fall asleep, what with their shoving and complaining and, finally, their snoring and smells. Everything and everyone in the soap works smelled of the rancid beef fat that had to be rendered and added to the lye.

As I labored to fall asleep, I tried to imagine the lives of my friends. I wondered if Claudia was back yet from Saxony, and whether it was hard for her to be living in a cloister again after the balls and soirees of her family's life in the country. After the castles and hunts, the masquerades and garden parties. After the fitting sessions with the dressmaker, and her trips to town with her mother to pick out the silks and velvets and lingerie for her trousseau.

I thought about Giulietta traveling the wide world with her young lover. I thought of her playing her cello in some cheerful atelier while he painted and birds sang and the yellow sun poured like honey through their window.

I thought of Marietta on the stage of the Teatro San Grisostomo. I pictured her in a magnificent costume, dripping with jewels, her eyes outlined in kohl, and her hair studded with pearls. I saw the flowers strewn at her feet as if she stood in a garden.

I thought sometimes of Sister Laura and how she would be telling some other girl to call her *Zietta,* some other girl she'd favor with an apple or some praise or even a kiss on the forehead.

My sleep was haunted by a nightmare during the many months I lived and worked in the laundry. It was always the same. The great wooden spoon slipped out of my hands. Sister Laura stood over me, crying out, "Grab it—grab it before it's too late!" And then la Befana came up behind me and shoved me, so that both my hands went into the lye, and I knew—I knew in that moment of searing pain and horror—that I would never play music again, that it was lost to me, lost to me forever.

Dear Annina,

Where were you for the opening? I saw everyone else, but I couldn't see you anywhere! When I came to the parlatorio and asked for you, Maestra Evelina said you weren't receiving. Are you ill? I'm going to ask my future mother-in-law to send you a chicken.

Oh Annina, you must have heard by now that my debut was an absolute triumph—far more wonderful than even I had ever dreamed. I only had to consult the prompter a couple of times, and my voice was as strong and good as it's ever been. And, oh, my costume! I thought I would die of happiness when they brought it to me for the dress rehearsal.

Handel's patron, Prince Ernest of Hanover, was there. He kissed my hand when he met me, and swears he's going to come to every performance as long as I'm singing Poppea. And Handel says that, as far as he's concerned, there should be a law passed to bar anyone but me from ever singing Poppea. Isn't that sweet?

They're really terribly shy, these Saxons—they can't seem to just say what they want to say (no less do what they want to do!). Instead they waste one's time and pots of ink writing poetry, or else they stand about casting sidelong glances and making faces, till one wants to ask them whether they ate something bad that gave them indigestion.

Handel has written the most divine hymn to the Virgin, "Ah! Che troppo ineguali!" He asked me to sing it at a private concert at the palazzo of the Marcello brothers. Everyone there adored it, and yet the composer couldn't even face me when it was done—and, I kid you not, the man was wiping tears from his eyes as he hurried out of the room. Tomasso guffawed in that annoying way of his and said that "il caro Sassone" had better sniff up someone else's skirts.

Tonight will be our fifteenth performance of Agrippina. There's no end in sight to the enthusiasm of la Serenissima for this opera. People are buying up tickets and selling them for three times their price.

I adore singing on the opera stage. This is the life I was born to live—I've always known it. Thanks to Tomasso's family and their riches, I am able to live it without the sordid struggles that attend the efforts of so many other artistes.

How can it be that there is not a woman who plays in any one of the opera orchestras—and yet we are allowed to sing on the stage? It seems so unfair that the four ospedali are the only places in this benighted city where someone such as you can perform—hidden away, where no one can see you!

You can't imagine how glorious it is to be seen and heard and known! I am only truly happy when I am performing thus, with everyone's eyes upon me. All the rest of life seems like nothing more than a collection of boring details.

I am practically brought to the theater now under lock and key. Tomasso's mother makes a great show of protecting my virtue.

What is virtue, Annina, but a sham? Every woman among the nobility, as far as I've been able to see, has her lover. My future mother-in-law herself says that it's the height of poor taste to be seen around town with one's husband.

I've been able to find out one thing more since I wrote to you last. I made off with a bottle of wine after the party on opening night and stashed it in my cell here in the cloister. Making use of it later, I got my old stinky nun liquored up sufficiently to have a nice little talk with me about the history of San Francesco della Vigna and some of the odd things that have happened here over the years.

Turns out there was a group of musicians from the Pietà who came here to make their devotions, late in anno Domini 1694. One of them—a young noblewoman traveling under an assumed name—stayed behind, supposedly for a year of silent retreat. But then she was spirited away in a gondola in the dead of night some eight months after her arrival.

One story has it that she gave birth to a baby and then drowned it in the canal. They say that some of the nuns can hear its ghost on rainy nights, crying out for its mother. Another version of the story says that the young noblewoman took her baby away with her. But in each version of the story, she was a daughter of the Foscarini.

Before you get your hopes up, I think you should bear in mind that no one from Tomasso's family would ever in a thousand years own up to such a scandal. And, anyway, dozens of girls of the Pietà could make an equally plausible claim to be the outcome of that par-

ticular story. But I thought I'd better tell it to you, just the same.

When the show has had its run, I will find a way to slip out in maschera. I'll come get you, and the two of us, you and I, will see, hear, and taste the best of what Venezia has to offer. We'll both dress up as soldiers or something equally rakish and fun.

By the by, the wench who serves my future mother-in-law—a priceless gossip—let slip that she carries letters almost daily to and from the Pietà. And now I'm wondering if that great oaf, Tomasso, is courting another girl there. Wouldn't that be just like him to have a spare virgin for when he grows tired of me!

Please try—try your hardest—to come hear me sing. I'm sure Matteo would help you, if all else fails.

Baci ed abbracci,

Marietta

It was, naturally, Paolina who gave me Marietta's letter—although I noticed a reticence on her part and even a note of resentment that I had no coins to give her for her trouble.

I failed to make any new friends in the *comun*. All of the girls there knew where I came from, and they delighted, I think, in witnessing my fall from grace. Paolina was always cordial, but I rarely got to see her, as the pressing room is at the opposite end of the building from the soap works.

I carried Marietta's unopened letter inside my chemise for a day and a half before I found a time and a place where I could read it without being seen. And then I read and reread it so many times that I committed it to memory.

For every day that I measured ashes and stirred the vat of lye over the fire, I felt the flame of my own life dying away.

It is not only food that feeds us, and it is not only prayer that lets us walk in God's light.

I saw the autumn turn to winter while living like a ghost among the *figlie di comun*. I went with them to the church at Christmastime to hear the oratorio performed by my peers. It reminded me of that night on the balcony of the Ca' Foscarini, when the heavenly sounds of the *coro* wafted up to me and I looked down upon them as a spirit looks down upon the living from the land of the dead. Only when I ceased to be Anna Maria dal Violin did I come to understand exactly who I was and how I was meant to live—but it was too late. That life was lost to me as I labored and languished in the soap works of the *ospedale*.

Unlike many of the others, who had worked in the laundry since the age of ten, I was closely watched by the mistress in charge, who had no greater love for me than the girls who worked under her. The door was barred at night, and the *portinare* who guarded it seemed content to sit there, gossip with tradesmen or servants, and bark at any of their less privileged fellow inmates of the Pietà who tried to steal a look at the world outside.

In the refectory, very soon after my arrival, I asked Paolina whether she could carry a letter for me, if I managed to find a way to write one. But she only looked offended and shook her head no.

I wanted to ask Silvio if he could help me—but to do what? How far would I get if I ran away? Without the locket, I had nothing of value to buy my passage or pay for bread.

I wondered what had become of the locket and the small collection of private things I'd kept under my bed—the quills and ink, the sealing wax and sand, the seal with my initials. I wondered, too, what the other girls had been told. Gross insubordination was usually kept a secret, lest it encourage others to rebel. Maybe they thought I was ill or that, like Giulietta, I'd run away. Maybe they thought I was dead.

I felt bad that I hadn't been able to give the locket to Silvio, as I'd intended. Did another girl have it now? It made my guts writhe to think of it clutched in Bernardina's freckled fist. Had it been confiscated by the Prioress? For all Silvio knew, I'd made it back safely to my room. He might be sending me messages even now—messages that would never reach me.

I wondered if Marietta might be able to help me, but I also knew that all her thoughts were on the opera and her upcoming marriage, and I firmly believed then that she was not a person to risk her own well-being in the service of someone else.

Thoughts of Franz were always with me, but I knew there was scant hope, in the real world, of ever seeing him again.

As the days turned into weeks, and the weeks to months, all my desires were distilled into a single wish: to hold my violin again and make it sing. I no longer wondered who my parents were or what different kind of life I could have if I found them. I wanted my old life back. I wanted only to be, once again, Anna Maria dal Violin.

I lived and breathed despair. I felt sure I would be there forever among the *figlie di comun*, sifting ashes and stirring fat and lye until I was too maimed to work or simply died of sorrow. With my friends gone, and with Sister Laura turned against me, I was sure as well I'd been forgotten. Even the maestro would have found another violinist who could try out new compositions as he wrote them, whose name he would scrawl in his florid hand across the top of the page. God had spurned me because I had squandered the gifts He'd given me.

I had to ask for paper, ink, and a pen half a dozen times before they were granted me. And then I wrote both to the Prioress and the governors, swearing that I had seen the error of my ways and that all I wanted, for the rest of my life, was to be able to play music again as a sage and modest *figlia* of the Pietà.

When I had gone over the letters many times, making sure they were as perfect as I could make them, I gave them to Signora Zuana, the *carica* in charge of all of the girls and women who worked in the soap works and laundry. She looked almost kindly at me when she took the two neatly folded letters from my hand, and she said that she would see that they were delivered. I tasted hope again.

I had already gone out the door when I decided to turn back and thank Signora Zuana again for her willingness to help me. I knew that she had no cause to do so, and my heart warmed at this unwonted act of kindness.

It took me a moment to understand what I was seeing when I entered the room. Signora Zuana was kneeling down beside the vat of lye. With one hand she shielded her face from the heat, while, with the other, she fed my letters into the fire. The flames flared up, bright green at first, then yellow, till the yellow died down into a mournful display of orange sparks. I watched in helpless silence as my words and all my hopes for a reprieve were reduced to ashes.

CHAPTER 14

A SORT OF DULLNESS set into my soul. The days stretched into weeks and the weeks into months. When I lay down to sleep, I looked at my hands and wept because they did not even seem like my hands anymore. My fingers were reddened, rough, and chapped. Especially as the weather grew colder, the fingers of my left hand felt too stiff for even Vivaldi's slowest passages. I tried to regain the suppleness in my hands when I realized that it was gone, practicing my fingering and bowing in the air. But I was always too exhausted at night to keep this up long enough to get any good from it.

My bedmates disdained me because I had no interest in gossiping with them, so intent was I on thinking about music, hoping to keep it alive inside me. More than once I overheard them gossiping about *me*—mocking my exercises and my foolishness in thinking I would ever play music again.

In the spring, Signora Zuana told me to report to the infirmary.

"But I'm not ill," I told her. I could never look her in the eye after that day I saw her burn my letters.

"Nonetheless, you're wanted there."

I came as I was, sprinkled in the ashes that nearly always covered me now, so that I looked more like a gray-haired lady than a fifteen-year-old girl. The attendant at the infirmary door led me across the main sickroom, past the coughing and quietly groaning, past the glassy-eyed patients and those who were fast asleep. We knocked and were admitted to another, smaller room with a window that looked out over the wintry courtyard and the rain.

Sister Laura was lying in a bed there, although I hardly would have recognized her. Her face was bloated. Her skin was gray. Her blue eyes were rimmed in red, as they had been on that terrible night. And yet they lit up at the sight of me, filled with all the kindness and affection she'd always shown me. I was overcome with remorse, remembering how I'd spoken to her.

The doctor attending her took me aside. "Do you know her well?"

"She was my first teacher," I told him, "and was ever a friend to me." I said nothing of the last time she and I had met.

He shook his head. "You'd best say *addio* to her, and wish her Godspeed on her journey. The priest is on his way."

"Why?" I asked him. "What has happened to her?"

"Inflammation of the lungs, fever, and delirium. Our remedies didn't work this time. She has been asking for you."

I knelt and took one of her hands—it was cold, as if she'd died already. "*Figlia!*" she said to me in barely a whisper before her whole frame was wracked by a fit of coughing.

I held her hand until the coughing passed and then kissed her forehead as she had once kissed mine.

Thus I knelt there, half paralyzed with dread, while other people came into the room, some of them bearing the objects needed for Last Rites: a little table covered with a white cloth, candles and incense, a bowl of water, and vessels of holy oil. These were followed by a priest—not the usual priest who heard our confessions and gave us Communion, but someone of higher rank and unknown to me.

The Prioress and several other *maestre* came in, along with a couple of noblewomen draped in black from head to toe and heavily veiled. The priest sprinkled holy water around the room in the shape of a cross. He wiped his fingers on a piece of bread and then, dipping pieces of snowy white cloth in the oil, he anointed her, again marking the shape of the cross. And as he did this, he prayed.

"*In nómine Patris, et Fílii, et Spíritus Sancti, extinguátur in te omnis virtus diáboli per impositiónem mánuum nostrárum, et per invocatiónem gloriósæ et sanctæ Dei Genitrícis Vírginis Maríæ, ejúsque ínclyti Sponsi Joseph, et ómnium sanctórum Angelórum, Archangelórum, Mártyrum, Confessórum, Vírginum, atque ómnium simul Sanctórum.*"

I stood with the others in a half-circle around the bed, and we prayed for the immortal soul of Sister Laura, reciting the seven penitential psalms and the litany of the saints.

She seemed to have a surge of strength as she kissed the cross the priest held for her and he bent close to hear her confession.

When this was done, her eyes glazed over again, and the priest turned to all of us who stood around the room. "Which one of you," he asked, "is called Anna Maria?"

He knew me by my startled look, I suppose. "She wants you to play for her. She wants this to be the last sound she hears before she passes to the next world."

How could I play when I had not touched a violin in half a year? How could I hope to play with these hands that had been scalded and waterlogged, my calluses gone, my dexterity gone? I burned with shame at the thought of such sounds as I would make now being the last sounds that Sister Laura would hear.

Someone else was sent to fetch my violin. I knelt by my dear teacher, my kind friend, and kissed her hand. She drew my own hand to her mouth and I felt the dry touch of her lips, so burning hot that I expected to see a mark from them on my skin. She said, very softly, "*Figlia mia!*"

I wanted to say something in return, to thank her for her attentions to me throughout my girlhood. Of all the *maestre*, she had always been the one who seemed to care the most about my progress. I was crying, but not only because of Sister Laura's misfortune, nor only because I knew that I would fail her in this final hour. I cried because I feared she would carry to her grave my last chance of finding my mother and knowing her.

I knew it was a selfish thing to ask her in this moment when surely all she wanted to do was cleanse her soul. And yet I could not help myself; I thought only about the urgency of my own need.

If there were any one moment in my life I were given the chance to do over again—to discard it as badly done, something I would consider more thoroughly, prepare for more assiduously, and then perform anew with the depth and insight it deserved— this would be the moment I would choose. But life gives us very few second chances—and death gives us none.

I put my lips close to Sister Laura's ear and whispered, "Please, for the love of God, tell me how to find her! Take pity on me, *Zietta*!"

She looked in my eyes and murmured the same meaningless words over again. Then she turned her face to the wall.

"... *in nómine Dómini: et orátio fídei salvábit infírmum, et alleviábit eum Dóminus: et si in peccátis sit, remitténtur ei; cura, quæsumus, Redémptor noster, grátia Sancti Spíritus languóres istíus infírmæ, ejúsque sana vúlnera, et dimítte peccáta, atque dolóres cunctos mentis et córporis ab ea expélle, plenámque intérius et extérius sanitátem misericórditer redde, ut, ope misericórdiæ tuæ restitúta . . .*"

The room was close with the smell of incense, and I myself felt close to fainting.

Someone placed my violin in my hands. It was la Befana, looking as strong and vital as Sister Laura looked weak and spent. "Play, Anna Maria!" she said to me so harshly that I winced, associating with her voice, as I did, the sting of her baton upon my flesh. I thought of the joyous shouts of the people in the Ghetto who had gathered around me, so many months ago, and I refused to look at la Befana, even though she was so close that I could feel her breath upon my ear. "Play her into the next world!"

I took the instrument from her and bought time by tuning it, even though all the notes were true. It was my old violin, and I nearly wept from the joy of merely holding it again.

I spent longer tuning than I ever had before, trying in vain to get the bow coordinated with my left hand. My two hands seemed as if they belonged to two different people, and neither of them me. It was like a nightmare. I was filled with terror at the weight of responsibility before me, and my overwhelming doubts that I could do it justice.

When I realized, from the subtle noises and movements of the people around me, that I could delay no longer, I began to play. I chose the maestro's A-minor concerto, the *grave e sempre piano* of the middle movement, which had always been one of Sister Laura's favorites.

The notes of the first few bars wobbled horribly, and I felt my face grow hot. La Befana was watching me. She was not rubbing her hands together, but she might as well have been, so great was her look of triumph. I willed my muscles to remember—and then something changed. It was as if the violin itself remembered for me.

I was playing again. I was myself again, the violin a part of my body.

With barely a pause, I followed the A minor with the largo from the maestro's F-major concerto in the same series. The music formed a bridge of sound for me: I walked across it from the world of the dead to the world of the living.

I remembered how I used to imagine, during nearly every performance, that my mother was in the audience. That if I played with enough sweetness and skill, she would rise up at the end, her eyes shining. She would hold out her hand to me and say, "Come away from this place, Anna Maria. It is time to go home."

I played hoping to move Sister Laura with my music, since I had been unable to move her with my words. I played hoping that she would rally, as is sometimes the case with those who have seen the Angel of Death—that she would stir herself to live and tell me what I needed to know. I played with all the home-sickness and longing that had filled my heart from the moments when I first understood how utterly alone I was in the world, and so unlovable that even my own mother, if indeed she lived, refused to know me.

I held the last note as long as I dared, not wanting to let go. When the strings were silent and, looking up, I lowered my bow, everyone in the room was crying—and Sister Laura was dead.

I can only remember with imprecision what followed. Someone tried to take the violin from my hands, and I struggled to hold onto it. Finally, I was led away to the laundry again, where I lay in my bed, for several days, unable to take solid food. During those days I envied Sister Laura.

Paolina came to see me once while I was ill. She brought me a freshly laundered handkerchief, a bowl of soup, and a letter from Marietta.

Dear Annina,

Maestra Evelina finally told me what has happened to you. Cara! It seems so unfair for you to be banished to the comun! I hope they have not given you too odious a task there.

My God, though, how I roared when she told me how you socked la Befana! Brava! I didn't think you had it in you. It was certainly time that someone punched that old bitch. My only regret is that now you have to suffer for it.

If the maestro had still been on staff, believe me, you would never have been chucked out of the coro. He valued you too highly ever to let you go. We've had no tidings of him here, except that he spends a great deal of time in Mantua.

I'm not sure how I can find you a husband now, but I'll try to find someone who can wrench you out of that place. Tomasso has a lot of friends who are usually too drunk to care whether a girl comes from the coro, the comun, or a brothel. But I would only find you one such who would give you his name. Never fear!

The more I find out about Venezia's nobility, the more amazed I am. They are like a perfect-looking piece of fruit that one cuts into only to discover maggots and mold.

Even the Foscarini have far worse things than Tomasso and me to feel ashamed of. In the dead of night a week ago, I was called out of my bed at the convent and told to put on a set of clothes that was brought to me, all of black silk, and a fat pearl necklace I'm only allowed to wear at family occasions. I was popped out the water gate and shoved into one of the family's gondolas, all ablaze with candles encircling a coffin. The coffin itself was covered in red roses as if the sky had opened up and rained flowers. I tried to ask who the stiff was, but no one—not even Tomasso—would tell me.

All of them were weeping, although they tried to hide it. Mam-

ma Foscarini was the one weeping hardest. Papa and all the sons
and daughters I'd already met were there, and so I figured it must
have been a kid they'd kept hidden away—although it wasn't a
kid-size coffin.

We went like that—with all of them crying and none of them
giving me so much as a hint—all the way to the Cimitero San Mi-
chele, where all the stiffs are buried. It was highly creepy slogging
half asleep through the grass to the family plot and having it dawn
on me that that's where I'll be buried one day.

Even though whoever it was who died was being kept secret, the
funeral was as full of pomp as one would expect of such a family.
A cardinal officiated, plus my Lady's private confessor, who is evil
enough to be la Befana's long-lost twin. He has twice taken time
out from his prayers to touch my bottom.

Only at the very end, when everyone had thrown down their
clod of earth, I heard Tomasso whimper, "Antonia!" I'm guessing it was one of his siblings. Whatever happened to this Antonia, you can bet that everyone in the family feels pretty guilty
about it.

I keep sending messages to Tomasso, asking when the date will
be set for our wedding. And he says that his father is making sure
first that my own mother and her brood are moved away and set
up in Vicenza. I don't know how big a payment she was able to
wrest from him, but I'm sure it was substantial. Rather than making her crew beg under bridges, she's going to set up a sort of agency
where matrons and their housekeepers can come and hire children
to work in their household and on their lands. I'm sure my mother
will consider it to be the best bargain she's ever made. I've promised myself I shan't miss her. But, in any case, I will have money
enough to go visit her, if I feel the need.

I've been singing, of course, here among the nuns, but the rep-

ertoire is even more boring than it was at the Pietà. I'd run away if
my mother-in-law hadn't promised me that I'll be able to perform
in an opera again as soon as I'm safely married.

Flowers still arrive here for me sometimes. But my adoring public, for the moment, has forgotten me, now that Agrippina has
come to the end of its glorious run: twenty-seven performances,
each one hailed as a triumph for all of us involved.

Don't lose hope, Annina! I'm going to work on getting Papa Foscarini to use his influence to see you reinstated in the coro even
while I talk you up to Tomasso's loutish friends. Believe me, if I
have anything to say about it at all, you will not be stuck in the
comun much longer.

For now, I've sent a chicken and two gold coins. I will not abandon you, cara, although all the rest of the world has.

Sending you baci ed abbracci,

Marietta

ate that September, I was called before the Prioress.
I registered her look of surprise when I walked in.
"Sit down, dear—you look so tired!" The passage of time seemed
to have softened the edges of her anger toward me. She looked,
if anything, quite sympathetic—and yet I was wary. "The governors met yesterday, Anna Maria, and took several decisions."

I thanked her and sat down. I did not know if I had changed or
if everything around me had changed. Balestra's "Annunciation"
seemed almost a different painting to me. The Virgin's eyes had
the look of someone betrayed.

The Prioress waited until I was looking at her again. "In spite
of the numerous and dire problems facing the Ospedale della
Pietà, the governors took time at their meeting to consider the

case of your demotion. I want you to know that I myself wrote a letter to them on your behalf, as did several of the other *mae-stre*."

I braced myself for the bad news. I knew I was about to be consigned to spend the rest of my life in the *comun*.

The Prioress of those days is dead now. Although she was the cause of so much pain for me, I have come to understand, over the years, how good she was at her job. She was harsh, but she was honest. I truly believe now that she based all her decisions on the evidence before her, and that she did her best to provide the governors with an unbiased view of the daily goings-on at the Pietà.

She looked at me in silence for a moment, and then spoke again. "Just before their meeting was adjourned, the governors voted to reinstate you as a *figlia di coro*."

It took me a few moments to take this in. And then I wept freely. My pride was gone. My anger and despair were gone. All I felt was gratitude.

She let me cry, and then she spoke again. "Further, I think it will interest you to know that the governors voted to reinstate Don Vivaldi as our *maestro di violin*. He has been authorized to look for suitable new instruments for several of you. Until Maestro Vivaldi finds just the right violin for you, you may use the violin that belonged to Sister Laura. It's a fine instrument, as you know. She would have wanted that, I'm quite sure. Here, child—stop that! Here's a handkerchief. There's one thing more."

The Prioress stood up and unlocked a little drawer in her credenza. She took out a sealed letter and handed it to me. "Normally, I would have read this first to ascertain that there was nothing in it that would harm you. However, Sister Laura asked me very specifically to give it to you without breaking the seal. I am sure that, since it comes from her, there can only be good in it. She loved you well, Anna Maria. You were her favorite student, and she always had the greatest hopes for you. I know you'll do your best to see those hopes fulfilled."

The Prioress pressed my hand as she gave me the letter, and I realized in that moment that she was also fond of me, though I had never known it before. "If Sister Laura was ever harsh with you, it was only because she wanted for you what she felt that she herself failed to achieve. She was always her own harshest critic. Let us both remember Sister Laura in our prayers and hope that she has, at last, found peace."

Figlia mia,

I have ached with every particle of my being to say these words to you and have you hear the truth in them.

My dearest daughter, my only child, born of a love that should never have been. Pray for me, my daughter! Pray that the flames of Purgatory will burn away the sin I visited upon us both!

Figlia mia. *Finally you can know how I have treasured the letters you wrote me. You made paper and quill into yet another musical instrument that sprang to life beneath your fingers.*

I have felt pride where I should have felt shame. Watching you, helping you, guiding you in any small way I could, I have never been able to make myself feel the remorse that could cleanse me of the sin of making you.

I had some small talent as a violinist, but you have the divine spark in you. And if the Creator chose to place it there, how can I doubt that He smiles upon your existence?

I heap sin upon sin.

How I longed to claim you! Yes, it's strange to write these words knowing that I will be dead when you read them. I have seen how the doctor looks at me—how they have isolated me from the others, and how they have given up hope. I've seen others with this illness, and I do not expect it to go any differently with me. My life is ebbing. Even now, I can only write a little while before I have to stop and rest.

I've read and relished those words in your letters that I knew I could never hear you say, "Madre mia carissima."

It's a hard thing to fathom, Annina. Death. We sing of it, we're taught to fear it. And yet it's truly difficult to believe that it will ever come. That this body we know so well—these hands, these eyes, these ears—will cease to contain us. Our hands will open, our souls will fly out, and our eyes and ears will close forever.

Fifteen years ago, my own mother and her Confessor made me swear on your immortal soul that I would never, as long as I lived, make myself known to you. Only that promise would buy me the right to live near you and watch over you, rather than abandoning you to the care of strangers. Only my lies about who fathered you made this possible—my lies and the complicity of the one other—Maestra Meneghina—who knew the truth and kept it safe. Never for a moment did she allow me to forget that she did it for love of him and not for me.

When you read these words, my promise will no longer bind me.

I have loved you, Anna Maria, more than I have ever loved anyone or anything. More than I have loved music. More than I have loved God.

I watched with fear as you became more and more beautiful. I watched over your maestro in the hours he spent teaching you and your friends. And I felt such relief to know that his eyes were too fixed on his own success to ever fix them on you. I praised God for Vivaldi's selfishness and Vivaldi's ambition.

I noted as well the influence that Marietta had upon you. Marietta, a conjuror if ever I saw one, more skilled than any other girl I have ever known—either here or on the outside—in bending other *people to her will. Marietta who will soon be, if she is not already, your aunt.*

But perhaps she will make as good a wife as any woman could ever be to that foolish middle brother of mine, who is as gullible and profligate as our brother Marco is learned and wise.

When Marietta duped Tomasso—and you unwittingly helped her—I could hardly contain my outrage. It was my mother who argued the wisdom of allowing Marietta's scheme to be fulfilled.

She is no fool, your grandmother—and I am hoping that she may yet be of some service to you in your life and career.

I was so afraid that you would run away with nothing but the clothes on your back and your violin. I have lain awake at night, thinking of you at the mercy of the world and with no means to pay your way. I encouraged the Prioress to lock you up as often and as long as possible. I exaggerated your trespasses in my struggle to keep you safe.

The locket was the one thing of value I had that had not come to me through my family. It was mine and mine alone, although I was naturally not allowed to keep it with me at the Pietà. Still, it was mine to give away, and it would not lead you back to me and thus imperil your soul. How I seethed when I found out that Tomasso had stolen it!

I have been such a fool. My mother could not protect me from love, even locked up in this place with no men around but men of God.

Figlia mia, *forgive me for betraying you that early dawn. I could not bear the thought of you sacrificing your tremendous talent on the altar of love. And now I cannot forgive myself for the result of my act of betrayal. I have pleaded with the Prioress to let you return to the* coro. *And she has promised me now that it will be done.*

All men are inconstant, Anna Maria. They believe everything

*they say, and yet they will say it another time to someone else
and believe it anew. I believed that my lover loved me. And yet he
turned to me only after he was spurned by another who loved him
and yet had the strength to resist him.*

*I have realized, lying here for such long hours in this bed, that
you are a woman now—and, as a woman, you will make your
own choices. I cannot tell you what to do with the gifts you have:
that is between you and God.*

Of course, I pray that you will make good choices.

*I never abandoned you, Anna Maria. I have always been with
you, and I will ever be with you.*

*I will sign this letter as you signed your letters to me, with a
thousand kisses.*

Your loving mother,
Antonia Laura Foscarini

CHAPTER 15

Madre mia carissima,
I had to write those words one last time.

*How different is it, after all, writing this letter and knowing that
it will never reach you? I had no certainty about the other letters
I wrote you—and yet you read them. Perhaps, my dearest teacher,
my dearest mother, you will have found some magic beyond the
grave for hearing me speak my heart, even as you found that magic
pathway while you lived.*

*I will not dwell on my misfortune in losing you—because I had
you all along. I know that now. I know that it was love for me that
made you keep your secret all these years.*

*I am angry, but not at you. I feel cheated, but not by you. And
both these troubled feelings are well smoothed over by my sense of
feeling rewarded.*

*I used to ask myself what it was that allowed you to always be
so calm and serene and kind within your cloistered existence here,
when you could well imagine that other life you might have had,
living in a palazzo, surrounded by everything lovely the world has
to offer a well-married* zentildonna nobile. *And now I know: I
was the reason. Being close to me—helping me, teaching me, guiding me like the best of mothers—was enough for you. You didn't
require credit or recognition for doing so. The simple fact of my existence made you happy.*

Knowing this has changed everything for me.

I suspect that it is just as easy to be unhappy in a big place as a small one, or to feel fettered while blessed with a thousand freedoms. For a winged creature to feel earthbound—for a bird to fail to see that the door to its cage is open.

It would have been easy for me to become such a creature. But instead, because of you, I feel my wings and see the open door. I feel my strength, and I will fly if it suits me. For now, though, for now I can think of no higher calling than to be music's handmaiden here.

I know that my life brought you happiness—and this does much to comfort me for my failure, at the end of your life and the beginning of mine, to see what was right before my eyes.

Of course, I wish I could live those moments over again. When you whispered those words, figlia mia, I would have given you a daughter's blessing instead of torturing you, in your last moments, with my selfish, stupid questions.

And yet (I have told myself this many times since reading your letter), perhaps it would have been horrible to you if I had, at the last, acknowledged our kinship. Because then all the self-restraint and discipline you'd shown over all those years would have been in vain. Your vow would have been broken, and you would have feared not only for your own immortal soul but also for mine.

Even in your last request to the padre, you were wise—because I played for my mother as you lay there dying. I think you knew that I would play for her, and thus I would play, with all my heart, for you.

I look around me here and see a thousand girls and women who have never known a mother's love, and I feel so blessed among them. Would that I could give back, in some small way, some part of what I have myself been given. If I am made a figlia privilegiata someday, and am allowed to take on private students from a young age, perhaps I will be able to do so.

Your mother came to see me in the parlatorio *soon after I was reinstated in the* coro. *She gave me the little silver casket lined with pale blue silk and filled to the brim with letters—some written on note paper and some written on music paper—tied together with a darker blue silk ribbon. She didn't say anything about them, or even whether she had read them, but simply that she thought I should have them now.*

I will seal this letter and add it to the others, and tie the ribbon again.

You will ever be in my heart, Sister Laura. I will pray for you. And I will freight every note I play with the love and strength you've given me.

Anna Maria

ll of my spare time was taken up, in the first weeks following my return, with embroidering an apron as a wedding present for Marietta. Just before it was done, I slipped the locket inside the hem and sewed it fast there. No one had disturbed the locket, or the other little things that I'd hidden under my mattress—or, more likely, no one had found them.

Marietta came to the *parlatorio* to receive her gifts on the day before her wedding. The Prioress herself was there. All of us had come down to the *parlatorio* to give our gifts to the bride. I asked for permission to give her a kiss as well, and the Prioress nodded that I might.

We bent our heads close together, with only the filigree of wire between us. "Give the apron to Silvio!" I whispered. "Do not fail me!"

Marietta's eyes glowed green. "And what is your present to me, then, you cow?"

"This," I said. I kissed her then.

"If you were not a girl," she said, "I would quite fall in love with you!"

"Greedy pig!" I whispered. "You want everything!"

"And I shall have it!" laughed Marietta.

My conscience was set quite at ease, knowing that the locket would be where it belonged—and that it could be of help to Rebekkah and Silvio if they needed it. With my arms wrapped around my music and music wrapped around my heart, I knew that I would want for nothing.

*B*ernardina's lessons with me recommenced, rather to our mutual surprise, very soon after my return.

It was hard at first for both of us. As a confirmed member of the *coro*, she hated having to submit to instruction from me—unconfirmed, lately disgraced, and always her rival. As someone who had come, over the years, to regard her as my greatest enemy among all the *figlie*, I hated having to pay such close attention to her, and especially since she might—by means of my instruction—eventually surpass me in her skill.

The scrutiny of private lessons casts a powerful light on student and teacher alike. I had to learn to know Bernardina—her fears, her weaknesses, her strengths—in order to teach her well. As I learned to know her better, my antipathy for her melted away. I came to see her as just another lonely girl, like me, who had tried to find the best ways to survive in a place where love is hard to come by and everyone is plagued by the same deep fear of being, essentially, unlovable by virtue of being here.

The Prioress was wise to throw two such sworn enemies together in such a delicate relationship. If she hadn't, I never would have become Bernardina's ally.

For all that she resented my help and suggestions, we both

heard—everyone could hear—that her playing was becoming much lovelier and more refined as our lessons continued.

The maestro met with me sometimes, just the two of us, to speak about the methods that have worked best for him as a music teacher.

I hadn't ever thought before about the gratification to be found in helping another person play better. I've always had a good set of ears, and now they served me well. But I was careful not to perpetuate the habits of my worst teachers. I always found laudatory things to say before offering any criticism. Like Vivaldi—who was ever my favorite teacher, despite his moods—I kept my expectations exceedingly high.

Perhaps it was partly competitiveness, but Bernardina played far better in my presence, and under my tutelage, than she'd ever played before. And it wasn't just her technical performance that improved, but also her willingness to infuse the music with the range and depth of her true emotions.

Of course, like me, she was growing up—and so it's difficult for me to say how much real influence I had upon her as a musician. We each had our share of joy and suffering, and our music was the better for it. I'd found and then lost my mother. And Bernardina—all unbeknownst to everyone but her—was slowly losing the sight in her one good eye.

It was not six months after we'd started our lessons again that she came to me, her whole face blotchy and her one eye rimmed in red, to tell me that she would be resigning from the *coro*.

I looked at her a long time before responding, certain that she would take such a decision only for the direst reasons. "And yet, if you stay, *cara*, you are sure to become a *maestra*." I paused, thinking, before I continued. "I do not think that life in the *comun* would suit you. You are, like I am, a *figlia di coro*: you belong here."

She turned to face me—which meant, for Bernardina, holding her face at an angle, so that she could look at me with her good eye. "I may have once, but there will not be a place for me here before long."

"Tell me what you mean."

"Tell me if you're smiling now."

I was sitting at the spinet with my face washed in light from the window, not an arm's length away from her. Without thinking, I crossed myself.

"I could see that," she said. "I can see movement well enough. It is the smaller things—the expression on a face or the notes on the page—that have become increasingly difficult to read. And when the light is low, I cannot read them at all."

We both sat in silence then, with our faces turned toward the window. I remember looking down at the gondolas and other boats with their various cargoes, brightly dressed people, and the shimmering reflections of everyone and everything on the water. I tried to make myself think about what it would be like to live in a world where everything was shrouded, all the time, in fog.

"I am your teacher, Bernardina."

"Are you also a witch? Because, otherwise, you cannot teach me if I cannot see the music."

It took me a while to convince her that she could learn to do it, just as I had. The sun was already setting—and we were both late for our prayers—when I'd explained to Bernardina the method I'd devised, out of desperation during my months in the soap works, for seeing music by hearing the sounds of the notes, all without having the music before me or even having an instrument in my hands. How I'd learned to construct an entire written score in my mind's eye and then to read it there.

It was too late to begin by the time I'd talked her into at least giving it a try before she gave up music altogether. We'd already used all the time allotted for our lesson. But it was better this way, because it gave me time to think it through and make a plan.

From then on, at all our lessons, I taught Bernardina by playing her part, phrase by phrase, until she had no need to read it and could find her way to any place in the music almost as well as any sighted member of the *coro*. I've used the method since then with other *figlie* who, for whatever reason, have trouble reading. But Bernardina is the one who showed the greatest gift for learning by sound alone.

Of course, it was obvious in other ways that she was going blind. But everyone except the meanest-spirited among us banded together to help her, guiding her in the hallways, lending a hand when it was needed, and keeping her from harm. There are certain advantages to living in a place with so many other people. After all, we are, in the *coro*, rarely alone. Bernardina was safe with us. And as a musician, she continued to excel.

We were both chosen to perform in a select group, along with four others—including the maestro—late that September, in a concert at San Francesco della Vigna, the convent that had lately harbored Marietta, and where I myself had gulped my very first breaths of air. It was my first time outside the walls of the Pietà since my performance in the Ghetto, and my first performance as a soloist for the *coro*, even though I still hadn't been confirmed and had begun to doubt I ever would be.

Marietta was there at the festivities, along with her husband— now my uncle—and my mother's parents, who ignored me.

It was an odd thing, being in that place where I was born. I had no memory of it, of course. But the sense that I had been there before was very strong, and I felt my mother's presence in the stones of the church walls, on the marble balustrades where she'd placed her hand, and in the empty spaces where her voice had echoed. I was filled with a sense that in this place she had first looked at me, and nursed me—and now I knew, by her own words, that she had looked at me with love, glad that I was born.

I played the better for knowing this. Bernardina played like an angel, and I felt as proud of her as I felt of myself. Everyone said that the concert was one of the most amazing they had ever heard.

We performed three of the concertos from *L'Estro Armonico*, which Vivaldi had finally published the year before, in Amsterdam, with a dedication to the Grand Prince Ferdinand III de' Medici—one of our greatest fans and patrons of the Pietà. The Prince himself was in Venezia at the time, seated with his entourage among the other nobles in the audience.

Vivaldi played the *violino principale* for the G-major concerto. But he'd held an audition for the violin solos in the fifth concerto, the A major, and Bernardina and I had won out over all the others (probably because we had so much practice in imitating and echoing, by ear alone, solo passages of great complexity). I felt like an athlete of ancient times as we played the two allegros, with all their cadenzas and breathtaking multiple stops. The audience gave us a standing ovation.

The maestro was first *violino concertante* and I was second for the A minor. Signora Pelegrina—who had taught Giulietta— played her *violone*. Signora Maria Ricciuta, named thus for her wonderful blond curls and to distinguish her from our other Marias, played viola. And Signora Dianora sat at the cembalo. Many in the audience wept. Prince Ferdinand presented each of us with a gold *Luigi*, and God knows what riches he had already rained upon Vivaldi.

Silvio was also there, although I only saw him afterward, during the party. He was *in maschera* and well disguised, although

dressed this time as a man. Slipping in among the throng of
well-wishers who came up to me after the concert, he put his
face close to mine, opened his brown eyes wide, and crossed
them before disappearing into the crowd, leaving me there, giggling like a schoolgirl.

*H*ow I have treasured Silvio's presence in my life, from
the very first days when we found each other in the
comun! Even in middle age, he is as winsome and handsome
as ever. He's as slim as a youth and his hair is still blond, although I suspect he uses some nostrum to keep it so. His cheek
is smooth, his hands are slender and nearly unmarked by time.
He can afford now the rich silks and velvets he always favored,
and he wears them well.

Silvio understands the transience of beauty, and more than
anyone knows what a will-o'-the-wisp it is. It is he who first
sees *la piavola de Franza,* the doll dressed in the latest fashions,
down to the last detail, and sent to him by post chaise once a
week from Paris. One or another of his handsome apprentices
puts the doll on display in the window of Silvio's shop in the *mer-
ceria.* All the ladies of fashion—and those who merely aspire to
become ladies of fashion—come to gaze at it and take notes and
then send urgent messages to their dressmakers. Butterflies, all
of them. Venezia is filled with butterflies. And Silvio supplies
them with their favorite food.

He has done well by himself, to be sure. But unlike many
who are wealthy, he is also generous. Every year or so, he sends
enough silk from his own factory to make new robes for all of
us in the *coro,* and I suspect he makes frequent donations to the
comun as well, although one would never know it from speaking
to him. In fact, I don't know how he manages at all as a man of

business, because he still likes nothing more than to winkle the satire or silliness from any situation.

And yet, inside, he is the person, man or woman, of the most exquisite sensibilities I've ever known.

To mark my birthday in the year after my mother died, he sent me a little branch of *finocchio*—which is, of course, the word that's rudely used to describe men such as Silvio, as well as the licorice-flavored plant. Stuck fast to that lacy branch of fennel was a pair of cocoons.

I didn't even see them, at first, or know what they were. They looked like nothing more than part of the plant itself, two places where the stem was thicker and a paler shade of green—two slender, lozenge-shaped packages swelling out from the stem, half-hidden among all the feathery dark green leaves. It was Maestra Olivia, with her deep knowledge of gardens, who—though almost blind even then—put her ear up close to the branch and smiled. "You must watch them carefully, Anna Maria, because they are almost ready."

"Is it some fruit?" I, in my ignorance, asked her.

"Yes," she said, smiling her toothless grin that was as sweet as a baby's. "Yes, a sort of fruit! Put the branch in a warm place straightaway, where the sun can shine upon it, and you will see it ripen."

I put the branch in a patch of sun in my window. And, directly, I saw the little lozenges begin to writhe. Whatever fruit was inside their skin had come to life. What magic was this that Silvio had sent me? Were there fairies in the branch of fennel?

I put my ear up close to them and heard a rattle and then a tearing noise. And then I watched, and time stood still as the fabric of their prison ripped open and—first one and then the other—two creatures wriggled out, new and panting and wet. They looked like ladies in ball gowns suddenly released from a net, tumbling bottom-first onto the dance floor, all enfolded in their silken skirts. And then their wings unfurled, as bright and bold as Joseph's coat of many colors. I crossed myself, because I had never seen a miracle before.

I do not know how long I stood there watching them as they flapped and dried their glorious wings. I know I watched—hardly daring to blink my eyes—until they'd found each other, found their strength, and flown away.

I had fallen so in love with them, in so short a time—and yet they were gone from me, gone forever.

So it is with everything we love, and with everything that is most beautiful in this world. I keep telling myself, "Drink it in, Anna Maria! Drink as deeply as you can while there is yet water in the well."

I see my butterflies sometimes in the moments before sleeping and waking. Sometimes I think they've come to me again, in just the same way that sometimes I feel the touch of Franz's hand caressing my hair, or the brush of his lips against my cheek—just as soft, just as fleeting.

ANNO DOMINI 1711

Dear Annina,

You were brilliant at the concert. I felt quite jealous to be in the audience merely watching you with all the dullards from my family, who couldn't begin to appreciate how difficult the concerti are, or how fabulously well you played your solos. The only compensation was having the prince come home to sup with us afterward. I got to sing for him, and I can't tell you how wonderful it was to be heard, for a change, by someone who truly appreciates the finer points of music.

How someone like you sprang from the Foscarini is quite be-

yond me. There's not a singer or player among the lot of them—and they're all, except Tomasso, a terrific bunch of snobs. I felt like slapping my mother-in-law when she snubbed you yet another time. And yet, after we were all safely tucked into the gondola, she couldn't say enough about how pretty and graceful you've become, and how you're obviously the maestro's favorite and destined to become a maestra *yourself, before long. My darling mother-in-law is, without doubt, the biggest hypocrite I have ever known.*

You and Bernardina seem to be as thick as thieves these days. Is she really blind now, in both eyes? However does she manage? She has even more freckles now than she used to—but I suppose it doesn't matter what she looks like, stuck inside that hole. Oh—sorry, cara! *I promise, I'm still working on the question of a husband for you. Are you still giving lessons to Bernardina? Do you get paid?*

To be absolutely honest, I hate being married. Tomasso is utterly revolting. He stinks and he snores and he never trims his toenails, and yet he insists on coming to my bed at least once a week. And now I'm pregnant again. Oh, dear Mother of God, I asked him not to, but he wants nothing more than to get a son. "What of my career?" I asked him. "Career!" he said, and then he squeezed my booby. I hate him! I have to keep a basin close by me at all hours, even though they call it morning sickness. My face is bright pink when it's not green, and my tummy is swelling up like a dead dog.

The latest horror is that my own lovely Virgilio has been sent into exile for being a sodomite. I had no idea he went that way! And here he is, written into the marriage contract as my official cicisbeo. Mamma *Foscarini says, too bad—one only gets one* cicisbeo *per marriage. "But he's been sent into exile!" I told her, "and he's a* finocchio *besides." I think she knew all along, because she's looking terribly self-satisfied about the entire business.*

I've heard that you're to be the soloist in another concert this coming January in the Basilica. Is it true? How is it that things were never so exciting when I was in the coro?

I'm going to ask Papa if he'll put my name in for election by the board to serve as a visitatrice for the Pietà. At least, as a volunteer, I'll be able to spend some time with all of you, although the governors will probably think I'm too young to stand for the job. And I won't be able to do it, anyway, until I'm done having this wretched baby.

Sometimes, I'll tell you, Annina, it's a curse being so clever. I'm in a gilded cage now, but just as much imprisoned as I was at the ospedale.

I'll come again next visiting day with another letter. Be sure to wear your big sleeves.

Congratulations, cara. Would that I were doing half so well as you!

Your best friend always,
Marietta

CHAPTER 16

*T*HE MAESTRO has nurtured bitter quarrels with other impresarios when his work, in their hands, has failed to meet with success. And his relentless suits for patronage—his fawning and petulance—must surely try the patience even of those who most appreciate his talents. But since championing the career of Anna Girò ("the Red Priest's Annina," they call her), Vivaldi seems to have more enemies than friends, especially among his brothers in the clergy.

No one was more curious than I when he finally brought his young protégée, two years ago, to the Pietà.

Of course, the rumors had been dogging him since he first installed her as his prima donna. How could there not be rumors adhering to a situation as sticky as this one: a priest, traveling with a young woman and her older sister, who was still hardly old enough to serve as a proper chaperone.

And yet the situation never struck me as particularly odd: the maestro had for decades been putting a good deal of his time and energy into writing and producing operas. It seemed only natural that he would care greatly about the success and welfare of his favorite contralto. Singers here hate her, of course. How could they not? I myself felt jealous of the attention he gave her.

The maestro had me stay behind, after one of our rehearsals, to play the continuo for Signorina Anna while she tried out some new solos destined for his latest opera, an adaptation of Apos-

tolo Zeno's drama *Griselda*. He had spread himself particularly
thin that year, and it was showing in his face, which had begun to
look quite careworn. He was wearing out his health—and giving
much more money than he liked to porters and gondoliers.

The librettist he hired showed real grace when introduced to
me. But la Girò merely waved in my direction. I was nothing to
her—a middle-aged, de-sexed factotum. "*I* am the Red Priest's
Annina!" I wanted to say to her. But of course, I said nothing.

The diva's sister was apparently considered so unimport-
ant that no one bothered introducing her at all. Some fifteen
years older than Anna—around my age—Signora Paolina was as
modest and quiet and generally squashed-looking as Anna was
vociferous, fiery, and proud.

I knew from gossip that Anna was twenty-five, but she looked
younger. She could have been eighteen, with her glowing skin,
her large, expressive eyes and cascade of lustrous dark brown
hair. I've always wondered what it would feel like to have long
hair. Her face was not beautiful. But there was an undeni-
able beauty and drama simply in the way she held herself and
moved.

While the diva conferred with Vivaldi, her sister sat in the
corner, working a piece of lace.

The maestro put the music before me, when they decided
where they wanted to start, and I played the introduction. Anna
never even looked at me, but she heard her cue nonetheless.

From the first moment when she opened her mouth and began
to sing, I thought the maestro had lost every quality of discern-
ment that had made him great, both as a teacher and composer:
his cherished diva's voice was as thin and frail-seeming as her
person. Her pitch was true, and her gestures were graceful. But
I couldn't imagine how she would ever make herself heard at the
back of the theater.

Not five bars into her first aria, Anna threw down the music
and addressed Vivaldi in what struck me as a most disrespectful
manner. "The words don't allow for any movement at all! What
can I possibly do but just stand there and sing?"

I saw the librettist suppressing a smile.

Here the maestro was, fifty-seven years old and at the height
of his career. He'd just been reengaged by the governors as
Maestro de' Concerti, and was enjoying the patronage of several
crowned heads of Europe. And yet Vivaldi looked quite cowed by
this frail young woman. None of us had ever dared to talk to him
with such impudence.

He took in her comment, then turned, in a slightly blustering
way, to the poet. "Well?" he said.

Signor Goldoni smiled graciously at both of them. "My apologies, Padre. I was under the impression that this section was for
a singer not a dancer."

La Girò shot a murderous look at Vivaldi and stomped her
foot.

I'd never seen him look so foolish or flustered. He didn't
want to offend the poet, who was even then considered to be the
very best among the new crop of librettists, following his triumph with *Bellisario*. But Vivaldi was also clearly terrified about
displeasing Signorina Anna.

The competing strains of his two careers had taken their toll
on him, as had his frequent travel and general health, which had
always been indifferent, at best. Anna, on the other hand, looked
radiant, despite her unpleasant ways. I concluded, as everyone
else did, that he must be madly, hopelessly, ridiculously in love
with her.

"Sir," Vivaldi ventured. "We'll need new words here—words
that will allow Miss Girò to act as well as sing." He stole a look
at her to see if she approved, and I burned with shame for him.

This is what happens, I told myself, when a musician lets other things matter more. "Let's carry on with the other arias to see if they are … suitable. And we can meet again tomorrow, if that will not be too soon, to try out whatever new texts you manage to write by then."

"I'll write them now, Padre, if you'll give me pen and paper."

The maestro merely made dismissive sounds at the possibility of the poet pulling text that would be good enough out of his sleeve, even when the young man protested that it could and would be done. He finally grabbed a piece of paper off my music stand, tore off the lower half, and bowed to me. "Signora, would you be so kind as to provide me with a quill?" He looked at Vivaldi. "Must I write it in my own blood, Padre, or will you lend me some ink?"

Vivaldi gave in, but had scant expectation, I'm quite sure, that the poet could come up with anything but drivel in such short order. He conferred with Anna for a few moments, consulted his schedule, and talked a bit with me about some of the people we both know. Marietta had just given birth to her fifth child—another daughter, which was a great disappointment to her family and an extreme source of annoyance to Marietta, although I know she loves her girls to distraction. She hasn't sung on the stage since *Agrippina,* and I think she knows she never will again.

The poet came up to us with his half-sheet of paper all scribbled over. Vivaldi put on the spectacles he uses now for reading. He half-read, half-sang the words, then looked up with tears in his eyes. "Dear Sir! My dear fellow!" He threw his arms around the poet. "This is brilliant! This is beautiful!" Then he shoved the paper under my nose. "You saw—you saw it just as I did. He wrote this in not fifteen minutes—absolute poetry!" Then he turned to Anna. "It's perfect!"

She looked away, her nose in the air. I don't think she liked his effusions for another person's talents.

"It is perfect for you!" He was whispering, almost begging.

It didn't make sense to me then—not yet.

*S*ilvio had his gondola waiting, as always. Everything was quiet in the lowest reaches of the *ospedale* when I made my way down the stairs to the water gate. The *portinara* pretended to be asleep. The gondolier greeted me almost as an old friend. I left as easily and unnoticed as a bird that might have flown in by mistake among the rafters and now flew out again.

I could see, even in the starlight, the pain behind Silvio's smile.

"*Caro mio!*" I told him as he took my hand and helped me step aboard the gondola. "I'm so very sorry about Rebekkah."

She had been aunt, adopted mother, and teacher to him, all in one. She was the one thing in the world, I think, that made him feel that he belonged. I had envied him that, over the years. And now I grieved with him that she was gone.

Silvio kissed me. "She had a good death, if there is any such thing."

"She had a good life," I told him.

"As good a life as was possible here. And from what I've heard, far better than it might have been elsewhere. In any case, the Hevrat Ghemilut Hassad'm did their job well." He explained in response to my puzzled expression, "The Jewish burial society. Everyone in the Ghetto contributes to it, although I had assured Rebekkah during those final hours that she would have the finest procession money could buy. Between their efforts and mine, we had over two hundred torches and yet avoided every bridge and passageway from which *Veneziani* might have thrown their rubbish and curses upon the funeral of a Jew."

I saw tears in his eyes—the first, I think, I'd ever seen there.

"I will be your *zietta, caro!*" I tried to say it while making the same face that he had once made while saying the words to me.

I don't have Silvio's gift for mimicry—but my ineptitude itself was funny, I suppose, and he was smiling again by the time we settled ourselves onto the gondola's cushions and arranged the rugs over us. Once all this was done, Silvio reached into his breast pocket and handed me a tiny velvet pouch. "Annina," he said with his usual look of mischief, "Rebekkah left this for you. It was given into her keeping, many years ago, by your mother."

I thought I'd already been given all the gifts my mother had to give me. I opened the little pouch with more of a sense of curiosity than need. What message was this that she was sending me from beyond the grave? And whatever it was, how odd of Rebekkah to have waited so long to give it to me!

I should have known, of course: the pouch contained the key. It was exactly as Rebekkah had described it to me, that night—my first night—in the Ghetto. I held it up for a moment against the velvet of the sky. The three sapphires looked like the stars in Orion's belt.

I hadn't forgotten Silvio's promise that we would open the locket together, if he ever found the key. "You don't still have it, do you?"

Silvio laughed. "I came close to selling it more than once, when money was scarce for us. But Rebekkah always found a way. And, well, you know how my own business has flourished since then."

"I'd say so! I've heard it said that you're one of the hundred richest men in Venezia."

He didn't argue with me, and I let the subject drop. "Where are we going?"

"To the Lido."

I'd never been there before, and why would I have been? The
Lido, the bewitched island that is the final resting place of *la
Serenissima*'s Jews. I knew that Rebekkah would be buried there
in a freshly dug grave, no doubt side by side with the sister she'd
so greatly mourned.

I tucked the little pouch into my bodice and settled myself
back against the velvet cushions, next to my friend. The journey
to the Lido is a long one, but I knew that I would travel, with
Silvio, in luxury. We ate French pâté and drank champagne as
we crossed the *bacino* and rounded the customs house at the
point of Dorsoduro. Silvio had ermine shawls and tumblers full
of hot buttered rum for us when we entered into open water and
the wind blew colder. He lay back beside me on the cushions,
beneath the height of the baffles, and we stayed like that, in
companionable silence, gazing at the stars.

Sometimes it seems to me that a piece of Heaven must have
fallen out of the sky, crumbling as it fell, to make the islands
of *la Serenissima*. I've heard it said that there are more of them
than anyone has ever counted. They are as numerous as the stars
and as impossible to mark on any map. Whole islands, small
but perfect, rise and then disappear beneath the waters of the
lagoon between two risings of the sun.

The poets tell of a certain flower that pushes out of the soil of
these temporary islands, blooming and dying in a single night,
with leaves the color of sea foam and petals the color of wine.
Their perfume is sought by wise women, witches, and necro-
mancers, who say that it can raise the dead or cause someone to
fall in love, irrevocably, through all eternity.

Everyone who lives here, or visits here, catches the faintest
whiff of it, now and then, lingering in the air. It is the smell of
youth and love and music and longing and a tinge of decay. I've

gone whole years without smelling it, and then I find it again—
or it finds me—and I breathe deep and savor the memories it
brings. I think I would like to smell that smell at the moment
when I pass from this world to the next.

I counted and wished upon three falling stars on that journey,
the same wish every time. The Lido hove into view—an unpre-
possessing shoreline of sand and scrubby trees, and so long that
it was hard to think of it as an island at all. Silvio gave the gondolier a handful of coins, telling him that we would be awhile.

We walked for a long time between sand dunes, and then
along a wooded pathway, and finally through a gate. The white
Istrian stone of the monuments was even whiter for the moonlight washing over them. The headstones leaned every which
way, as if the dead were gossiping with those they loved in life and
pulling away from those they loathed. Some pairs of headstones
leaned against each other, melted together, in death, into one.

The older stones were grown over with trees and vines and
half-covered with brambles. Walking among them, I felt the
spirits of the past hovering round me.

Time has a very poor memory. We each of us do what we can to
be remembered—but most of us are forgotten.

If someone had asked me, that night on the Lido, who,
among all those I'd ever met, I thought would live on in some
way, I would have been hard pressed to name more than half
a dozen. Vivaldi, surely. My uncle Marco Foscarini, if he lives
long enough to become Doge. Gasparini and Handel. Scarlatti
and, the only female among them, Rosalba. The various popes
and royal personages—time always saves a place for these in her
guest book.

But what of all the rest of us? I knew that each one of those
blocks of stone in the graveyard stood for a life that was lived.
Within each grave beneath them reposed and rotted the mortal

remains of someone, like myself, who yearned, who wept, and laughed and loved. Not one of them ever believed that what they strived so hard to achieve or avoid—the person they held most dear, their fondest dream, the secret they kept, the one thing that inspired their devotion: all of it would be as forgotten as surely as yesterday's rain.

The legends on the tombstones are eventually worn away as the stone is eroded by rain and wind and centuries. Better to slip away quietly after having lived as fully as one can, doing the very best one can with the gifts one has been given. What more can a mere musician possibly hope for?

Music cannot be kept or captured. It unfurls in one miraculous moment in time, and then it's gone. The glorious sound of Marietta's voice in a cantabile aria will be forever lost after she is dead and all of us who ever heard her are dead, too. No matter how well I manage to play, my playing will be forgotten when all those who have heard me have died.

As Silvio and I walked through the Hebrew cemetery of San Nicolò di Lido, the sand worked its way into my shoes, so that I knew I would carry a small part of these graves back with me to the cloister. It is tonic to be reminded, once in a while, that we are but specks in the world, and as easily swept away.

We stopped, and Silvio held the torch close by a single headstone that stood apart from the others. I knelt to read the legend, which simply said, EBREI 1631. "All the hundreds of Jews who died in the Plague are buried here in this one grave."

As we walked, we cast shadows on some of the graves, and revealed the legends and symbols of others: stone drapery held aloft by the small, rigid hands of putti. A plumed helmet. A two-headed eagle. A deer in a basket, like Moses in the rushes. The moon, the stars, and a rooster with a palm branch clutched in its claws. Hands joined in prayer above a crown.

Silvio explained to me that all of these are symbols for Jewish families from disparate tribes and cultures, who live as far apart from each other and as separately as they can, within the close quarters and limited space of the Ghetto.

Before that night in the graveyard, I had thought the Pietà to be the only place in Venezia where people who would never have mixed on the outside all sleep together in the same place. But I was wrong.

We stopped at yet another grave, this one marked by a ladder and a scorpion. "My grandmother's teacher is buried here—a poet and philosopher who was famous both inside and outside the Ghetto, and throughout Europe as well." Silvio held the torch so close that it nearly singed the headstone of Sara Copio Sullam. "Some say that the dead dig their way from here, under the sea, and all the way to the Holy Land, to be there on Resurrection Day."

"The Holy Land cannot be half so beautiful as this place. I think I could spend eternity quite happily here!"

"Well, you can't, *cara*—so you'd best reserve another bed for your final slumber. Being buried here is one of the very few things a Jew is allowed in this pestilential world that a Christian is denied."

Silvio took my hand before a headstone topped by an angel playing the violin. Rachel's name was inscribed on it both in Italian and Hebrew, with some verses Silvio translated for me from the *Cantico dei Cantici*, "The Song of Songs"—

My beloved speaks and says to me:
"Arise, my love, my beautiful one, and come away,
for behold, the winter is past;
the rain is over and gone.
The flowers appear on the earth,

the time of singing has come,
and the voice of the turtledove is heard in our land."

The words were half-covered in ivy and moss. There beside Rachel was Rebekkah's shiny green marble headstone, simply inscribed with her name and the years that bracketed her life, and the phrase, ZIETTA DI SILVIO. "It's what she wanted," he told me.

The fence nearby was covered in late-blooming roses the color of ripe apricots, glowing now in the moonlight. It was a lovely, peaceful place. Silvio knelt there, and I was silent because it seemed that he was praying.

"Do you pray as a Christian or a Jew?" I asked when he looked up again.

"I pray as one who hopes to win a bit of God's mercy in any way he can."

I thought of what Vivaldi had said to Rebekkah, that night in the Ghetto. "Surely God listens gladly to our prayers, in whatever language they're spoken."

"Hah!" said Silvio. "Tell that to the Magistrates of the Inquisitors Against Blasphemy. As far as they're concerned, all Jews are damned from the moment of their birth—and, under Hebrew law, as Rachel's child, I am a Jew."

"And yet you were baptized at the Pietà."

"Yes, Saint Peter is going to scratch his head mightily when I show up at Heaven's gates. I rather like that I can be either Christian or Jew, depending on which suits the situation."

I kissed him on the cheek—in truth, Silvio looks more like an angel than any grown man I have ever known. I could not imagine that God would not want him in His Heaven.

We sat down on the other side of the headstones then, out of the wind, supported by the two sisters who had given Silvio life and nurtured him. I wished I had my violin with me so that I could play for Rebekkah a final time—but, then, I truly believe that the dead can hear us wherever we play. And when we play well, we lop years off their term in Purgatory. I dearly hope that someone plays for me after I have gone to my grave, because my term will be a long one, and I will need a lot of music, well played, to set me free.

Silvio turned to me. "Are you ready, Annina?"

I nodded and fished the little velvet bag out of my bosom. He rummaged in his clothes and brought out the locket, just as Franz Horneck had done, so many years ago, when he gave it to me. I missed him then—but I always miss Franz. There is rarely a day that goes by when I don't think of him.

"How odd of Rebekkah to have waited so long to give this to me! Do you have any idea about what might be inside?"

"A fairly good idea, but not based on anything but a sense of affinity."

"Affinity for what?"

"For you, of course. Here—you do it." He held the torch closer so that I could see where to put the key. "It's usually the men who have to poke it in."

I laughed then till he squealed at me, in that *finocchio* way of his, to hurry up.

The key turned easily, the lock gave way, and I opened the tiny jewel-encrusted door on its little hinges. There was nothing inside—or, at first, so it seemed. But then, looking harder, we could see some writing inscribed into the gold.

It took a long time to decipher it, because—alas—our eyes are not what they used to be. I said each word out loud, syllable by syllable, as I strained to make out the inscription, "*Unending— love—forever—secret—forever—*' Very repetitive, whoever wrote this!"

Silvio continued for me. "Forever ours—my darling—Laura ..."

We read the last two words out loud together: "Bonaventura Spada!"

He was laughing. I was crying.

"I knew it! My own little sister!"

I'm sure that Rebekkah was laughing, wherever she dwells. And I'm equally sure that Rachel must have wept for the perfidy of her lover. Still her lover had given a gift of great price to his two bastard offspring by two different mothers. Deprived of them, Silvio and I nonetheless had each other. We always had—but now I knew that not only friendship but also blood bound us together, and had done so all along.

I understood immediately why Rebekkah had chosen to wait until after she was gone. It was a final act, beyond the grave, of nurturing her beloved nephew. Of letting him know that he is not alone.

It was the most beautiful piece of news I'd ever learned, because it wasn't too late this time. It wasn't too late to throw my arms around him and tell him how happy I was and how grateful. I sat there in the moonlight, among the graves, sobbing in my brother's arms, mad with joy.

*O*ne does not need very many thrills—nor to be thrilled too often—to feel that one's life is quite thrilling enough to be perfect, in its own way.

I'm sure that if I lived anyone's life but my own—in any other place—I would overindulge on the thrills that here, in this life, are few and far between and yet of such surpassing beauty that I am filled by them and fed by them through all the times of quiet and routine.

No—my life in the cloister suits me well.

Every year, since I came of age, I've had at least one proposal of marriage. And every time, I've considered my suitor and turned him down. By now, it is a joke here. The governors, I've been told, have a pool to see whether I will ever marry, although they would be loath to see me do so, I think.

They need not fear. No lure of riches, or even a handsome face, has ever been strong enough to draw me away from what I love. And I have recognized for a long time now that I am too old and settled in my ways to start life someplace else.

The Pietà is my home, after all. I have much more freedom here, as a *figlia privilegiata* and now as *Maestra di Coro*, than I would have in any house as someone's wife. What husband would tolerate a bride who lived and breathed music in all her waking hours? And, anyway, I know myself. If I did love, I would not be able to live a divided life. And if I let music die in me, I would die as well. I know myself well enough to know that this is true.

I do not live in perpetual exile from family life. I spend at least a week every summer at the Villa Foscarini Rossi on the Brenta. There I live quietly among the sometimes antic goings-on of my relations, enjoying the chance to amble in all that greenery and under all that blue sky.

I can only laugh at Marietta when she throws up her hands in despair at her daughters' bad behavior. "They are no worse than you were, *cara!*" I tell her. In truth they are, each and every one of them, a holy terror.

They are as beautiful as well. Marietta herself has grown rather fat, naturally enough, and she's furious with me for keeping my figure. I tell her that there have to be some compensations for remaining a virgin.

I've never told her about the reappearance of Franz Horneck in my life. I've never told anyone, nor ever shall. It is the one secret I will carry with me to my grave.

I have the mask that Silvio made me for my occasional forays into the outside world. It's a beautiful creation, as all his creations are, of silk and silver filigree, fashioned to look like a butterfly. He made two such masks so that we can always recognize each other if we have gone out separately or lose each other in a crowd.

Marietta likes to bring costumes of her own devising, although we have not gone out together *in maschera* for years. She still visits me every week in the *parlatorio*, except when the doctor makes her stay in bed.

I never know when Franz will come to me again, except that it will be during one of the months of Carnival. He always engages the same gondolier, except—last year—it was that same gondolier's son who came to call for me at the water gate.

We are faded butterflies, Franz Horneck and I—but we are no less beautiful in each other's eyes. He has grown sons now, in that other life of his in which he's a God-fearing, good husband.

We've gone to crowded places to wonder at the marvels there— the fireworks, the slaughter of the bulls, the human pyramids, and the daredevil who slides down a rope from the top of the Campanile to the *Piazzetta* in a gondola made of candlelight. And we have gone to those islands that only exist for a single night, where the waters of the lagoon wash over every trace of us and the island itself disappears beneath the waves by dawn. There we've smelled those magic flowers that unfurl like butterflies in the darkness, whole meadows filled with them, pumping their fragrant wings.

Those islands don't last long enough for anyone or anything to ever grow old there, and our visits are not long enough, nor frequent enough, for us ever to grow tired of each other. Each kiss is the first kiss, and there is not time enough to ever quench one's thirst completely.

Lucky for me that Franz, as a man of the world, is wise in its ways, and I have never come to harm.

In truth, I feel watched over in this life: I have always felt watched over by the Virgin even though I know that, later, I will be punished by God. This life of mine, in all its wealth, will have been worth whatever punishment is visited upon me.

*T*he maestro just left me. He looked more worn than I have ever seen him look, even during those times when he's afflicted by his breathing difficulties and chest pains. At first I thought it must be his excitement over the success in Verona of his latest opera. That and the rumors that he will not be allowed in Ferrara this Carnival season. It seems that certain cardinals there are none too happy about the Red Priest's activities as an opera patron and impresario.

It is, of course, all because of Anna Girò. The Church does not take kindly to priests who are rumored to travel with their mistresses and never say Mass—although he has always protested that he doesn't say Mass only because he doesn't have the breath for it. I think he doesn't have the time for it, either, what with everything else he tries to do.

He seemed feverish to me, and as if he'd been suffering from lack of sleep. I offered him a glass of wine and we drank together. I saw he had something to tell me, but I never would have guessed—or perhaps I would have, if I'd thought about it properly. After all, his story is my story as well.

He paced back and forth between my desk and the window, started speaking, and then interrupted himself with several observations about trivial things that I knew had nothing to do with what he wanted to say. I was meanwhile looking over the piece of music he had given me.

"You wear glasses now, Annina?"

"Yes, for reading. But only when the light is low."

He sat down, and I poured him another glass. Outside my window, the sun was setting over the Canal. "I will always think of you as a young girl, far too young for reading glasses."

"Then you are living in a dream, dear Maestro."

"Yes, I suppose I am." He drank—he drank it all down in one gulp, I noticed, and then wiped his mouth with the back of his hand. "I want to ask your advice."

"Indeed, Maestro. You know you can trust me."

"Precisely. I know I can entrust you with my secret. And I know of no one better suited to help me decide. It is a question of enormous delicacy."

I got up and cracked the door open to make sure there was no one lingering and listening in the hallway. "We are safe here, Sir, and I will help you if I can."

"It is about Signorina Girò."

This, of course, came as no surprise to me, but I have to admit that I found the situation more than a little uncomfortable. As much as I have always valued the marks of distinction Vivaldi has shown me, I did not relish the idea of being his confidante in this matter.

"I have erred greatly, Anna Maria."

"Hush, Sir! I think you had better speak to your Confessor than to me."

He shook his head and, much to my horror, started weeping. "Who but you can understand?"

Did he know my secret? I was too stunned to reply.

"I am a sinner, but my sin is not that for which I have been blamed!"

"You confound me, Maestro."

He looked exasperated. "You've heard the rumors, surely!" I nodded. "And you've seen my Anna."

What did he want from me? I hated hearing him call her "his" Anna.

"You don't believe them, do you? Please, Anna Maria—tell me you don't believe it's true! It would be an abomination."

"I do not mean to sound cynical, Sir. But it no longer shocks me to hear of a priest who has broken his vows of celibacy."

"Only once, and that over two decades ago. May I have some more wine, please?"

"I think I'd better have some more myself. I'm utterly confused now."

He took his refilled glass and drained it, again, in one go. "I do not know how I can speak more plainly. Anna Girò is my daughter."

Priests! Surely it was not God's idea to throw His anointed into such hypocrisy.

"I only learned of her existence a decade ago. I have been trying to make amends ever since. And yet these rumors hound us. These evil rumors!"

I thought of my own father and his prolific career. "Does she know?"

He shook his head. "How can I tell her? How will she feel when she learns that I am not only her teacher and protector but also her father—I, an ordained priest?"

"I have misjudged you!"

"Everyone has."

We looked at each other in silence, and then he looked away

from me. "Shall I be remembered as a lecher—I who have lived in probity among virgins all these years? You know the sort of man I am, Anna Maria. I have lived for music, and I have faithfully served both God and the Republic. Does not an entire lifetime of musical achievement weigh more in the scales of justice than a single night of indiscretion in Mantua?"

"I do not know, Maestro. But I am sure that your music will never be forgotten."

His eyes were overflowing again. "I wanted to ensure that someone knows besides myself, in case something happens to me. But I don't want Anna to learn the truth before the time is right for her. She must feel safe enough, and strong enough. And she must know that I would have given up all of it—my fame, my gold, my reputation—for love of her."

I advised him—I urged him—to tell her the truth without delay. I'd had enough pain in my own life over having the truth kept from me.

But all he could do was shake his head and pull at his hair—now faded to a pale gingery gray. "She will hate me for it. At least now, she is fond of me, and I can be near her. Oh, my love for her robs me even of my hope of salvation! How can I feel remorse for bringing her into the world?"

Yes, he was right to come to me, although he refused to heed my advice.

All I could give him, in the end, was my promise to tell no one but Anna, and only after Vivaldi is dead, if he dies before me.

My poor maestro! I will keep my promise to him. It is the very least I can do, considering everything he has done for me.

I have come to understand how complex a thing the truth can be, as well as the companionability of a well-kept secret, protected and nurtured till the time is right for its unmasking.

❧ ❧ ❧

*L*a Befana's influence here has been durable and strong. Though I have been teaching these many years, I was only elected *maestra* this past August—and, by the same vote, *Maestra di Coro*. It would not have happened if Maestra Meneghina still held sway.

I was never made a *scrivana*, and would never take that job, in any case. The *libri della scaffetta* would be open books to all the foundlings were I in charge of them.

But there is another book of secrets for which I am both the guardian and the scribe.

For many years, this book resided in a locked desk in my room. It started life as a blank book—vellum pages caught between gilded leather covers. It was a present from my grandmother, one of two such books she gave me.

Both are nearly filled now, although this one I filled very quickly over the course of these past few weeks since my promotion.

The other I have been filling slowly ever since my return to the *coro* so many years ago.

It is a second Golden Book for Venezia—not filled with the names of every noble family, but inscribed with a list of ignoble deeds. The girls know to come to me whenever they have been misused by her. When I reached the last page, I knew the time had come.

I gave it to Marietta and she gave it to my grandfather, who presented it at the governors' meeting.

A truly good teacher can mean the difference between a happy life and a tragic one. A truly good teacher can see the hidden light in eyes that may seem hooded to the rest of the world and even to him or her who possesses them.

But evil teachers—those who derive joy from inflicting harm, who want others to suffer because they themselves have suffered—deserve to be punished, not only in the next world, but in this one as well.

℘lena has just poked her head in at the door.

When I looked up from my writing—in that first moment before my eyes had adjusted—I thought it was Giulietta. They have the same smile. And of course, Elena is the same age as Giulietta was when I saw her for the last time.

"*Zietta,*" she said, "I'm ready for my lesson. How beautiful you look in this light!"

We both looked out through the window, my window over the bacino, where the late afternoon light, golden-hued, was pouring through like a blessing.

Elena has been in my care since the age of three. I could not love her more if she were my own daughter. She works hard, too—and she's a very talented violinist. I keep wondering if she'll find a way to continue, once she's left here. Her parents have planned all along for her to marry. I know she will be a credit to them, and to me as well.

I smiled at her and said, "Give me five minutes to finish what I'm doing, *figlia mia.*"

I've lit the lamp for these last words and Elena's lesson. I've filled every page in this book now—and I think I've said everything I needed to say. Holy Mother of God, I beseech you to preserve these papers from fire, flood, and decay. I've written the entire story here. I was writing it even when I thought it was my own story, and not Vivaldi's as well. All that remains for the truth to come out is the passage of time. *Sancta Maria, Mater Dei, ora pro nobis peccatoribus, nunc, et in hora mortis nostrae. Amen.*

Anno Domini 1737
Venezia

ECAUSE OF THE SCANDALS that dogged his name,
Antonio Vivaldi became persona non grata in Venice,
the city he loved so well. He was indeed undone by his love for
Anna Girò, although I think I am the first to suggest that she
might have been his daughter rather than his paramour. No one
has yet determined the true nature of that relationship.

The Red Priest died at the age of sixty-three in July 1741 in
Vienna, where he was buried in a pauper's grave (coincidentally,
the young Joseph Haydn was one of his pallbearers).

Vivaldi's music immediately fell into utter obscurity for
nearly two hundred years. If he was mentioned at all in books
about Venice, or even in musical histories of Venice, published
before the 1930s, it was as "a freakish violinist and eccentric
cleric" rather than as a composer (Michael Talbot, *Vivaldi*). The
rehabilitation of his music began, albeit slowly, when schol-
ars recognized the direct and profound influence of Vivaldi's
compositions on the music of Johann Sebastian Bach. Little by
little, and sometimes by great leaps, the Red Priest's prodigious body of both secular and sacred music is being brought
to life again.

New scores by Vivaldi are still being discovered, and much of
his music remains to be recorded. Many of the exquisite choral
works he composed for the Pietà, from around 1713 until 1739,
have recently become available on compact disc from Hyperion
Records Limited of London, England. I listened to these *sans*

cesse while writing this novel, except when I was studying the music played by Anna Maria and her mates in the *coro*.

Since the explosion of his popularity in the 1960s, Vivaldi's resurrection has been nothing short of spectacular. His *Four Seasons* is now the most widely played and most recognizable piece in the classical music canon.

Bonaventura Spada was indeed a priest-musician who taught at the Pietà during the period in which I've placed him there. But very little else is known about him. The active love life I've made up for him is entirely a novelist's fancy—although priests of the time did, without doubt, father children.

There were four different internal violin teachers at the Pietà named Meneghina, one of whom "was stripped of her privileges and permanently demoted to the status of a *figlia del comun* on June 9, 1752, for maltreating a child in her care" (M. White, *Biographical Notes*).

I made up the story about Tiepolo and Giulietta, although similar tales have been in circulation about love affairs between Venetian painters and cloistered musicians of the *ospedali*.

An actual young man named Franz Horneck was in Venice during the time described, procuring scores for the Archbishop of Mainz and enjoying himself (we have a traveler's account of this) as much as possible. He was an avid student of the violin, and it seems that at some point he may have copied scores for Vivaldi. There is no historical record of a relationship between Franz Horneck and Anna Maria.

Indeed, we have only the merest biographical sketch containing the main events in Anna Maria's highly successful musical life (and that thanks to the tireless research of Micky White). The only facts that are even vaguely personal in White's compilation are that Anna Maria was put on a special diet (of chicken) on January 23, 1728, and was granted two extra measures of oil weekly on October 7, 1729.

We know from the accounts of many contemporaneous observers that Anna Maria was celebrated far beyond the boundaries of Venice as a consummate musician who mastered many other instruments in addition to the violin, and was a credit to the Pietà throughout her career. That she also may have been a bit of a scofflaw was suggested to me by the fact that her promotions lagged far behind and came much later than those of her peers.

Anna Maria enjoyed the unusually good health and longevity that seem to have been a special privilege of the *figlie di coro*, who always had sufficient food and medical care close at hand. She lived to be eighty-six years old in a century in which the average life expectancy in Europe was around thirty-five.

Some sixteen years after Anna Maria's death, in 1797, Napoleon's army walked into Venice without any resistance from the once-mighty defenders of *la Serenissima*. With Napoleon's signing of the Treaty of Campo Formio, Venice became part of the Austrian-held kingdom of Lombardy-Venetia.

The Venetian tradition of wearing masks during Carnival—recorded as early as the mid-thirteenth century—was brought to an end with the fall of the Republic. It was not until the 1970s that some of the traditional mask designs were put into production again, and a much shorter but no less showy version of Carnival was revived.

The original Church of the Pietà, on the Riva degli Schiavoni, was torn down in the 1740s—during Anna Maria's lifetime and after Vivaldi's death—to make way for the present-day magnificent Palladian structure designed by Giorgio Massari. Even in the "new" church, though, one gets a very good sense of how the members of the *coro* must have looked, half-hidden and half-revealed, behind the lacy metal grillwork of the choir lofts.

The buildings that housed the foundlings of the Pietà are still standing, hidden behind a gate, just across from the Hotel Metropôle (in the lobby of which one can see two pillars from the original church). The well and the courtyard, the vaulted windows of the room where the governors met, and the original water gate are all intact and very evocative of the cloistered world where the foundlings of the Ospedale della Pietà played and sang the music that kept *la Serenissima* in God's good graces.

ACKNOWLEDGMENTS

*M*icky White, an independent scholar and resident of Venice who has dedicated her life for decades now to seeking out the history of Vivaldi and the *figlie di coro* of the Ospedale della Pietà, is in the process of writing a monograph about Anna Maria, to be published with the sponsorship the Istituto Italiano Antonio Vivaldi at the Fondazione Giorgio Cini. I am enormously indebted to her for the work she has done so far and her kindness in meeting with me, despite her inherent distrust of novelists. Micky quite literally opened the door to the Pietà for me, so that I could see it with my own eyes.

Dr. Francesco Fanna, director of the above-named institute, has been the soul of kindness and generosity, sending me photocopies of hard-to-get articles, letting me use his Internet connection to e-mail work in progress to my editor until I figured out how to do it on my own in Venice, and listening with graciousness both to my odd theories and my very imperfect Italian. Vivaldi scholar Giuseppe Ellero was similarly helpful in guiding me back on the path when I became distracted with a highly evocative tidbit I found on the Internet having to do (as it turned out) with another Anna Maria of the Pietà.

This book would not have been possible had I not been able to refer to the meticulous scholarship of those who have studied and written about eighteenth-century Venice. Dr. Michael Talbot, Alsop Professor of Music at Liverpool University and a Fellow of the British Academy, is the ultimate authority on Vivaldi's life and work. I am indebted as well to the long-out-of-date historical effusion, so chock-full of juicy details, written by Philippe Monnier. The works by the late Jane L. Baldauf-Berdes as well as Micky White's "Biographical Notes on the '*Figlie di coro*,'" all cited in the bibliography, were my constant companions during the composition of this novel.

Laura McCreery shared her academic staff member access to the magnificent University of California Library, which allowed me to have all the rare volumes of research I needed at my fingertips for a full year. I was saved from numerous misspellings and grammatical mistakes, as well as given a great deal of encouragement, by the Italian journalist Caterina Belloni. Violinist Vivian Warkentin's insider's knowledge afforded some wonderful details I would never have come up with on my own. Lutenist and Vivaldi afficionado Howard Kadis and his colleague, Nadja Matisoff, at "The Musical Offering," provided invaluable help with the discography.

Marcus Grant's insightful suggestions at an early stage of the writing proved to be spot on. Judy McKay was my cheering squad, while her husband and my writing buddy, Matthew McKay, gave me untold hours of free therapy. Liz Stonehill, a great reader, was the first person I entrusted with the final manuscript.

I am grateful to the producer and writer Ron Levinson for his enthusiasm and belief in this novel when the project was at its earliest stages. Cedric Shackleton made it his business to get me to Venice so that I could begin writing the story that had been chasing me for more than a decade.

My agent, Felicia Eth, believed in this book from the get-go, helped me nurture it from a fifty-page fragment into a full-grown novel, and found precisely the right editor and publisher—of prodigious skill and literary sensibility—in Gail Winston of HarperCollins. I am immensely grateful for the enthusiasm and support given to *Vivaldi's Virgins* by my publisher Jonathan Burnham and his colleagues at HarperCollins, who have all made me feel like the luckiest writer in the world.

John Quick—toward whom I have so many reasons to feel grateful—was always ready to hold down the fort while I was away. And last, but certainly not least, our son, Julian, light of my life, helped me remember how to see the world from that middle place called adolescence.

GLOSSARY

abbracci: hugs

Accademia degli Impediti: "The Academy of the Impeded"—
   a short-lived Jewish musical academy in Venice whose
   existence was thwarted by various tragedies, including the
   Plague of 1630–1631

addio: goodbye (*adieu*)

"Andiamo!": "Let's go!"

ars musica: art music—i.e., music containing polyphonic harmonies

baci: kisses

bacino: short for *il bacino di San Marco,* St. Mark's Basin—the
   body of water where the Grand Canal, the Giudecca Canal,
   and the San Marco Canal all converge

bambina: (female) child

baretta: little hat

burattino: puppet (term of endearment)

bauta: silk or lace scarf, covering the lower jaw (worn while *in
   maschera*)

ca': Venetian dialect, short for *casa*—"house"

Campagnia dei Musici del Ghetto di Venezia: "Musicians' Society
   of the Venetian Ghetto," organized by Rabbi Leon Modena

campo: square (as in, a place surrounded by buildings)

cara (fem.) caro (masc.): dear; an affectionate term of address

carica (sing.) cariche (plural): senior member(s) of the *coro* who held the eight highest offices for the internal administration of the Pietà

il caro Sassone: the dear Saxon (i.e., G. F. Handel)

corbetta: measure of firewood, given as a reward for achievement

cornetto: sweet crescent-shaped roll

coro: literally "choir," but referring here both to singers and instrumentalists

dispensiera: the *carica* in charge of provisions and supplies

domino: all-encompassing black silk gown (worn while *in maschera*)

ecco: here (as in, "Here it is!")

figlie di comun: foundlings given a general education and occupational training (literally, "daughters of the common [group]")

figlie di coro: foundlings deemed to have musical talent (literally, "daughters of the choir")

figlia mia: "my daughter"; term of endearment

gnaga: white grotesque mask

iniziata (sing.) iniziate (plural): initiate(s) (female)

libro (sing.) libri (plural): book(s)

Madre mia carissima: my dearest mother

maestra (sing.) maestre (plural): teacher (female)

maestro: teacher (male)

maschera: mask; *mascherata:* (fem.): masked

moreta: a black velvet mask

ospedale (sing.) ospedali (plural): in modern Italian, hospital; in Venice of yore, a charitable institution for those unable to care for themselves, such as orphans, foundlings, and the chronically ill

palazzo (sing.) palazzi (plural): palace or building

parlatorio: the parlor or visiting room of a cloistered community

pazza (fem.): crazy

portinara (fem.): door-keeper

poverina (fem.): "poor thing"

Prete Rosso: Red Priest

priora: Prioress

putela: little one

putte: cupids, in modern Italian; in old Venetian dialect, virgin girls

scaffetta: a drawer fashioned in the stone of the church wall where infants were abandoned to the care of the Pietà

scrivana (sing.) scrivane (plural): the Pietà's official scribes (there were two at any given time) (female)

scusi (polite): "excuse me"

Serenissima: most serene (affectionate name, even today, for Venice)

signorina: miss

signor: sir

signora: madame

sottoportego: sheltered passageway between buildings

violone: fretted instrument with six strings (although some versions had five or, more rarely, four strings), generally tuned a fifth or an octave below the bass viol

visitatrice: female visitor (i.e., a volunteer)

zendaletta: capacious mantle (worn while *in maschera*)

zentildonna: in Venetian dialect, a gentlewoman or, with *nobile*, a noblewoman

zietta: "auntie"; a term of endearment

BIBLIOGRAPHY

Aikema, Bernard, and Dulcia Meijers. *Nel Regno dei Poveri: Arte e storie dei grandi ospedali veneziani in età moderna (1474–1797)*. Verona: Istituzioni di Ricovero e di Educazione, 1989.

Baldauf-Berdes, Jane L. "Anna Maria della Pietà: The Woman Musician of Venice Personified," in Cook, Susan C., and Judy S. Tsou, eds. *Cecelia Reclaimed: Feminist Perspectives on Gender and Music*. Urbana and Chicago: University of Illinois Press, 1994.

———. *Women Musicians of Venice: Musical Foundations, 1525–1855*. Oxford: Clarendon Press (Oxford University Press), 1996.

Barbier, Patrick. *La Venise de Vivaldi*. Paris: Bernard Grasset, 2002.

Calimani, Riccardo. *The Ghetto of Venice*. Milan: Oscar Mondadori, 1995.

Davis, Robert C., and Benjamin Ravid, eds. *The Jews of Early Modern Venice*. Baltimore: Johns Hopkins University Press, 2001.

Decroisette, Françoise. *Venise au temps de Goldoni*. Paris: Hachette Littératures, 1999.

di Robilant, Andrea. *A Venetian Affair: A True Tale of Forbidden Love in the Eighteenth Century*. New York: Vintage, 2005.

Fortis, Umberto. *The Ghetto on the Lagoon: A Guide to the History and Art of the Venetian Ghetto (1516–1797)*. Venice: Storti Edizioni, 1987–2001.

Hampl, Patricia. *Virgin Time: In Search of the Contemplative Life*. New York: North Point Press, 1992.

Heller, Karl. *Antonio Vivaldi: The Red Priest of Venice*. Pompton Plains: Amadeus Press, 1991.

Kaley, Diana E. *The Church of the Pietà*. International Fund for Monuments, 1978.

Labie, Claude, and Jean-François Labie. *Vivaldi: Des Saisons à Venise*. Paris: Gallimard, 1996.

Laini, Marinella. *Vita Musicale a Venezia durante la Repubblica: Istituzioni e Mecenatismo*. Venice: Stamperia di Venezia, 1993.

Landon, H. C. Robbins. *Vivaldi: Voice of the Baroque*. Chicago: University of Chicago Press, 1993.

Landon, H. C. Robbins, and John Julius Norwich. *Five Centuries of Music in Venice*. New York: Schirmer Books (division of Macmillan, Inc.), 1991.

Lang, Paul Henry. *George Frideric Handel*. Mineola: Dover Publications, Inc., 1996.

Laven, Mary. *Virgins of Venice: Broken Vows and Cloistered Lives in the Renaissance Convent*. New York: Penguin Books, 2002.

Mamy, Sylvie. *La Musique à Venise et l'imaginaire français des Lumières*. Paris: Bibliothèque nationale de France, 1996.

Martineau, Jane, and Andrew Robinson, eds. *The Glory of Venice: Art in the Eighteenth Century*. New Haven: Yale University Press, 1994.

Monnier, Philippe. *Venice in the Eighteenth Century*. New York: Chatto and Windus, 1910.

Norwich, John Julius. *A History of Venice*. New York: Random House, 1982.

Pedrocco, Filippo. *Ca' Rezzonico: Museum of Eighteenth-Century Venice*. Venice: Marsilio Editori, 2001.

Ribeiro, Aileen. *Dress in Eighteenth-Century Europe*. New Haven: Yale University Press, 2002.

Selfridge-Field, Eleanor, with Edmund Correia, Jr. *Antonio Vivaldi: L'Estro Armonico, Op. 3, in Full Score*. Mineola: Dover Publications, Inc., 1999.

Selfridge-Field, Eleanor. *Palade Veneta: Writings on Music in Venetian Society, 1650–1750*. Venice: Edizioni Fondazione Levi, 1985.

———. *Venetian Instrumental Music from Gabrieli to Vivaldi*. Mineola Dover Publications, Inc., 1994.

Talbot, Michael. "The Pietà as Viewed by Johann Cristoph Maier (1795)" in *Informazioni e Studi Vivaldiani 4, Bollettino Annuale dell'Istituto Italiano Antonio Vivaldi*. Milano: Ricordi, 2004.

———. *Vivaldi*. New York: Oxford University Press, 2000.

White, Micky. "Biographical Notes on the 'Figlie di coro' of the Pietà contemporary with Vivaldi," in *Informazioni e Studi Vivaldiani 21, Bollettino Annuale dell'Istituto Italiano Antonio Vivaldi*. Milano: Ricordi, 2000.

White, Micky, Giuseppe Ellero, and Don Gastone Vio. *Piccolo Museo della Pietà "Antonio Vivaldi": Musica e Vita Quotidiana delle Allieve (Figlie di Choro) al tempo di Vivaldi*. Istituto Provinciale per L'Infanzia "Santa Maria della Pietà" di Venezia, 2004.

DISCOGRAPHY

*T*HE FOLLOWING compact discs contain much of the music referenced in this novel. The reader should note, however, that many of the scenes involving this music are products of the novelist's imagination. I've played a bit fast and loose with dates and places: some of the music might be off by as much as a year in terms of when it was published and when I show it being performed. Also, the "battle of the bands" between Handel and Scarlatti occurred in Rome, rather than Venice, although both musicians were in Venice, and are likely to have interacted, during the time I place them there.

Vivaldi: Six Violin Sonatas (Opus 2, Nos. 1–6). Elizabeth Wallfisch, violin. Hyperion Records Ltd., London: 67467 (2004). [For the sonatas played by the *coro* in 1709]

Vivaldi: Sonate di Dresda. Opus 111: 30154. Fabio Biondi, violinist. [For the music evocative of the B-flat sonata dedicated to Anna Maria]

Rome 1709: Handel vs. Scarlatti. Stradivarius: 33623 (2002). [For the keyboard wonders performed by the two musicians in contest with one another, in my book at the Palazzo Foscarini]

L'Estro Armonico (Opus 3). Europa Galante, Virgin Classics Ltd. 45315. Fabio Biondi, violin, director (1998). [For the concertos Anna Maria and Vivaldi play in the Ghetto]

Music from the Venetian Ospedali. San Francisco Girls Chorus, on their own label (1998). [For a *Cum Sancti Spiritu* similar to what the girls and women of the *coro* might have sung under the balcony of the Foscarini palace]

Amori e Ombri: Duets and Cantatas. La Venexiana. Rossana Bertini (1998). Opus 111: 30182. [For vocal music by Francesco Gasparini, composer of the oratorio performed for the Doge by the *coro* of the Pietà]

Antonio Vivaldi: Six Violin Concertos for Anna Maria. Quaderno Musicale di Anna Maria: L'Arte dell'Arco. Classic Produktion Osnabrück 777 078-2 (2005). Federico Gugliemo, violinist. [For the D-minor concerto written for Anna Maria, Bernardina, and Giulietta's aborted confirmation party]

Arte dei Suonatori, La Stravaganza: 12 Violin Concertos (Opus 4). Rachel Podger, violinist. Channel Classics: 19598 (2003). [For the *grave e sempre piano* movement of No. 4, and the largo movement of the F-major concerto, which Anna Maria plays in the deathbed scene]

Antonio Vivaldi: Concerti (Opus 3, No. 8). *Interpretati Veneziani.* [For the A-major—with its two allegros—and the A-minor concerti, which Anna Maria and Bernardina perform with Vivaldi at the concert at San Francesco della Vigna]

Vivaldi Sacred Music—9. Choir of the King's Consort. The King's Consort. Hyperion Records Ltd.: 66839 (2003). [I listened to this almost constantly while writing the book, along with *Sacred Music 5 and 7,* from the same series.]

THE HISTORY
BEHIND
THE STORY

How This Novel Came to be Written

Nineteen years ago, at an open market on the streets of Budapest, I bought an engraving. I wasn't by any means an art collector, and I didn't have a lot of money; I was in Hungary doing research for an entirely different book. But something about this engraving spoke to me. Entitled *Vivaldi*, it shows a young composer writing with a quill on a musical score propped up against a baroque keyboard. Utterly engrossed in his work, he is surrounded by what I took to be angel musicians, who are presumably playing the music as he writes it. The engraving is numbered 73 in an edition of 100 printed by the artist, who signed his name Pituk J. V.

When I returned to California, I had the engraving beautifully framed. Again, this was not at all typical for me at that time. (The reproduction turn-of-the-century posters I brought back with me from Hungary got mounted on foam core.)

The funny thing was that I was living on a sailboat at the time. The only art I could possibly hang on our walls were greeting-card-size reproductions, and so *Vivaldi* went into storage. Over the next decade, *Vivaldi* moved in and out of storage as I moved from house to house and from one stage of my life to the next.

And then somewhere I read or heard a tidbit of history that lodged in my mind. One of the Italian composers whose name began with a V (I thought at first it was Verdi) was also a priest who taught in an all-girl orphanage.

So many miscellaneous facts we hear are like fireflies that glimmer and beckon and then disappear. But for whatever reason, this sparkly nugget stayed with me. I found myself at dinner with a gentleman who was an expert in the history of the lute. "Oh, it wasn't Verdi!" he told me, when I thought I'd tap into his musical expertise. "It's Vivaldi you're thinking of—Antonio Vivaldi, the Red Priest of Venice."

I went to the library and checked out all the books I could find on Vivaldi. Coincidentally, I'd already started studying Italian, which helped me when I went to the more specialized music library on the Berkeley campus of the University of California. From the sketchy information I was able to find about the Ospedale della Pietà, the institution where Vivaldi taught, I started writing a story. At its center was a foundling adolescent girl I called Pellegrina. She was a violinist and one of the maestro's favorites. She was telling her story through letters written to a mother she didn't even know existed.

When my own mother passed away, I used every penny of the money she left me to make a down payment on a house. *Vivaldi* emerged from storage. And then—finally, as I hung the picture in my bedroom—I understood. Those weren't angels standing around the composer, serving as his muses. Those were the orphans—or, more accurately, the foundlings—of the Ospedale della Pietà.

A good friend of mine who is a great traveler offered to give me some of his frequent flyer miles so that I could actually spend some time in Venice and begin to build a fully textured world to hold my story. By the time I got to Italy, I'd discovered that there was an actual foundling of the Pietà, a violinist named Anna Maria, whose profile was a near exact match for the girl I'd created.

From there on, the story seemed to write itself. I can say with complete honesty that every day I worked on it—about three years in all—was a joy.

Albeit beautiful and beloved, Venice is a rather closed city when it comes to exposing its more arcane cultural treasures to the curious gaze of outsiders. The archives and academic libraries are in themselves difficult to find and more difficult still to penetrate. I had to call upon every skill I'd ever learned as an actor and investigative journalist to talk my way into the stacks of the Conservatorio Benedetto Marcello, where Anna Maria's part-book is housed. I found out the etymology of the *Terra degli Assassini* by talking to someone setting up tables and chairs at a restaurant on the square. The flirtatious locution *"Una bella mozzarella!"* was something I heard from a cheeky gondolier as he passed by the perch where I was scribbling in my notebook. Everything I heard and saw during my three trips to Venice—and everything I read about la Serenissima—became material for the novel.

Back at home, while running laps at an outdoor field, I collared an Italian soccer player and asked him to help me come up with an appropriately sinister nickname for a hated teacher at an all-girls school (five minutes of conversation yielded "La Befana"). My interactions with my son, deep in his morph at that time from child to teenager, helped me remember and record the resentment, pain, and drama of adolescents everywhere.

I was more in the eighteenth century than in the twenty-first during those three years. Sometimes, after a day of writing, when I bicycled over to my neighborhood market to buy ingredients for dinner, I would look in befuddlement at the U.S. currency in my wallet, perhaps expecting to see ducats and *soldi*.

The book's working title was "Anna Maria dal Violin, Student of Maestro Vivaldi."

"Too Italian, and too long!" Gail Winston, my editor at HarperCollins told me. "You have to think of a better title."

I filled a couple of pages in my journal with possibilities. I could think of titles in other languages that sounded great—but nothing seemed to work in English. And then one morning I woke up and saw, as I see every morning, J. V. Pituk's picture on my wall. "Vivaldi's Virgins," I heard in my head and then said out loud.

And that is how this novel came to be written. It chased me, and finally caught me. To whatever force in the universe made this happen—and to the spirit of Anna Maria and also Vivaldi—I send my thanks for the honor of being the one to tell this story.

The lighter side of **HISTORY**

✻ Look for this seal on select historical fiction titles from Harper. Books bearing it contain special bonus materials, including timelines, interviews with the author, and insights into the real-life events that inspired the book, as well as recommendations for further reading.

AND ONLY TO DECEIVE
A Novel of Suspense
by Tasha Alexander
978-0-06-114844-6 (paperback)
Discover the dangerous secrets kept by the strait-laced English of the Victorian era.

DARCY'S STORY
Pride and Prejudice Told from Whole New Perspective
by Janet Aylmer
978-0-06-114870-5 (paperback)
Read Mr. Darcy's side of the story.

PORTRAIT OF AN UNKNOWN WOMAN
A Novel
by Vanora Bennett
978-0-06-125256-3 (paperback)

Meg, adopted daughter of Sir Thomas More, narrates the tale of a famous Holbein painting and the secrets it holds.

REVENGE OF THE ROSE
A Novel
by Nicole Galland
978-0-06-084179-9 (paperback)
In the court of the Holy Roman Emperor, not even a knight is safe from gossip, schemes, and secrets.

THE CANTERBURY PAPERS
by Judith Healey
978-0-06-077332-8 (paperback)

CROSSED
A Tale of the Fourth Crusade
by Nicole Galland
978-0-06-084180-5 (paperback)

ELIZABETH: THE GOLDEN AGE
by Tasha Alexander
978-0-06-143123-4 (paperback)

THE FOOL'S TALE
by Nicole Galland
978-0-06-072151-0 (paperback)

THE KING'S GOLD
by Yxta Maya Murray
978-0-06-089108-4 (paperback)

PILATE'S WIFE
A Novel of the Roman Empire
by Antoinette May
978-0-06-112866-0 (paperback)

A POISONED SEASON
A Novel of Suspense
by Tasha Alexander
978-0-06-117421-6 (paperback)

THE QUEEN OF SUBTLETIES
A Novel of Anne Boleyn
by Suzannah Dunn
978-0-06-059158-8 (paperback)

THE SIXTH WIFE
She Survived Henry VIII to be Betrayed by Love...
by Suzannah Dunn
978-0-06-143156-2 (paperback)

REBECCA
The Classic Tale of Romantic Suspense
by Daphne Du Maurier
978-0-380-73040-7 (paperback)

REBECCA'S TALE
by Sally Beauman
978-0-06-117467-4 (paperback)

THE SCROLL OF SEDUCTION
A Novel of Power, Madness, and Royalty
by Gioconda Belli
978-0-06-083313-8 (paperback)

A SUNDIAL IN A GRAVE: 1610
A Novel of Intrigue, Secret Societies, and the Race to Save History
by Mary Gentle
978-0-380-82041-2 (paperback)

THORNFIELD HALL
Jane Eyre's Hidden Story
by Emma Tennant
978-0-06-000455-2 (paperback)

TO THE TOWER BORN
A Novel of the Lost Princes
by Robin Maxwell
978-0-06-058052-0 (paperback)

THE WIDOW'S WAR
by Sally Gunning
978-0-06-079158-2 (paperback)

THE WILD IRISH
A Novel of Elizabeth I & the Pirate O'Malley
by Robin Maxwell
978-0-06-009143-9
(paperback)

Available wherever books are sold, or call 1-800-331-3761 to order.